THE TRAITOR'S MERCY

STARIAN CYCLE #1

IRIS FOXGLOVE

THE STARIAN CYCLE

The Traitor's Mercy

(Coming soon)
The Duke's Demon
The Prince's Vow
The Exile's Gift
The King's Mage

THE TRAITOR'S MERCY (Starian Cycle #1)
IRIS FOXGLOVE

Edited by M. Fee

Cover design by Paper and Sage (paperandsage.com)

❀ Created with Vellum

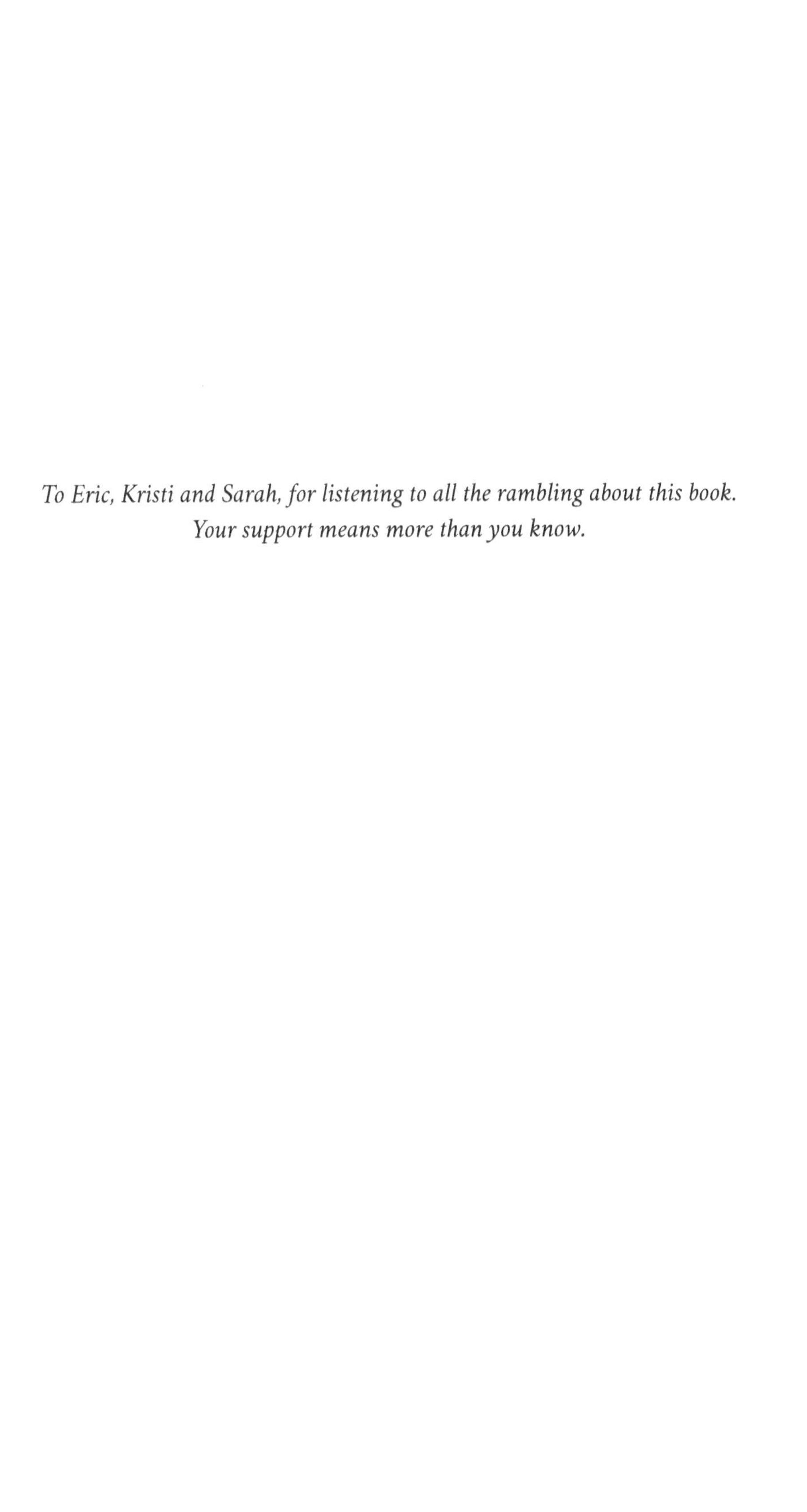

To Eric, Kristi and Sarah, for listening to all the rambling about this book.
Your support means more than you know.

AUTHOR'S NOTE

Please be advised that the biological imperative kink element to this story is intended as fantasy, **and is not intended as a factual representation of BDSM as practiced between consenting adults in real life**. The dynamics portrayed in *The Traitor's Mercy* (as well as other titles in this series) are entirely fictional, and should not be considered a guideline for the safe practice of any activity described herein.

Thank you for reading!

CHAPTER 1

"Sabre. Darling. Head up."

Sabre de Valois opened his eyes. His mother, her long, red-brown hair draped with ribbons even as she stood in just her cream underdress and bare feet, lifted her chin a fraction. The executioner's rope lay snug around her bare neck.

Sabre took a shaky breath and raised his head.

The crowd that had gathered to watch his family die looked more like they belonged at a street fair than a hanging, with vendors lining the plaza and children running about underfoot. Some of them held bits of bright cloth in their hands—pieces of Sabre and his family's clothes, his mother and sister's gowns, his own suit, stripped and tossed into the crowd as souvenirs. Sabre could hear bells ringing further down the hill, the sound of heralds delivering the news to the lower city; That the de Valois family had been discovered conspiring against the crown, and were dragged out of their own summer ball to face the king's justice.

The executioner fitted the rope around Sabre's neck. It was heavy and coarse, and when it was tightened, Sabre glanced at his mother, who was staring into the crowd. Her gaze settled on the raised stairs where King Emile de Guillory sat, watching them as though he were nothing more than one of the hundreds of commoners crowding the square, and her bound hands twisted and clenched behind her back.

When the executioner fitted the rope around his sister Elise's neck, Elise let out a soft sob, and Sabre turned to her. She was trembling, hot tears in her eyes, her blue shift clinging to her legs.

She'd only turned sixteen that morning.

"Elise," Sabre said. "Ellie." He looked at the executioner, a lean, expressionless man in a dark suit and rough leather gloves. "Sir. If you could let me hold her hand."

His mother made a soft sound beside him, a warning, and the executioner slid his dull gaze over Sabre.

"Please," Sabre said. "Just her hand, that's all I ask."

The executioner turned from him, and Elise took a ragged breath. She raised her chin high, like her mother, and closed her eyes.

"*Please,*" Sabre said, one more time.

"Sabre, that's enough." His mother always held an unnatural dominance in her voice—Sabre's father said it came from the fact that she was a distant cousin of the royal family, inheriting the power of their bloodline. But Elise's dominance was a soft thing, and Sabre was as much a natural submissive as his mother was a dominant, so blood could only go so far. As it was, Sabre went still, and Elise clenched her hands tight behind her back.

"Look at him, Sabre. Elise." Their mother's voice was sharp as a blade, cutting through the chatter of the crowd. "Look at the man who would kill his own kin to keep his power."

The king shifted on the steps, leaned back on one arm, and raised a hand. Sabre tensed, prepared for the floor beneath him to give way, but nothing happened. The executioner stepped to the edge of the platform, and a young girl in a page's livery raced through the crowd like a minnow through a school of fish.

"Sir," she said, bowing smartly. "His majesty the king requests to speak with the prisoner Sabre de Valois."

"What?" Elise twisted to stare at him, brown eyes wide.

"Elise." Their mother barked out the order like a commander. "Eyes front. Be *silent.*"

"I don't understand," Sabre said, as the executioner slipped off the rope around his neck. A susurrus rose from the crowd, hundreds of voices whispering and calling out as Sabre was taken by the arm and wrenched away from his mother and sister.

"Wait," he said. "Wait, shouldn't they—Shouldn't you let them—"

"The king asked for you," the executioner said. "By name."

"Mother," Sabre tried to twist to look back, but the executioner was surprisingly strong for his size, dragging him behind a row of the king's guard. The crowd pushed against them, seeking a better look. "Mother, should I ask him—"

"Ask him for nothing," his mother said. "Any promise he makes will come at a cost too dear to pay."

"Ask him to let Mother go," Elise shouted, as Sabre was pulled out of sight.

The line of the king's guard shifted and flowed like a tide against the shore as the crowd surged to break through, and Sabre was close enough to the palace steps to see the litters where the noble houses of Staria were being held. Every noble he'd ever met was there, watching him as he was dragged, barefoot in just an undershirt and thin gray trousers, to the steps where the king was sitting. The only one missing was Prince Adrien. Had he known? Was he the reason Sabre was being pulled off the gallows? Sabre was almost glad he couldn't see him in the throng. He didn't think he could handle knowing that Adrien was there to watch him die.

King Emile had none of his son's sympathetic nature. He looked more like Sabre, or his father, another cousin in a tangled web of royal breeding. They had the same reddish hair, a sturdier frame than Adrien's willowy, beanpole shape, the same line of their jaw. The only difference lay in the king's eyes—blue, clear and pale as a winter sky.

The king didn't even glance Sabre's way when Sabre was dropped at his feet and pushed to his knees. He kept his gaze fixed above him, to the platform where Sabre's family stood, waiting.

"So," he said. "The submissive of the de Valois. I haven't seen you since the winter solstice. Dabbling in treachery, are we? And here I thought your hobby was…dancing? Swordplay? A little of both, I think."

"Your Majesty," Sabre said, twisting his hands behind his back. "We weren't conspiring against you, I swear."

"Now, that's a lie." The king turned his gaze to Sabre, and the only thing that stopped Sabre from shrinking into himself was twenty years of dealing with his mother's flares of dominance. The king was nearly as strong as she was, but not quite. Perhaps he knew it. "Your mother has been conspiring against me since we were children. It's healthy, they say, to keep an enemy or two around. It's like hunting. Do you hunt, Sabre?"

"I've…once," Sabre said. "Not since my father—"

"I wasn't asking for your life story, boy, I *know* that. The point is, if you hunt all the deer to extinction, you'll be proud of yourself for a season, and then you'll come back the next and find nothing satisfying to shoot. Leave a doe or two be, and you'll have enough sport to last for years to come."

Sabre swallowed around a dry throat.

"Your Majesty, if there were a trial, you would—"

"Have to listen to lawyers? Yes. Odious business. There's a simplicity in a hanging." The king smiled down at Sabre, and Sabre quickly looked away. "But no, I don't think you knew of any treason. You were too earnest when you asked after my health, last we spoke, and your mother and sister are…bold personalities. It can't be helped if a submissive bows to the pressure of their dominant family."

"Please, Your Majesty." Sabre leaned over his knees, half bowing. His mother had muttered about the king often enough, but treason? He certainly couldn't think it of Elise, who only wanted to catch the eye of her lady's maid, who Sabre caught reading poetry to her just a week before. "I can prove our innocence. I'll do it myself, if I have to. I'll do anything, Your Majesty."

He bowed, pressing his forehead to the ground. It made his stomach churn to do it, to bow as a submissive would to their dominant before a king who ordered his family to the gallows, but he kept his forehead pressed to the stone.

"Oh," the king said, and Sabre shivered at the light brush of fingers over his hair. "To inspire such devotion."

Sabre grunted as the king pressed a booted foot firmly on his back, holding him down. "Tell the executioner to let them hang."

"No." Sabre struggled to rise, but the king was a powerful man in more than just his dominance, and he couldn't wriggle free from under his foot. Sabre could feel his breath go hot on the stone beneath him. "No, Your Majesty, please, I beg of you. I *beg* of you."

There was a sound of a door slamming against stone, and the crowd erupted in a collective gasp. Sabre closed his eyes as the nobles around him began to applaud, polite and scattered like the first pattering of rain on a roof, before the applause rolled over the crowd, building up into a storm that drowned out even Sabre's broken, gasping sobs.

They said Laurent de Rue, former courtesan turned noble and proprietor of the House of Onyx, had a heart full of nothing but ash and silver coins. That all he cared about was the reputation of his House; the one nobles contacted in coded letters, sent by hired servants attired in unknown livery, for those desires the traditional pleasure houses couldn't satiate.

It was said that Laurent had ambitions to replace Jasque de Yvain, the noble who was ostensibly in charge of the pleasure district, and it was whispered in the ballrooms and drawing rooms of the Starian elite that it wouldn't be long before he did it. Laurent had earned his noble title by not only paying off his debt in the fabled House of Gold —the most exclusive of the pleasure houses—but by convincing King Emile to let him take over the near-defunct House of Clay and turn it into the House of Onyx, which catered to the stranger fetishes of the Starian nobility.

Or the commoners who could afford it, which made him something of an aberration; courtesans were typically an indulgence restricted only to the nobility. Staria understood that its thriving merchant class was wealthy, but they were still enmeshed in the old ideas, that money meant little without a title to hold it up. Laurent had met plenty of nobles who were trapped in the sticky web of genteel poverty, slowly starving in their crumbling manors, freezing to death in homes with ten or so hearths bereft of wood.

A silver coin was a silver coin. If a wealthy merchant from beyond the fabled Ring of Stars—the districts in Duciel that surrounded the palace—could afford the services of his House, Laurent had no intention of turning them away. He'd supplemented his own income in the House of Gold by fucking wealthy merchants on the side, those who resented the nobility with less coin were allowed a thing they were not. It seemed only fair he did not prohibit his courtesans from paying their debt the same way.

"It's a pity," Julien d'Albert said, examining his nails. "This poor noble. Did you hear he watched his family hang? Dreadful, just dreadful, so I heard. They thrashed on the gallows so long, I hear people left out of boredom."

Laurent pasted a bland, disinterested look on his face. "Mmm." He could hear the salacious eager tone in d'Albert's voice, as he pretended to be above petty court gossip even though they were anything but. Laurent had been chosen for the House of Gold by this man, who'd fucked him for a week or so after Laurent's First Night, until another pretty courtesan in training caught his eye, and Laurent was left to pay off his debt in peace.

He'd never paid Laurent for the privilege of suffering his rather boring, pedestrian attentions. It was his *right as the house proprietor* to take Laurent to bed, of course. The courtesans in the House of Onyx, however, were used to Laurent's professional distance, which was unusual for a proprietor in the pleasure district. He didn't impose on what little free time they had, and even if he did wish to hire one of his courtesans for an evening, he would have dutifully noted the usual cost on the ledger to account for it. So far, he had yet to indulge.

The man in the center of the gathered circle of House Lords was not enjoying himself. He was naked and collared, his reddish hair worn long, though free of the proper nobleman's ribbon—removed before they forced him to climb the steps of the gallows, Laurent imagined—and he was trembling on his knees, gasping softly, tears falling onto the marble ground of the open-air pavilion in the complex that made up the pleasure houses.

"He'll be off to the whorehouses in lower Duciel," said Lady Amalie de Reve, the proprietor of the House of Silver. "Taken by those who want a taste of what it's like to bask in the golden light of the king and his chosen stars, I imagine, until he's too used up and thrown to the brutes on the street." She snapped open a fan and said, in a voice throbbing with disingenuity, "what a sad end to his charmed life."

"Careful, darling," murmured Lord Marcel de Cuivre, proprietor of the House of Bronze, as he grinned at her. "Your claws are showing."

She shrugged. "We are nobles. His family were traitors to the crown. Am I supposed to feel sorry for him?"

Trembling there in the circle of unmoved lords and ladies, Sabre de Valois said something under his breath and tilted his head, letting his hair fall over his face. Trying to hide.

"It's not the whorehouses that await this one," Lord Julien said, dismissively. "King Emile's law was clear. If by nightfall he went unclaimed by the pleasure houses, by dawn he'd greet the quarry quart."

"How dreadful," said Lady Amalie, smiling in satisfaction. "Let him end his cursed life hauling stones for the baths in which he used to soak. I've seen enough." She snapped her fan closed and walked to the center of the circle, then tipped de Valois' face up to hers. "I hear it took your sister four minutes to die. I bet it felt like an eternity. They say she wet herself in fear. And your mother, watching you subjugating yourself before the king while she and her daughter swung and choked. She cursed you with her dying breath, did you know?"

"Lady Amelie, really," Lord Marcel said, indulgent. "The boy will be tormented enough, come dawn."

"How I wish I could see it," Lady Amelie said. "When your back breaks under the marble, and they let you die screaming in the sun." She kicked him, hard, in the ribs. And then again, so that Sabre curled in on himself and drew his hands over his head, either protecting it from further blows or trying to block out the words about his mother and sister's last moments.

"All of this because his mother never hired her again," Julien confessed to Laurent, under his breath.

"Starian nobility keeps their grudges ever at the ready, like an Arkoudai with their sword," Laurent responded, watching Amelie leave on Marcel's arm.

"Yes, but one mustn't forget, it's the young man's fault." Julien *tsked* and turned away, dismissing the crying young noble as easily as he did Laurent's fake moans of pleasure in his bed, years ago. "At any rate, I'm hardly going to put him on offer, my house has standards. Lord Laurent. Good day."

He, too, turned and left.

The guard sighed and turned to his companion. "Call the quarrymaster."

Laurent studied the miserable, shivering young man who'd been left there in the square. The king must have known none of the pleasure houses would want to take him, this son of a woman hanged for treason, even without the apparent personal grudge. King Emile had forced this poor noble to stand on the gallows with a noose around his neck, waiting to die beside his family. Then he'd offered the hand of hope, only so Aline de Valois could see her son bow in subjugation and beg before she'd hanged.

Now, unwanted and in disgrace, he would be taken to the quarries. It was back-breaking labor, hauling the marble used for the nobility's decadent homes, and men like Sabre never lasted long. If the unfamiliar work and dangerous conditions didn't end them, the others who were condemned to toil there did. It was a prison sentence for those who weren't born and bred for such work. Julien had threatened Laurent with it a few times, when his natural dominance showed on accident and insulted his client.

"Maybe we can have fun with this one, first," the guard said, sneering, as if Laurent wasn't there. The strict class divide in Staria caused quite a bit of pent-up frustration for those who weren't at the top.

Sabre, who was related to the de Guillory line itself, had quite a long way to fall. "Nice long, leisurely trip to the quarries. We can switch off." The guard's cock was pressing against his pants. He looked at Sabre like a starving beast might eye up a herd of weakened deer.

Laurent put his dominance into his voice, speaking sharply. "There is no need to call for anyone, and I'm afraid you'll have to sate your lusts elsewhere. I'll take him. You're dismissed."

For a second, the guard looked like he might argue. But Laurent's stare was unwavering, and the guard lowered his gaze after a moment and muttered, jerking his chin at his companion and wandering off.

Alone, Laurent approached Sabre, who hadn't moved from his position. He was curled around himself, sobbing, already turning red in the heat of the midday sun. Laurent went down on his haunches and laid a careful hand on Sabre's shoulder. The young man flinched hard and drew in closer, trying to make himself invisible.

"If you can get to your feet for me, I'll put my coat on you. It will be warm, but it should keep your skin from the sun and give you something to hide in."

Sabre didn't look up.

Laurent sighed. "My name is Laurent de Rue. I'm the proprietor of the House of Onyx. Come with me, and let's see what we can do about you."

* * *

SABRE DIDN'T THINK he could stand.

He wasn't sure he deserved to. Not with Elise dead, and his mother's last sight of him as a traitor, a coward who would kneel for the king who let them hang.

"You should go," he said. His voice was hoarse, low, his mother's years of elocution lessons lost the moment the platform fell.

"You'll find I don't have to follow your orders," said Laurent de Rue, sliding his hand under Sabre's arm. "Stand up. Can't have you crawling through the streets—they haven't been swept yet."

Sabre slowly pushed himself upright. He swayed slightly, blinking in the sun, and shivered at the memory of his mother's voice, sharp and commanding.

Head up.

"No, we're not doing that," Laurent said, grabbing him firmly by the arm as Sabre started to fold in on himself again. Sabre barely noticed when Laurent draped his coat over Sabre's shoulders. "Put it on."

Sabre responded automatically to the dominance in Laurent's voice, relieved, in some small way, to have an order he could follow. Something simple. He tugged on the coat, but it wasn't quite big enough to cover him all the way. Sabre was trim enough, for a noble, but his shoulders were a bit more filled-out, a weak shadow of his distant royal cousin.

"Thank you," he said, in that same soft, broken voice.

"You might reconsider that," Laurent said. He kept a hand on Sabre's arm, guiding him through a maze of familiar streets that warped and blurred as they walked, nothing but smudges of color against a pale sky. "Do you know what the House of Onyx is?"

"Yes." Sabre touched the collar at his throat. It was gold, made of clever interlocking scales that didn't catch at the skin. It had fit him perfectly, when the king locked it around his neck. Like it had been made for him. "I've been there. To the House."

"You have? I thought your family had views on the pleasure district."

"Yes, exploitation of the poor," Sabre said. He'd heard his mother's lectures on the subject often enough. "My friends wanted to go, but I...I paid the girl and went outside. She's probably still there, isn't she?"

"Probably, yes. So you know that we cater to more *particular* needs, then?"

"Yes." It was part of the appeal. If a noble had a desire that could lead to an awkward talking-to at one of the other Houses, they discreetly applied at the House of Onyx. If he'd known they had proper dominants there, Sabre might have actually stuck around, that night, found someone who could wield a flogger properly, not drop halfway through and leave Sabre to his own devices. He'd only heard about their resident dominant after his friends were done, and by then it was too late to run back in and change his mind. Now, he couldn't see the point.

"So long as you're aware of what you're getting into."

Sabre laughed hollowly. It sounded terrible. "The king set my debt at fifteen hundred crowns."

Laurent stopped in the middle of the street. There were pink rose bushes billowing up over a wall at his back, bursting with blooms. They framed him on either side like an unusual fur ruff. "Did you say…are you certain."

It wasn't a question.

"That's all he told me," Sabre said. He took a breath. He wasn't sure of the last time he'd done that. "I don't think I can stop walking. Sir. My lord."

Laurent took his arm again. "It's not far."

Sabre peered at the houses that lined the street on either side. He hadn't even noticed that they'd passed into the pleasure district. There was the House of Copper, with the stone lions at the gate. The House of Iron had a courtesan tied to one of the severe stone pillars, looking mildly bored. The House of Stone wasn't even a proper house, just a pavilion with a cellar they said went down three flights. Courtesans eyed them as Laurent guided Sabre past the main Houses, down a side street lined with small empty buildings. At the end of the street, the House of Onyx stood with a single violet light flickering at the door. Black curtains draped over the upper windows and trailed down almost to the street, and Laurent stepped up to the door and pressed a panel next to the frame.

The door swung open, revealing a young man in a raven mask, feathers curling around his round face.

"My lord," he said. "It's been dead today, thanks to the hanging, but Nanette has one of her regulars, at 1—oh." His green eyes blinked behind the mask. "Do you need help, my lord?"

"This is our newest," Laurent said. "He's a little rough around the edges, at the moment. Let us in, Yves. And stop wearing out the masks, you know they're for clients."

"Yes, my lord." Yves took off the mask, revealing a mess of pale hair, and stepped aside.

The last time Sabre had been in the House, he'd only stayed long enough to explain to the poor girl he'd hired that he was a submissive, actually, and hadn't paid much attention to his surroundings. Now, he passed through the entrance, where nobles donned their masks and were led by the host to their courtesan of choice, and into the main lounge. A courtesan was already there, a man a little older than Sabre with glossy golden hair, wearing nothing but a black loincloth draped with silver chains. He scrambled out of his ungainly sprawl when he saw Laurent enter, and pushed back his hair.

"No using the lounge during working hours unless you're ordered to," Laurent said.

"Yes, but no one's here except for the cat woman," the courtesan said. "They're all watching the traitors dance, aren't they?"

Sabre stiffened, but Laurent squeezed his arm once, a warning.

"It's been over for an hour," Laurent said. "And I suspect some of them may already be on their way. Easy," he added, softly, when Sabre's breath hitched.

Nobles. Coming to the pleasure district. Sabre knew his mother wasn't exactly an easy woman to love. His father was friendly enough, loyal to the king and a veteran of his army, but he died on a hunt with Elise when Sabre was fourteen. Too many nobles with a grudge would have no qualms taking it out on Sabre with his mother gone, and if they knew he was given to one of the pleasure houses—

"—a new courtesan in training," Laurent was saying, somewhere beyond the roaring in Sabre's ears. "When Nanette is done, send her and the others to my room. There are a few extenuating circumstances with this one."

"Is he sick?" Yves was pulling out a heavy black ledger that looked almost the size of his torso. He grimaced at Sabre. "Because you look sick."

"I might be," Sabre said.

"Not on the carpet, please." Yves set the book down on a plinth with a grunt. "I'm on cleaning duty."

"He'll keep that in mind," Laurent said. He gestured at the other courtesan and snapped his fingers. "If I don't see you at Nanette's door when I pass by…"

"Yes, my lord, at your service, my lord."

"Brat," Laurent said, but there wasn't any heat there. The dominance in his voice strengthened, filling the fog in Sabre's mind. "Come. Keep walking."

"Yes, sir."

"Courtesans call the proprietor of the house *my lord*," Laurent said, towing him up a set of plush, carpeted stairs. There were more violet lights scattered throughout, giving the dark walls the effect of a cave, glittering with precious stones just out of reach. "If I'm not a lord, clients won't treat me like one, and then they'll think *they* run the place. Do you understand?"

Sabre struggled to breathe again. It was never so hard, before. "Yes, my lord."

"I'll add you to the ledger soon. I can't mark your debt until the king sends a clerk to confirm it, but you won't be taking clients yet."

"What?" Sabre blinked slowly. They passed a closed door, and Sabre jumped at the sound of a smack and a squeal of pain. "I don't understand…I thought it would start tonight."

"Courtesans are trained, first, when they join the Houses," Laurent said. "I can't unleash an untrained whore on the world, can I? Well, I can, but it won't do either of us any good. You'll do this properly, which means no clients tonight." He caught Sabre with his gaze, shadowed in the dim light of the stairwell. "Repeat it so I know you understand."

"No clients tonight," Sabre said.

Laurent turned from him, heading up the stairs, and snapped his fingers twice. "Follow me."

"Yes, my lord."

Sabre's heart was hammering so loudly he could feel it in his *ears*. He stumbled up the steps after Laurent, forgetting a lifetime of dancing and fencing lessons, and shuddered when they reached a single door at the top floor. The door was outlined in silver, and there was a relief of a line of women winding up a mountain, carrying vases on their shoulders. A dragon appeared on the other side of the mountain, sinewy and wild as a snake, fangs bared.

"I don't trust you in your own room, yet," Laurent said, pushing open the door. "You'll be staying with me until I know you won't try to do anything rash."

"I don't think I *can* do anything," Sabre said. He touched his arms. He was shaking. He didn't know when he'd started that. "I even knelt for the king, when he…gave the order." His voice trailed off at the end, barely a whisper.

"Yes, I heard." Laurent sighed. Sabre would have called him lovely, a few hours ago. He had a delicate face, framed by long hair that looked almost violet in the light of his room, muted by a silver that suited him far better than some of the more fashionable nobles he knew. His eyes were the same gray, almost ghostly, and Sabre found himself holding his breath, waiting for him to laugh, or sneer, or admit that it was all a ruse to get the traitor's son alone.

"I won't pretend that what happened to you wasn't terrible," Laurent said, and Sabre frowned, slightly. "But you won't have time to grieve properly. Few ever do. It will be unpleasant, I imagine, but if you don't fight me, I'll see what I can do to keep the worst of it at bay."

"Why?"

Laurent shrugged. "Anyone can look at you and see you weren't a traitor before this started."

"Before?"

Laurent turned into his room, lavishly decorated in grays and blacks and silver. "You may not have enough time to grieve, Sabre," he said. "But I expect you'll have plenty of time to learn to be angry."

CHAPTER 2

*L*aurent had no idea if Sabre's parents were really traitors or not. It didn't matter, not in the grand scheme of things. The king was the king, and he was not known for being rational. He hated the Mislians for some fever-dream of his perfidious wife— the stories said he'd executed her himself, and made their young son, the Crown Prince Adrien, watch. And now he barely spoke to Adrien, though whether it was because his son and heir looked like his hated mother, or was a submissive, no one knew. And given he'd once executed his entire personal guard for speaking too quietly in his presence, it was unlikely anyone would ask.

Laurent wanted his noble title not because life was easier for him, but because it let him make life easier for others. He remembered being in the House of Gold, chosen for his odd looks—thanks to his foreign parentage, on whatever side—and shaking in his bed at night, fucked to an inch of his life and suppressing his own natural dominance so fiercely that he hated the feel of the silk sheets on his skin. Maybe it was the thing that made him so popular amongst Staria's elite, who were bored and jaded enough to find complacency too dull and an outright challenge too much work. He liked pleasure as much as any courtesan who was well-trained enough to enjoy it, but submitting went against every natural instinct he had.

The king had called for him only once, but Laurent was a popular choice with Isiodore de Mortain, the king's loyal advisor and, so it seemed, only friend. He was the only person who'd ever seemed to notice Laurent's dominance, and as one of the most notorious sadists at court, even Laurent wouldn't have quite known what to do with him if he'd been allowed to manifest his true proclivities.

It must be terrible, de Mortain had murmured, stroking Laurent's cheek with a knife. *To have to shove what you are, and what you think, so deep inside. Don't get me wrong, pretty thing. You're better at it than most. But it takes one to know one.*

One thing about de Mortain—he paid handsomely, and he always gave Laurent a bauble, some ring or piece of jewelry that he explicitly said should be sold off to someone instead of given to Lord Julien, as the custom dictated. And he gave Laurent *information*, tidbits about the court that proved invaluable because he was never wrong. Come to think of it, if de Valois' family were traitors, de Mortain probably knew. And probably turned them in for it, too. He might have been the reason Sabre was still breathing.

De Mortain liked to cause pain. Maybe a good choice for Sabre's first client, but not time to think about that, now.

"You should have a bath. Come with me." Laurent went to his private bathing room, which had a deep, sunken marble tub heated by taps, large enough for six people to comfortably swim in. There were heated floor tiles and soft cotton towels, and a smaller pool with cooler water cascading over a stone slab, allowing for a waterfall effect to provide a bit of relief from the heat.

It was absurd and unnecessary for one person, especially when the house itself had its own bathing room, full of floating lights, several waterfalls and benches for relaxation. Laurent knew what it was like to come back from an assignment and want nothing more than a nice, long, hot soak. Especially here, where clients tended to be a bit...more *intense* than the others.

"I used to be indentured in the House of Gold," Laurent said, as he led Sabre into the bath, gently guiding him to step in. "One of the courtesans there was a former orphan from the lower city, came from one of those crowded houses full of motherless children. A thieves guild, you might call it, where the kids were sent to some rich merchants' houses in the winter. He talked about how he was supposed to play it up, shiver and cry, so they'd let him stay the night, and so he could rob them blind in the morning. He did it until he was too old to look innocent, then he sold himself into debt to get off the streets. Someone asked him once if he nicked some silver from the nobles who hired him, but he said no. That it was honest work, and at least he had the choice to do it. There weren't many, for a starving child with no one to look after him."

Sabre lowered his head and stared at the water, shoulders drooping. There were freckles there, which wasn't common—so many courtesans used powder to hide them, thinking it made them look common, as if they saw the sun more than two minutes a day.

"So, in case you're worried, I think you are no more a traitor for bowing to your king to save your life, than that courtesan was a thief when he stole to keep himself fed and from freezing to death on the streets. I might be a dominant, but I know very well how little that matters in Staria, where true power is granted not by your status or your wealth or your talents, but by your name and the favor of your family. Your family lost their favor, and maybe they were traitors and maybe they weren't, but it doesn't change what happened, or that it would have happened anyway, if the king wanted it to. A whim could have sent you to me and your family to the gallows."

Sabre was gasping again, shaking. "They weren't...*I* wasn't—"

"This is going to get worse before it gets better," Laurent said, speaking over him, voice ringing with dominance. "I know, because I've been there. I've spread my legs for men I hated, I've buried my face between the thighs of women who I'd just as soon see dead. Do you know how many courtesans pay off their debt, little fox? Hardly any. Especially in the House of Gold, where you are the most expensive whore there is, and so is your debt to the house that offers your services. I was, oh, moderately popular for a while, but my requests went up when I let them see just a little truth in the lie. That's what you need to do, Sabre. They'll ask for you first out of curiosity, they'll do just Lady Amelie did, earlier, pick at you, poke your scars, want to tear at you so that you bleed. Some of them, here? Might put the rope around your neck again just to see what you do, feeling it there on your skin. Fall apart for them, bleed, cry...but never give them all of you. That's the only way you survive."

Sabre said, to the water, "I don't know if I'm glad. That I...that I didn't die. I wish I would have made myself watch."

"I think you won't mean that, in a year. Wash your hair, or I'll have someone come in and do it for you." Laurent's days of playing bath attendant were long over.

Sabre washed his hair, and the rest of him, while Laurent watched. He took a few mental notes as he did so, noticing the lean body, the broad shoulders, the submissiveness that was so pronounced he only glanced at Laurent a time or two while he bathed. He seemed perfectly at ease in the hot water, and did not protest when Laurent told him to go stand beneath the waterfall, where the water was much cooler.

He was a pretty man, wide-eyed and pale like most nobles who didn't venture much outside in their part of the city that was named for the sun, topped by their palace of gold. His eyes were the color of copper, or would be, if they weren't dull and empty as glass. He pulled his hair as he washed it, and stood a bit too long beneath the cold water. When he tipped his head beneath the stream of clear water, his hands clasped behind his back, twisting of their own volition. It must have reminded him of the gallows, because he startled like a rabbit caught grazing unawares by a hawk. His gold collar gleamed in the light.

"When you're done," Laurent said. "Come kneel here, before me."

Laurent waited patiently with a towel in hand—the thick kind, heavy woven fabric, kept above the brazier of coals that would make sure they were warm. Sabre was shivering when he knelt, and silent, though he was starting, Laurent imagined, to get lost in his head again.

Laurent took up a comb, braiding his hair after he wrapped the linen towel around Sabre to stop his shivering. He reached down and dragged his fingers over the gold of Sabre's collar. "I know what he meant this to be, do you?"

"Justice," Sabre said. "And that I live only at his mercy."

"Such as it is," Laurent murmured. "And yes, I'm sure you're right. Well. If that's the King's sigil meant to remind you of the bright light of his eternal, ah, regard...I chose *onyx* for my house because it's in direct opposition to the sun and the bright blazing light of our kingdom." His voice went sardonic as he finished the braid, urged Sabre to his feet and wrapped the towel around him. It did little to ease his shivering, but Laurent knew well enough the cold Sabre felt came from within. "It is supposed to represent not only harmonious relationships between people, as in submissives and dominants...but they also say it symbolizes being the person we are in the dark, in the shadows where the light can't reach. You're going to spend a lot of time there."

When he got Sabre back into the room, he found the cuffs and decided maybe to leave the ropes for the moment. That night was going to be hard enough for Sabre without them. "I'm going to put you under, then cuff you—wrists in front of you, and your ankles, and leash you by both to the foot of my bed. All right?"

Sabre's eyelids were drooping—he must have been exhausted. He probably needed to eat, but likely sleep was more pressing than anything. Laurent took the towel from him, gently knocking his hands away when Sabre tried to cover himself. "I don't think it will... work, being under. I..." He shuddered, hands migrating toward his back again, twisting his fingers together.

Laurent wondered if the only time he'd ever gone under, truly under, was when the noose was around his neck and the drumroll sounded, when he thought he was going to die on the gallows. Had it put him under for the first and only time in his life, being dragged through the crowd, demeaned, his clothes torn and his hands bound? The man who made a living out of catering to the strange desires of others filed that away for future consideration.

The man who was once just as vulnerable, just as helpless, submitting with a smile to a graceless noble who didn't know Laurent was a dominant and didn't care...that man understood.

Laurent said, "Has anything ever gotten you close?"

"Yes. I was flogged, once. It almost, almost worked."

"Good. Lay on my bed, and I'll see to you." Laurent had to help him do it, of course, lay sideways across the bed with his arms in the proper position, head turned to the side, braid pushed gently over one shoulder so it was out of the way. "The first lesson you learn in the House of Onyx is that no one, *no one*, comes without asking."

"I don't want to come," Sabre said, in a small, miserable voice. "I want to sleep, and I...don't want to dream." His fingers curled into Laurent's bedding, and he took a deep breath, tense and waiting, naked save his collar.

That might be impossible, but Laurent would do his best.

* * *

THE FIRST STRIKE of the lash was always too light.

Sabre didn't move when the strips of leather brushed his skin. He held himself still, fingers tense in the soft cotton of Laurent de Rue's bedsheets, and grit his teeth against the gentle warmth of his shoulders under the flogger, a comfort he didn't deserve.

He'd experimented some with other young nobles, gamely kneeling for them after fencing bouts or behind the gates of the Lord's Council, where noble liaisons were overlooked by their peers. He'd been flogged a few times, and spanked by Ginnie Halson, who complained that he wasn't enough of a brat to be worth the trouble.

"You're too well-behaved," she'd told him, with a groan of disgust that made Sabre smile. "Can't you say no for once in your life?"

Laurent flicked the lash cleverly, striking Sabre hard across the shoulders, and Sabre let out a faint gasp. Not enough. Not yet.

He held still as the strikes sharpened, as the pain turned from mildly pleasant to a burn that stirred Sabre's cock, pushing up against the sheets. He was only half hard, but the thought of giving in to pleasure with Elise dead in her shift in some unmarked grave was enough to keep him quiet, keep him still.

Most dominants stopped at this point, when the pain would make other submissives cry prettily into the sheets, rutting into the bed while they begged for more, for it to stop, for them to be fucked pliant. Sabre waited.

The next blow was strong enough to push a sound out of him, soft and helpless, and Sabre hissed in a short breath as the ends of the flogger slid down his back, over the curve of his ass. The soft lashes returned, but his overheated skin was sensitive, and his arms strained with the effort of not moving against the bed, arching into the pain.

"Is there a reason you're so still?" Laurent asked, and Sabre moaned at a bright flare of pain, twisted his hands in the sheets.

"You said I was to lie like this," Sabre said. "My lord. I wasn't given an order to move."

Laurent seemed to take a moment to consider this, and Sabre trembled beneath him, desperate for the lash.

"Next time you need this," Laurent said, "we'll try a cane."

"Yes, my lord," Sabre said, and bit down on his lower lip as Laurent fell on him, relentless and fast and sharp, pushing out short, broken cries of pleasure until the pain became almost too much. Sabre groaned as it fell over that edge, and his hips moved involuntarily, grinding a small circle into the bed. He stopped, panting into the mattress, and cried out as Laurent ran sharp nails down his back.

"Your body wants the release," Laurent said, lifting Sabre by the braid, and the pain of it left him dazed, staring up at him with his mouth gone slack and his hands still fisted on the bed beneath him. "But you won't ask for it."

Laurent twisted Sabre's hair in his grip, and Sabre moaned, ragged and broken.

"No, my lord," he said, and gasped when Laurent slapped him across the face.

Laurent dragged him off the bed by the hair, throwing him onto the rug, and Sabre lay where he fell, staring up at him. He could feel the fog in his mind closing over, the pain rolling through it like lightning in a summer storm, and he watched as Laurent fetched the cuffs, padded leather that fit too comfortably around his wrists and ankles.

"Climb onto the bed," Laurent said, when he was done leashing the ankle and wrist cuffs together. Sabre struggled to obey, stumbling over his own feet, but he finally made it to the foot of the bed, where he curled up on the cotton sheets and stared down at his hands.

Laurent tied the end of the leash to the footboard. Sabre was still too warm, but the pain in his back tingled every time he shifted, lulling him into the fog.

"Sleep," Laurent said. "It's inevitable."

Sabre thought he might have laughed at that, but then he was drifting, Laurent was no longer standing before him, and Sabre was curled up on his side with the ends of a blanket tucked under his arms. A pale light glowed in the distance, and there were voices, like the murmur of a dinner party at the manor.

"Poor bastard," someone said.

"And they just let him in? I had to give *references*. I had to fuck someone just to get them to give out references."

"It's not like it's a privilege to the likes of him," someone else said. Sabre squinted his eyes open. There was a woman lounging on the floor, dressed in a gauzy, diaphanous nightgown and fake pearls in her hair. She took a bottle from Yves, who had changed into a leather outfit with too many straps and not enough cloth to cover anything, and passed it to a younger woman with short-cropped black hair and nothing but trousers. No one seemed to mind her exposed breasts, or the smudged writing in ink over one of them, a refined script signed with a flourish. She rubbed at it, and her thumb came away blue.

"The king vouched for his innocence," Laurent said. He was sitting on his desk in the corner, feet propped up on his empty chair. "But he can't let the son of a traitor walk free after an execution. So he's been made an example for any other hapless nobles who might follow the de Valois' example. He's of the House, now, for better or worse, and no amount of, hah, patriotic zeal you feel regarding traitors will live up to what he's seen today."

"*I* never slept on your bed when *I* joined up, my lord," Yves said, flashing a smile. He met Sabre's gaze, and Sabre looked down.

"Because you gave me a weak lie about a sick brother and a two-legged dog," Laurent said. The others grinned and pushed at Yves, who lay a hand on his heart.

"I *could've* had one, my lord. You never know, my dear old Jacques—"

"I thought it was Michel," said the woman in the pearls.

"Oh, fuck off, Simone. I have a sick brother, you know."

"*And* a two-legged dog," said the woman with the bottle. "Definitely not a dear old mother in the country, doing perfectly well for herself while her son runs around calling nobles *daddy*."

"If I never have to milk a cow again, I will die happy," Yves muttered.

"Is he getting the storage room, then?" asked the courtesan Sabre had seen earlier, with the golden hair. "I have things in there."

"He'll be staying here for now," Laurent said. Someone whistled. "Unless one of *you* wants to make sure he doesn't strangle himself on his bedsheets."

"Poor lamb," said Simone. "He paid me for a night, once, did you know? I remember thinking he looked so like the king. Shaking like a newborn fawn when he was dropped off at my door, didn't know where to put his eyes."

"Was he good?" asked Yves.

"He paid me and apologized," Simone said. "Then he went outside to stand with the horses."

"Oh, no," said Yves. "They'll eat him alive."

"I'm not certain they haven't already," said Simone, and Sabre felt himself starting to drift again, their voices blurring together in a soft unintelligible murmur, as though Sabre were at home, a child falling asleep on the stairs as a dinner party faded into the distance below him, warm and bright and familiar.

He woke at dawn, tied to a stranger's bed in an unfamiliar house, heart in his throat. Just a day ago, Elise had stormed into his room to announce she was finally a woman, and therefore old enough to borrow Sabre's horse, thank you. He'd refused to even think about it until she stopped tugging at the bit like a beast, and had stolen her ribbons when she whirled round to report to their mother.

He curled in on himself, thinking of the way she'd shaken when the executioner cut the gown from her back, and jerked when a bare foot kicked him in the side.

"No," Laurent said, in a voice still thick with sleep. The bed rustled, and Sabre ducked his head as Laurent leaned over him. His silvery violet hair brushed Laurent's arm as he undid the cuffs one-handed, and he was close enough that Sabre could smell the oils he used on his skin, soft and vaguely sweet.

"Put on a robe and go downstairs," Laurent ordered. "Eat something. Then bring *me* something. You're in training, now, so you might as well be useful."

"Ah." Sabre sucked in a sharp breath. His stomach was twisted in knots, caught between anxiety and ravenous hunger. "Yes, my lord."

"Mm. Leave." Laurent flapped a hand and sank back into the bed, looking like a reclining nymph in the gallery at the palace.

Sabre climbed out of bed, uneasy on his feet, and headed for a closet at the far end of the room. He found a whole rack of robes, each more elaborate than the last, and dug through them until he found one that looked a little older, the dye faded and the shoulders stretched out. He slipped it on, but it only just covered his waist, leaving his chest exposed.

Well, that seemed to be a trend, there. He slipped out of the door and closed it carefully, then slowly made his way down the stairs.

The House of Onyx was quiet in the early morning, still recovering from the debauchery of the night before, and the only sound came from the occasional clank and clatter of pots far below. Sabre followed it to a small, functional kitchen with strings of dried peppers and baskets of fruit, with the short-haired woman from the night before moving pans around while another one, closer to Elise's age, sat on the counter with an apple.

The girl looked at Sabre and smiled. She had skin so dark she looked like *she'd* stepped out of a painting herself, one of the ones about the goddess of the night painting the stars, and her hair was pinned back out of her face, which was still round with baby fat. She swung her bare feet off the counter, and Sabre spotted her shoes just beneath her, pale blue like her dress.

"Oh," she said, setting the apple down. "Nanette, is this…"

Nanette—who was wearing men's clothes, a striped shirt rolled to the elbows and black trousers—gave Sabre a once-over. "Yep. Morning, uh…do we call you Sabre, or my lord, or…"

"I'm not a lord," Sabre said, hovering awkwardly at the kitchen doorway. He could smell the sausages cooking on the griddle, and a plate of scones with jam was already dotted with crumbs.

"Okay. Then hey, kid, I'm Nanette."

"Rose," said the girl. "But I'm trying out Violetta, or Tempeste."

"Just call her Rose," Nanette said. "She's an *actress*, it's a whole thing."

"Only an understudy so far," said Rose, reaching for a scone. She held it out to Sabre, who gingerly took it.

"So. Do you work here?" Sabre searched for a plate to eat on, sighed, and took a bite.

"What, officially? No." Rose took another scone for herself. "I help with the mending, sometimes. And the laundry. I fetch orders from the tailor. And Laurent lets me do the books on weekends."

"It's called nepotism," Nanette drawled, tipping sausages and mushrooms into a basket. "She's Laurent's little urchin."

"Urchin!" Rose cried, outraged. "No, I'm his put-upon, woefully unappreciated sister." Sabre raised his brows, and she sighed. "Yes. I know. He's so hideous, it's hard to see the resemblance."

"He adopted her," Nanette said. "Or she adopted him. It's hard to keep their stories straight with a *thespian* thrown in the mix."

"I'm just saying, it would be far more interesting if I *did* save his life from a jealous noble," Rose said, picking a mushroom out of the basket. "Are you hungry, Sabre? I've never seen someone inhale a scone before."

"I'll bring a mirror, next time," Nanette said, and they both smiled at each other. "Come on, kid, grab a plate. Haven't eaten since the, uh, thing, have you?"

"Oh," Rose said, softly. "I'm sorry. Here, sit down." She patted the counter next to her, and Sabre's chest ached. She would have been right at home with Elise's friends.

"Don't actually sit on the counter, we aren't heathens," Nanette said, grabbing a plate for Sabre. He tipped a few sausages onto his plate, and Rose passed him another scone.

"I said sit," Rose said. She had none of Elise's dominance, but Sabre was used to being bossed around by fashionable little sisters, so he climbed up onto the counter next to her. Nanette sighed.

"He's not being a bear about it, is he?" Rose asked. "He can get kind of growly with the ones in training, at first."

"It's a little too early to tell," Sabre admitted. "All he's asked me to do is bathe and get him breakfast."

"Well, that's easy." Rose swung her feet back and forth. "Since you were a noble, is it true you all have lessons on how to kneel properly and bow right?"

"Hypothetically, yes, but I never attended one."

"What a *waste*." Rose took a piece of scone off his plate. "I would have. I've already decided, I'm going to be a perfect submissive when I'm of age, and I'm going to be an actress, and I'm—"

"Going to have ten children," Nanette said.

Sabre blinked. "Why ten?"

"Because eight's an ugly number," Rose and Nanette said, at the same time. Rose rolled her eyes and dropped to her feet. "Come on, I'll help you bring breakfast to his royal highness. I've been feeling neglected lately, anyways."

* * *

TEN YEARS AGO, Laurent was an apprentice at the House of Gold, walking back from the market with an order for the house chef. He'd seen a woman with a young girl talking to one of the disreputable recruiters for the whorehouses of the lower city, called *minnow-*

catchers since they tended to take in people who were too young to even be considered by the pleasure houses.

They weren't picky, but apparently, they weren't interested in whatever the woman was offering. She was getting angry, but the recruiter shook his head and pushed by her, leaving the woman tearing at her hair and staring in fury at her young daughter.

She was four, with big dark eyes and a dirty dress, and Laurent had seen a thousand little kids like her before, since he started venturing into the city. But she was also smiling sweetly up at the woman—her mother, Laurent assumed—and trying to reach up for her in the gesture that all kids used for *pick me up and hold me.*

"No! You brat, I didn't want you anyway and—four more years before I can get rid of you?"

Laurent knew that Staria's social system was fucked, and it was hard especially on women—particularly those who found themselves solely responsible for children and no way to take care of them. It was how so many children ended up like his fellow trainees did, living in little gangs and stealing for someone ruthless enough to take advantage of small children's desperation to feel safe. He thought that would probably happen to her, this little one. Her mother would probably walk away, too fast for the smiling little girl to keep up, and she'd end up lost and alone on the streets crying for someone to help her.

Except as Laurent watched, the mother did something even worse than turn and leave—she waited for one of the heavy carts bringing in the marble from the quarry to trundle by, and pushed the little girl directly in its path.

Then she turned and ran.

Laurent could stop her, probably. Drag her before the courts, and then she'd end up hanged and her daughter would still be dead. Or he could save the child. So Laurent dropped the order he'd picked up, dashed into the street, and pulled her out of the way before she was run over like trash someone threw away.

She'd been confused, terrified, screaming for her mama—but she'd let Laurent pick her up and carry her, and while his order for the house was already snatched and carried off by opportunistic pickpockets, he'd had enough left to buy her some freshly-baked, warm flatbread with almonds and goat cheese rolled up inside. She'd eaten it like she was starving, then fallen asleep in his arms while he carried her back to the House of Gold.

Adding the order he'd lost to his debt added a couple of months. Adding a young girl who was too young to be a maid or a cook or a laundress, added two *years*. But he'd paid it without comment, because he remembered what it had been like, being unwanted and alone. And the girl, who took two weeks to speak to him, was sweet. Pretty, with her dark skin and dark eyes, and affectionate once she accepted easily enough that Laurent was her new big brother and responsible for her.

She'd had a different name, but she'd asked him if she could have another one, so he'd told her to go right ahead and choose one. She picked Rose, and a month after he'd brought her with him back to the House, she was telling him all kinds of stories. She'd climbed in the bed with him in his small room and snuggled close. "It's a good thing you found me, Laurent," she'd said. "Because the truth is, I'm really a princess. I'm here in secret. I was sent here, from the moon. By. By a turtle."

"A turtle, huh," Laurent said, charmed.

"Um-huh. And, I. One time my Mama, the nice one, the other one. She was made out of." Rose yawned. "Stars. Big ones, all bunched up together."

"Stars, huh."

"Uh-huh." Rose was silent for a minute. "The turtle brought me, and told me to find my brother. That's you. Because you're from the moon, too. You can tell who moon people are, because we're alone, and we have to find each other. And the turtle said, it said when I found you, I could live in a nice, beautiful big room in a *castle*."

The room they lived in was the smallest in the whole house, and this little girl thought it was a *castle.*

The little girl was now fifteen, fancied herself Laurent's personal assistant, and had yet to learn how to knock.

"Laurie, get *up.*"

Laurent groaned. "Don't call me that." He sat up, smirking and pushing his hair out of his face. "You met our newest house member, did you? Sabre, come in. This is my sister, Rose. I'm sure she had a wonderful explanation about how that worked."

Sabre didn't smile, but Laurent wasn't surprised. He didn't imagine he would see Sabre smile for a long time, not after yesterday.

"Saved you from an evil noble," Sabre said, a little dully. "We brought you breakfast."

"Scones. Get up! How can you still be sleeping, I've been up for ages."

Laurent got out of bed and grabbed his robe, slipping it over his silk pajamas. "Rose, I need to speak with Sabre and it's not appropriate for you to be here. But if you want to help, you can go and tell Charon to meet me in the Crescent Chamber in an hour. Then, you can go see about a wardrobe for Sabre, here."

"Oh! Okay, that's at least not boring. But later, you and me, we're gonna talk. I have to show you the lines I've been running. I'm getting so good, Laurie." Rose beamed, hugged him and waved shyly at Sabre before she ducked out of the room.

Laurent sat at his dressing table and motioned to Sabre. "Bring that tray over. Did you eat something, like I told you?"

"Yes." Sabre brought the tray over and placed it on the dressing table. He had that wild-eyed look again, but there was something different about it than yesterday. Something both more present and more horrified.

Laurent took one of the scones. "Kneel. Hands behind your back." He ate his scone. "Is there anything you want to ask me?"

Sabre went to his knees, and there was no real finesse there, not like Laurent would have done it back when he was serving in the House of Gold. But that wasn't going to be Sabre's draw, for the nobles that hired him. They would want him to shake, to tremble. To cry. They'd want him imperfect and falling apart, to see their own security in the way Sabre trembled and shook in their presence.

Maybe I would have done better by him, if I'd left him for quarry carts. None of the other houses had bothered to barter for him, but Laurent knew his was the only house that could take Sabre and help him actually pay off his debt. His clients would request Sabre, and pay handsomely for the privilege, but the challenge would be if Sabre would survive it, mentally, enough to have some kind of a life once the ledger under his name reached *zero*.

"Rose. She says she's your sister."

"Did she tell you how she's better looking?" Laurent laughed. "She says that, I'm sure. I adopted her, officially, once I left the House of Gold."

Sabre's shoulders were shaking. "I—she reminded me of—"

"Don't say it." Laurent wiped his fingers on the linen napkin and reached out, tugged Sabre's hair. "Keep something for yourself, of them. They're going to take all the rest from you."

"Who," Sabre whispered, and oh, this beautiful creature. If only he'd been free to come there, kneel for Laurent and beg so sweetly for the lash, to cry. He was going to break every time for all of them, every single client, and that was the horror of it. Laurent would make thousands of crowns, his house would flourish, and Sabre would one day earn enough to leave this world behind.

A broken shell of a man, made to live his family's death over and over again, for the cruel pleasures of nobles who might have been eager enough to throw their lot in with his family, if only they hadn't been caught.

Laurent smoothed Sabre's hair back, tipped his chin up, caught his breath at the tears spilling crystalline and beautiful over Sabre's sharp cheekbones. He wondered if that's what swayed the king, that this noble cried too prettily to be wasted on the hangman's noose. "The nobles who will pay me for a night with you. They will make you suffer it, over and over, and take their pleasure of you while they do it. They will want you to come, too. Degrade you in the worst way. I won't lie, Sabre. You'll make back your debt, but it might drive you mad."

Sabre's breath caught, and he made a noise too broken to be a laugh. "I think I. Already...did you ever read that story. About the man they caught for, for something, I don't remember, but they. They. Hanged him, and. He thought he escaped, ran home, and before he embraced his wife…realized it had all been. Just a fantasy as he fell, the seconds before his—his neck—"

Sabre started to weep.

"I missed that one," Laurent said, who hadn't learned to read until he came to the House of Gold. If he hadn't been beautiful and strange, *exotic*, he would have gone somewhere worse than the most exalted of the pleasure houses. "It sounds like something they'd write in Katoikos. They do like their melodrama, I'm told." The top earner in the House of Gold, Absolon Sonnerie, had been fond of Katoikos melodramas. They usually involved an Arkoudai soldier carrying them off and ravishing them to the death, at the end. Literally.

"I feel as if that is me," Sabre said. "And any moment, the rope will snap. And at least it will be dark enough that I don't see them, anymore, when I close my eyes."

"Ah, pretty thing, but you should have been taken from your family long ago, given to someone who could keep you as you deserve. Hurt you, fuck you, break you and put you under, then put you back together again." Laurent stroked his fingers over Sabre's mouth. "Would you like me to send you to them? Your family. I will mix the herbs myself, I swear you will feel nothing. You will sleep and it will be over."

Sabre hauled in a shaking breath, and somehow, even that was still beautiful. "Yes. I want that so badly I ache."

Something clawed at Laurent's chest, kicked around inside him, hot and unpleasant. "If that is truly what you desire, I'll see it done." He knew how, he'd mixed them before once or twice and heard about it, every so often. There were courtesans in the houses who could not make their debt, and when they fell out of favor with the nobles their houses would release them by selling their debt elsewhere. Faced with the choice between either the harsh labor of the quarry camps, or the brutish whorehouses in the lower cities, they chose the drink that sent them sweetly into death.

"Why? You should have no love for nobles, not after that long serving them." Sabre blinked up at him, face wet, copper eyes so lovely and bright. "I heard what happened, the exploitation you undergo, here."

"Sabre, we're not talking about me." Laurent's voice was gentle, but full of dominance. "I'm no monster and you're no traitor, but I would have you understand what it means, to stay in my house, to serve clients. The kind we have, they want the things that skirt the darker edges of pleasure. And the thing is, I think you might like those things. And I'm not sure that won't make it worse."

Sabre turned his face into Laurent's head, because he was clearly eager for touch. "And you'd let me…leave? Wouldn't they, wouldn't you be charged with murder?"

Oh, this poor little fawn, thinking he mattered enough for that. "No," Laurent said, stroking his face, his jaw, ignoring the slow burn of heat at how Sabre responded to his touch. "But there is something you should consider. The nobles, they talk. Learn to break for them and put yourself together again, and you'll learn things. Secrets. They hand them out like candy, thinking you harmless. If you want to die and join your family, I'll help you. If you want to live and find out the truth…I'll help you do that, too."

"That is treason," Sabre said, shaking.

Laurent shrugged. "I may be a noble, but too many of them will never think of me as anything other than a whore. The truth, Sabre, is that I've found whores to be far more honorable." He smiled. If Sabre were a little less traumatized, he'd lean down and kiss him.

"Do you know what happened to my family," Sabre whispered. "Who framed them."

Laurent wasn't entirely sure that they *were* framed, but he'd prefer Sabre at least try and put some distance between himself and his mother and sister's execution before choosing to follow them into the dark. "I don't, sweet thing. But I know some who might, nobles who talk in their sleep, you might say. There is no better way for you to find the truth, if you really want it. But keep in mind, bright eyes. It might not be the truth you want."

"I know it wasn't true. I know they weren't guilty." Sabre might have been a submissive, but he was the son and heir of a noble line, and for a moment Laurent saw the shades of it there, the mysterious *noblesse oblige* that gave some the right to rule. "If I could prove it."

It was unlikely that it would matter, but at least he'd be alive at the end of it. "Earn out your debt and search for your answers. They want you to choose an easy death, and I cannot say I'd blame you if you did. But if you want to try, I'll do what I can to help you."

"Why?"

Laurent smiled. "A good question. Maybe one day I'll tell you. You'll have to choose to trust me, Sabre. Let me guide you. I'll teach you how to make it better, how to survive it. If nothing else, it will make them all angry. Spite is a powerful motivator."

Sabre breathed out, then tilted his chin up. Something sharp flashed in his eyes. Some untempered steel, but it would be enough, Laurent thought, to start with. "Save your herbs. For now, anyway."

"A wise choice," Laurent said, then gave in, leaned in, and pressed a soft kiss to his forehead. "Now, let's go. I've got someone to introduce you to. He wasn't here last night, because he's one of my most popular courtesans. Charon is a dominant, a sadist, and the best, most amazing cuddler I've ever met."

"What," said Sabre, blinking as he got to his feet. "Did you say —cuddler?"

"You'll see," said Laurent, and went to dress. "But first, we'll have to make sure you apologize profusely for waking him up."

CHAPTER 3

Sabre wasn't exactly sure what he'd been expecting.

His family didn't go in for hedonism. There were rooms for playing with their various partners, if they ever brought them home—which Sabre didn't, not after his mother terrified the last one —but those rooms were generally kept locked up in favor of more practical ones, like their private sparring courts or the library, or the circular room with a map of the world painted on the floor, where Sabre taught Elise how to dance.

The Crescent Chamber was set next to the baths, which were currently in use by a pair of courtesans with long, honey-blond hair and a stack of books propped dangerously close to the edge. One of them Sabre recognized from his first night, or he thought so—The courtesans could have been twins, if not for the slightly more pronounced nose on the one reading from a book so worn the title had lost its gilding.

"Oh, I like this one," he said, as Sabre was pushed firmly toward the connecting door. "*Our hearts beat as one in a maelstrom of desire.* Write that down."

"Should be a hurricane," the other said.

"What? No. Maelstrom's *romantic.*"

Laurent closed the door to the Crescent Chamber after Sabre, leaving them in the dark. "That was Percival and Gwydion," he said, and snapped his fingers, activating a ring of magelight globes fixed throughout the room. "Don't let them drag you into one of their productions, and you'll be fine."

Sabre's breath caught as his eyes adjusted to the light, and Laurent smiled.

The Crescent Chamber was a windowless room, with wooden paneling on the walls and a cold tile floor, scattered with cushions. Hooks hung from the ceiling and walls. A swing, a complicated mess of straps and cushion and little cuffs Sabre assumed were for feet, swayed slightly nearby. There were multiple flogging stations, a wall of canes, whips, floggers and other tools Sabre didn't think could be used in play before that moment, a chair with—

"Oh," Sabre said. "Those are stocks."

"That's the first thing you notice?" Laurent asked, and Sabre felt his cheeks burn. His gaze skittered over the cage next to the stocks, the worrying drain in a patch of empty floor, and settled on a bench padded with leather, with straps attached and a frame with phalluses on either side.

"This room is available to any of our courtesans during off hours," Laurent said, as Sabre touched the edge of the bench. There was a lever there, with marks at different angles. He pulled it to the lowest mark, and jumped as the phallus started *moving*, thrusting into the empty air. "Not yet, precious."

"Fuck." Sabre pushed the lever back.

"Is there anything you haven't seen before?" Laurent asked.

Sabre still felt dazed, and more than a little distant from his own body, after his talk with Laurent in his rooms. He'd come so close, so close to ending whatever plans the king had for him, and he could feel the pull of it low in his gut, a wrongness that told Sabre he was still on borrowed time. A few days ago, Sabre would have paid half his own wages from the family allowance to have Laurent use one of those flexible canes and *possibly* the stocks on him, but it wouldn't *be*

Laurent, when the time came. It would be one of his family's enemies, striking him until he bled just to see him break.

To think that would be what it took to get someone to see to him properly. His mother used to complain that Sabre was too much of a slave to his desires, submissive to a fault. He wondered if she'd seen that in him, the yearning for pain that went beyond what others thought acceptable.

"I haven't seen most of this," Sabre said. A small part of him hated how *dull* he sounded. It was like he was already dead, dragging his body around after him. "What does that do? That saddle, in the corner?"

Laurent's eyes flashed with heat. "Another machine. Tests your endurance."

"My endurance is very good, I think," Sabre said, and looked down as Laurent met his gaze. "Physically, I mean. I could have gone longer, last night."

"That's only half of it," Laurent said. "And yes, I noticed."

"Charon," Sabre said. "He knows about the other half?"

Laurent's shadow slid over Sabre's feet, and he gripped Sabre by the chin, making him look him in the eyes. Sabre's gaze kept dragging away. "He's skilled at breaking nobles."

Sabre took a shivery breath. "Why is it I think you are, as well, my lord?"

"That's not what I'm known for," Laurent said, which wasn't an answer. He hooked his fingers in Sabre's collar, running his thumb over the scales, and Sabre felt, for a moment, like he was being dragged back into his body, a kite on the end of a string, scraping over the rocks.

The door swung open, and Sabre startled like a deer before the bow. Laurent sighed and drew back, patting Sabre's cheek as a giant of a man darkened the door.

"Oh, no," Sabre said, softly, and Laurent *laughed.*

The man walking into the Crescent Chamber looked like he could feature on the cover of every one of the terrible Katoikos *Illustrated Feature,* which Sabre had hoarded as a young man and usually included drawings of muscular Arkoudes slinging pampered nobles over their shoulders and bending them in half. It was a popular publication with Starian nobles, who liked to see Katoikos nobles get fucked within an inch of their lives or *wanted* to have an Arkouda break them six ways without trying, and Sabre had an entire collection of them before his father found them.

"Sabre," he'd said, slowly feeding the comics to the fire as Sabre wilted in front of his desk like a mortified violet. "I can assure you that there's a very, *very* low chance that you'll even meet one of these people, let alone be…" He'd read one of the pages, grinning to himself. "Goodness, where *did* his arm go?"

Years later, Sabre looked up at an Arkouda man with a gallery of tattoos on his bare skin, and grabbed the edge of the bench for support.

"Charon," Laurent said, sounding far too amused. "Sleep well?"

"Ask me when I've slept," Charon said. His voice carried a dominance as powerful as Sabre's mother, if not more, and Sabre cursed under his breath. His dark hair was braided back out of his face, and when he looked at Sabre, he lowered his brows and started forward. It was like being glared down by a dragon.

"Why is this submissive clothed," Charon said, in a dangerous tone. "And standing."

"Sorry," Sabre said. He dropped to his knees, banged his elbow on the machine, and cursed. Laurent covered his eyes with a hand. "I. Should I."

"Did I give you permission to speak," Charon said, in a voice like thunder, as Sabre started dragging off his borrowed robe.

"No. Should I not have? Was I supposed to answer just n—"

"Did your lord give you permission to speak," Charon said.

Sabre looked at Laurent, desperately. Laurent just leaned against the wall and raised his brows.

"Is this part of the training?"

Charon sighed, tipped up Sabre's chin with a finger, and backhanded him so hard he toppled to the tile. Sabre lay there for a second, breathing hard, pleasure jolting through him in a way he didn't think possible, even when writhing under the lash the night before.

"Were you given permission to speak," Charon said.

Carefully, still lying on his side, Sabre shook his head.

Charon rolled him onto his back, and Sabre's pulse quickened, pounding in his ears. "You think this one's a masochist. A proper one."

"Possibly," Laurent said.

Charon stood over Sabre, his face shadowed by the light at his back. "Mm. I don't think this one knows, himself." Sabre opened his mouth to protest, and Charon leaned down to gag him with his thick fingers, filling him, pressing down on his tongue. "We will see how far you will bend for me, little noble. First, you will apologize for making me come here when I could be on my balcony, having a good morning, not having to break Starian nobles who think they might be a masochist. And you will thank me for the privilege."

* * *

Laurent settled back against the wall, watching as Sabre tried to catch his breath.

Charon was an asset to the House of Onyx, and one of Laurent's top earners even if the masochists who so eagerly came to see him never lasted beyond half an hour at most before they broke. Still, there was no shortage of nobles who thought they could handle Charon's attentions, even if it had yet to happen. Laurent suspected the true reason was that the man had a talent for aftercare that none in the house could rival—he gave amazing hugs, and seemed to know exactly how to bring a sobbing submissive gently back to himself or herself. There was a noblewoman who booked time with him simply to have him spank her until she cried over enough layers that it wouldn't leave a mark, then the majority of her session had Charon hugging her, bathing her, and brushing her hair.

Some came with visions of being the first true masochist to handle the full extent of Charon's sadism, but it had yet to happen. For all that he made good coin, he seemed utterly disinterested in paying off his debt. Unlike the others, who put the majority of their tips and trinkets toward their debt, Charon used his to fill his rooms with historical artifacts, old maps, and books. He was particularly interested in the Lukoi, the Wolf People of the far northern island, and discovering the mystery of the kingdom that had exiled them there so long ago. Some mornings, Laurent would find him on his balcony sipping his one indulgence—the strong, distinctive Arktos tea he imported without a thought for its price against his debt—and reading books about the Lukoi, trying to learn the language. The only thing he'd ever mentioned wanting when he left Laurent's employ was to have enough money to take an expedition there and see it for himself.

Laurent assumed Charon wouldn't go back to Arktos—he didn't know why Charon left and had never asked, but Arkoudai didn't immigrate, ever. He assumed Charon must be a fugitive, but that wasn't any of his business.

"Look at you," Charon said, now, to Sabre. "I have many come to see me, wanting to feel the back of my hand. They pretend to fight, sometimes. They cry, always." He stepped back. "Get up and we will see what you can take of my hand, my lash. Hurry, boy. I have better things to do than waste my time with you, today."

Sabre looked as shocked as Laurent imagined he must have, when the king pulled him from the gallows—the story was already everywhere, of course, he probably had a stack of requests already for Sabre's company on the desk in his office—as he scrambled to his feet and stood shaking before the implacable force of Charon's quiet command. Charon moved him around like he was nothing, stripping the robe from him, shackling him to the hooks on the ceilings.

"If you come without my permission, rabbit, you'll be very sorry."

He used the old Senex word for *rabbit*, which was the insult the Arkoudai called the Katoikos.

Sabre didn't say anything as Charon positioned him, checking the cuffs and ensuring he wasn't up on his feet too much to cause a strain. He'd known all of this when he'd presented himself to Laurent for a position in the house, and Laurent had a feeling whatever Charon did before, in Arktos or perhaps elsewhere, it involved doing much the same thing, only very likely for people who weren't supposed to like it.

"Hmm." Charon studied Sabre with his usual calm disinterest, but he ran a hand down Sabre's back, gentle as he planned out exactly how to wreck him. "I know there are obvious things that would work, my lord. But that isn't what you want to see, is it?"

"No," Laurent said. He knew what Charon meant. A man who'd nearly hanged to death would be easy to ruin with a belt around the neck, or Charon's hand. And later, perhaps, they'd get to that. But that took no finesse, only brutality. And Charon was as careful a man as Laurent had ever met.

"Fear, for you, I think," Charon said. He turned and left Sabre strung up there, rustling through some items that he kept specifically for a very sort of client—military veterans or Misthrotoi mercenaries with too much guilt over their kills, he'd told Laurent. And the only reason Sabre was hearing him at all, was because Charon was letting him. "If you had a choice, rabbit, which would you choose to make you suffer? To be beaten with bare hands, to be whipped until your spine showed through, or pierced with the sharp blade of a knife?"

"The—the lash." Sabre's voice was a quiet tremble, but he answered immediately, no thought given at all to what he'd choose.

Charon set a whip aside, the long single-tail kind, the one that could make a submissive weep just from the crack of the air and the sound of it. "And then?"

"Someone's hands."

"Yes. All right." Charon picked up a knife, gleaming in the soft light of the room. "Then we will begin with the knife. That is what you fear. Sharp pain, pointed, that you cannot get lost in."

Sabre pulled against the cuffs, shaking like a leaf.

"They put your hands behind your back, on the gallows," Charon said. "If I wanted to terrify you, I would have done the same. Do you know the difference, between terror and fear? You will need to. That's what they'll want."

"Please," Sabre sobbed, but Laurent wasn't sure if he knew what he was asking for.

"Terror, that is of little use to anyone. It makes the body shut down. Impossible to do anything, react." Charon moved to press the tip of the knife against Sabre's back, and smiled when Sabre jumped at the press of it. "Fear, little rabbit. That's different. The heart races, the breath comes too fast. You flinch at the slightest sound."

Laurent did love watching Charon work over someone.

"You are not terrified, not of me, now, I would imagine. You know you are not here to be slaughtered, cut down to bone. But there's a fear there, even if you know that. Fear, and for you, it is something else, too, eh?" He looked over at Laurent, dark brows raised.

Laurent, who could see what this was doing to Sabre, said, "Yes, his body is certainly reacting."

Charon walked in front of Sabre, traced the tip of the knife over his face, the corner of his eye. When Sabre jerked reflexively, Charon dropped his hand and smacked him, hard, with the other. "Be still. You don't need both of your eyes to serve these nobles who will want you. Just one, so you can see the pleasure they take in frightening you." He placed the tip of the knife against the corner of Sabre's eye, and this time, Sabre did not move. Charon nodded. "Good." He dropped the knife down, over the curve of Sabre's throat—Sabre moved his head back, just a bit, to allow Charon to trace the knife above the collar.

"You don't fear this, enough," Charon said. He reached out and caught Sabre with his free hand, squeezed his fingers.

Sabre began twisting, legs kicking.

"That is fear," Charon said. He tightened his hand and lifted Sabre, bodily, and Sabre made a terrified sound that turned in a gasping, choking noise. Then he froze up. Charon nodded. "That is terror." He put Sabre back down, smacked him hard on his cock, and said, "We'll try something else. You are a pretty man, little noble, I would like, I think, to see you cry. If my lord will allow it."

"He certainly will," Laurent said, warmly.

"The lash, because you took that well, I think." Charon picked up a strip of black cloth. Every other dominant in the house, including Laurent, used a blindfold for this. Only Charon did the strip of black cloth. "Where I am from, Arkoudai only cover the eyes for those we care nothing about. You are exiled for crimes against the state, but for treason, it is death. Arkoudai believe that to watch the light fade from someone's eyes as they die, this is sacred. The light must be seen to leave. A myth, perhaps. But it is why we cover the eyes of those we condemn."

The strip in his hands was one of the few things Charon brought with him. Laurent watched as Charon tied it with something like reverence around Sabre's head. "I could do anything I wanted to you, like this. That's it, writhe for me, pull on your chains. The nobles won't have my deft hand with it, but we'll teach you to like it. There's no better way to ruin their plans, rabbit, than to turn your throat to the knife. Shudder in ecstasy from the pain. They'll like it enough, and you won't lose yourself."

Charon patted him on the shoulder. He must like Sabre, Laurent thought, to be so solicitous of him. "I will hurt you now, as you should be hurt. Scream if you want, pretty rabbit. It won't stop until I'm ready to let you down."

Charon looked at Laurent, who was insanely curious but who knew enough not to bother his prize sadist at work. He nodded, and Charon took up the single-tail. The noise and the crack of air was enough to make Sabre jerk in his chains, body thrashing, but nothing drew a sound from him. Charon looked pleased, but his voice was even when he said, "Do you know Senex, the old tongue?"

"I, yes, Lessons, not for—please," Sabre babbled, twisting.

"I asked one thing, you answer one thing. This one, he'll need lessons I cannot give. Protocol, for your submissives, here. Arkoudai submissives are, ah. They fight you. Make you earn it. The proper way to kneel, they'll tell you, is how they look on their knees when you earn the right to put them there."

"Mm," Laurent said. "I think we need to revisit Yves' thought about a themed Arkoudai and Katoikos ball. Sonnerie, from the House of Gold. He's part Katoikos, he must be, or he looks it well enough. You can toss him over your shoulder and carry him around."

Charon snorted, quietly, and turned back to Sabre. "The point remains, my lord. You will need him to learn the pretty lessons—maybe Yves. He could use a task. Always bothering me, asking for my tea. He charms those men who like obedience."

Laurent chuckled. "He does indeed. Sabre, answer only what is asked of you."

"Count in Senex," said Charon, and raised the whip.

Laurent enjoyed the way Sabre thrashed beneath the whip, but it still took him until five to make a sound, and Charon was putting increasing strength behind the blows. At eight, he bloodied Sabre's back, and Sabre moaned.

"Hmm," said Charon, and went back to work. He caned Sabre's upper thighs, which got only a gasp, and then lower, where there was more muscle and where it was traditionally used as a punishment. That got him another moan, and Charon switched again. He left the blindfold on as he attached the weighted clamps to Sabre's nipples and his balls, and one to his tongue, then flogged him until he got more of those gasps that seemed torn from him, while Sabre finally started to grow louder and louder and his cock, Laurent noticed, harder between his legs.

For the last, Charon took the clamps away and unhooked him, dragged Sabre by the hair to his knees and fastened him unceremoniously to the clips on the floor. He kicked him in the ribs, once, watched carefully as Sabre curled into himself. For all his moans and gasps, he still didn't cry. Charon was silent as he removed the strip of black fabric, placing it reverently back in the small chest that contained all of his personal implements. He took out a pistol, one favored by the Starian nobility for their duels, nothing like the rifles carried by the ranks of dark-eyed, impassive Arkoudai soldiers.

Charon went and stood above Sabre, who was shackled to the floor with his wrists on either side of him and his ankles behind him while he knelt. He blinked up at Charon, who pressed the tip of the barrel to Sabre's mouth. "Open, take it."

His dominance was so strong that Laurent felt it, too. His own mouth was a little dry as he watched Charon start to fuck Sabre's mouth with the gun. And he couldn't deny his cock was growing hard watching Charon work Sabre over so well. It took all of his trust in Charon, however, not to object when Charon very deliberately cocked the hammer back.

He knew it wasn't loaded—Charon fucked nobles with the gun, sometimes. Maybe a different one. But it was still something, to see it.

"In Arkoudai we execute our traitors by firing squad. Eyes covered, so no one sees the light leave. Are you afraid, little rabbit?"

Sabre nodded, or tried. His eyes were wide, and when Charon slid the gun in deeper, he started to choke.

"Maybe, eh, maybe I am here because I am a traitor, too." He slid the gun in and out, starting to fuck his mouth. "Maybe I've been bribed by the king's men, to make you feel safe, to make you moan in pleasure before I shot you."

Before Laurent could blink, Charon pulled the trigger.

Sabre's entire body shook and he cried out around the gun, eyes reflexively squeezing shut but of course there was no bullet in the gun. When Charon pulled the barrel free, Sabre was sobbing, softly.

"There, that's fear, little rabbit. Not knowing when it is coming for you." He stroked the side of Sabre's face with the tip of the muzzle, which was wet. "Kiss it. Thank me for instructing you."

Sabre turned his head, pressed his mouth to the barrel, and hiccupped something vaguely *thank you* sounding out.

Charon cleaned the gun and let Sabre kneel, crying, then came to stand before Laurent. "That is, as surprised as I am, the only true masochist I have ever met in the noble court of Staria."

There wasn't really much about it that was noble, but Laurent kept that to himself. "It would seem so. Thank you for that. It was, ah. I see why you make me so much money."

Charon gave him a small, rare smile. "It isn't often I get to show off for you, my lord."

"Why don't you do it for me some more, and take his mouth,"

Laurent offered. "Then you can find Yves, and later, if you wouldn't mind...show our Sabre what else you're known for, in our house."

"As you wish." It was obvious Charon was aroused; He was a big man, and his cock pressed against the loose-fitting trousers he wore. He crossed the floor and took Sabre by the hair, pulling his head back. "You will choke on my cock like you choked on the gun, cry for me, make it wet and messy. Make me come."

"Yes, my lord," Sabre mumbled.

"Ah, rabbit. I am no lord." He ran a thumb over Sabre's bottom lip as he freed his cock with his other hand; Laurent remembered how he'd told him, once, that all Arkoudai learned to use both hands in case they lost one in battle. They were as dramatic as their Katoikos cousins, in their own way. "You are under, and if you must, you can call me *sir*, as they did once, where I am from."

"Yes, sir," said Sabre, and opened his mouth, eyes sliding shut as Charon fed him his cock.

Laurent let himself rub a hand over his own cock as he watched, enjoying the simple pleasure of seeing two attractive people in the midst of natural power exchange. And then he made himself focus instead on Sabre's technique, which was sloppy but in a way that Charon clearly liked, given how hard he started to fuck Sabre's mouth.

It was enough that Sabre was making ugly choking sounds and Charon was on edge, moaning, holding Sabre close as he fucked his throat. Laurent had learned to suck cock like it was a dance done before the court, but the sorts of clients who came to Sabre would like this rough, unpolished desperation he showed, his lack of trained technique. But he could use some lessons on how to tilt his head, hold his tears until the client earned them.

"Come on his face," Laurent said, his dominance roused, unable to help himself.

Charon did so, holding Sabre by the hair and coming all over his tear-streaked face with a quiet little moan.

"Spit in his mouth," Laurent said.

Charon didn't even have to tell Sabre to open his mouth or hold it open, Sabre just did it and let him, swaying on his knees, limp and looking just as satisfied even though his cock was still achingly hard and he hadn't come.

It was obvious that he wanted to do something, caretake like he always did, but he acquiesced to Laurent's wishes and went to find Yves.

Laurent went to where Sabre was kneeling, and went to his knees in front of him so he could get him out of the cuffs. "I will clean your face, let Yves give you some lessons in protocol. But for now, I want to know how you feel. If you're under. What put you there. And if you do that, I'll make you come for me, let you beg for it, and give your body what it wants."

* * *

SABRE STAYED ON HIS KNEES, holding himself up with his hands on his thighs, and stared down at the tile beneath him. He wasn't shaking. He had felt the pull of the trigger in his *throat*, in his stomach, in every piece of him, like swallowing thunder. Now he was silent, the way a storm made the city silent, rain obscuring the lower circles as Sabre leaned against his bedroom window to watch it all disappear.

"I have an instructor," Sabre said. "My father's old friend, who served with him in the army. Isiodore. He taught me how to fight, with fists, and the sword. My father approved of the latter. Not so much the former."

He almost smiled, just for a moment, thinking of the day he'd come home after his first bout, twelve years old with his eye swollen shut. *He says he's sorry you didn't teach me how to duck.* His father had groaned, pushed away from his chair, and stormed off to have a word with Isiodore himself. He came back only to clear out the drawing room so he could teach Sabre a few tips of his own. It became a tradition, a friendly competition with Sabre caught in the middle, and it ended with Sabre knowing far more about how to win a fight than was reasonably proper.

Laurent crouched before him, his pretty face unreadable.

"He taught me how to be still." Sabre's voice sounded…more like himself, like this. Like who he was. His accent was richer, less dull and short. "I didn't like being still before. I'd stand there and he'd lunge, bring the sword just here." He touched his ear. He could still feel the silky rush of air against his face. "Closed my eyes. I learned to like it, being still. This is like that. There's a blade somewhere, in the dark, but I'm here, too."

"And what brought you here?" Laurent asked. He stroked the side of Sabre's head, and Sabre leaned into it like a pleased cat.

"Fear," Sabre said, and this time, he actually laughed. It startled him, foreign and strange, and Laurent pulled at his hair until Sabre was back in that place again, the stillness. "I was under, I think, when he took out the gun. I went deeper, after."

"The threat was part of it, wasn't it," Laurent said. "That he might be here to hurt you, beyond what you need. To make you suffer."

"Yes. The blade in the dark."

"Well." Laurent tugged at his hair again. "Now you know it can be done. And do you want to come, now that you've earned it, pretty thing?"

"Ah. Yes. I think so. Yes, my lord." Sabre slowly met his gaze. It was difficult—he wanted to look down—but he thought Laurent might like it, to be seen. Admired. "If you want me to."

"That's how you beg, is it?" Laurent's tone was hard, but there was amusement there, in his unnatural violet eyes.

"How would you like me to beg?" Sabre turned his head to kiss Laurent's fingers, and Laurent's eyes widened, just a fraction. *Make me come?* Too demanding. You should do what you want with me."

"He's too submissive to ask to come," Laurent said to the air. "Yves will teach you that, as well. You're desperate, I can feel it." He ran his fingers over Sabre's hard, flushed cock, and Sabre shivered. "Show me that desperation. Clean that mess off your face, show me your throat."

Sabre responded instinctively to the dominance in Laurent's voice, raising a hand to his face. He ran his fingers through the mess there, tasted it, gasped as Laurent wrapped his fingers around Sabre's cock.

"You won't come until you beg me for it," Laurent said, and oh, but

Sabre was too close already, and he had to tense, his breath short, eyelids fluttering closed.

"Please," Sabre said. "Please, my lord, if you, if you wish it, please may I." He moaned, felt a tremor roll through him. "May I come, my lord?"

"Yes," Laurent said, and Sabre shuddered as he came, head thrown back, hands grasping. He could feel Laurent's gaze on him as he panted for breath, and he leaned forward, reaching for him.

Laurent waited only a moment before he rose to his feet.

"Ah." Sabre raised a hand as he stepped away.

"I'm not leaving you," Laurent said, in a bemused voice. He went to a tap in the corner and pulled down a pair of clean cloths hanging above it. He wet them and took down a vial as well, which he set down next to Sabre before he knelt in front of him again. Sabre was quiet as he cleaned his face, but frowned slightly when Laurent dotted the second cloth with something from the vial and made him turn around.

"The skin broke," Laurent said, pressing the cloth to Sabre's back. "I know you masochists love to keep your bruises as souvenirs, but an infection is another matter. It's shallow, at least."

"Oh." Sabre tried not to sound disappointed, but Laurent snorted inelegantly behind him.

"Yes, tragic."

There was a sound of splashing in the other room, and a pattering of feet on tile. Sabre looked up as Yves entered, dressed in a black shirt that glittered faintly and. Well.

"You don't *have* to wear what your clients give you, Yves," Laurent said.

Yves snapped the band of his…shorts…which clung to his thighs like they were painted on. "At least it doesn't have his name embroidered on it, this time."

"Small favors," Laurent drawled. He patted Sabre on the back. "You're done. Yves, Sabre is recovering from Charon at the moment. If you could show him how to kneel properly, what to say to a dominant when they give him orders, I can go make sure no one is setting the house on fire."

"Yes, my lord, of course," Yves said. His gaze flicked over Laurent. "You said *Charon?* How far did he get?"

"He fired a gun in my mouth," Sabre said, pleasantly, and Yves stared.

"Huh. That's nice."

"And you can show him how to clean the toys, as well," Laurent said, smiling down at Yves as he passed. "Sabre, report to Charon again when you're done."

Yves waited until he was out the door before he let his face fall.

"Sorry," Sabre said.

Yves shrugged. "It's fine. I was in your shoes a few months ago, anyways. I mean, not really, but I was still new, you know? You're gonna do so much laundry, you have no idea. Your *life* is gonna be laundry."

Yves sat down in front of Sabre. He had a mass of freckles under his olive skin, and he was wearing a silver necklace with an elaborate pendant, which swung heavily when he moved.

"Okay," he said. "Show me how you kneel."

Sabre blinked at him. "I am."

There was a long, heavy silence.

"Well, you're on your knees," Yves said, in the way Isiodore would say, *You're still standing,* after Sabre failed to dodge a blow. "Wow. You're actually noble? Don't they know these things?"

"I'm the only submissive left in my house," Sabre said, and frowned. "And Cousin Adrien, I suppose."

"Cousin—" Yves dragged a hand down his face. "You call the crown prince *Cousin Adrien.*"

"Yes, he's a little shy, maybe, but…" Sabre grimaced. "Oh. I suppose I shouldn't, anymore."

"You didn't sound so posh before, either," Yves said. "What did Charon—No, don't say it. I know. A *gun. Masochists.* So how about we start small, okay?"

Yves spent a short time teaching Sabre, with varying levels of success, how to kneel, how to look up at someone from under his lids, how to say *yes my lord,* and *please, my lord,* almost like he meant it.

The fake moaning, though, that was a little harder to manage.

"Look, you never faked it before?" Yves asked, after a minute of it. "You've been with people before. Some of them had to suck."

"All of them," Sabre said. "Except, ah, here, they're very..." He waved a hand, vaguely.

"Yeah, Charon had me sobbing in half a second on my first demo," Yves said. "Have you ever seen a gorgeous, twenty foot sadist and just burst into tears? Thank goodness I left the country." He kissed his fingers and raised them to the sky. "Anyways. So you had to pretend to like it, right, to make the shitty ones think they did okay and leave happy?"

Sabre stared at him.

Yves sputtered out a laugh. "You just. You didn't even. You just *left* them there."

"I couldn't *lie,*" Sabre said, blushing hot.

"You're kind of precious," Yves said. "Wow. *Wow.* I am speechless. You've actually rendered me speechless."

"You're still talking, though."

Yves scoffed. "Details. Right. We'll just have to keep working on it, yeah? Give it time, and you'll be moaning and fake crying with the rest of us. No problem."

Sabre was still drifting by the time they were done cleaning off the toys, but Yves was almost comforting to have around, with his slight country burr and his endless stream of gossip about the various clients who wanted to hire him as their personal, private sugar baby.

"Two of them almost dueled over who got my first night," Yves said, as he led Sabre downstairs. "That's, you know, your first client. They pretend they deflowered you, and you act all timid and shy like a noble at their first—oh."

"It's fine," Sabre said.

"That's never not gonna be weird, though." Yves knocked on a door at the end of a narrow hall, which opened to reveal Charon, still massive, still covered in tattoos, but not nearly as…chilling, as he was with his hand on Sabre's neck. He gave Sabre a considering look.

"One weird-ass masochist, just for you," Yves said, and patted Sabre on the back. "How're you stocked on tea, by the way? I have some in my room if you want to—"

"Thank you, Yves," Charon said. Yves smiled brightly.

"Any time."

Charon gestured for Sabre to come in and closed the door on Yves. Sabre only got a glimpse of a high bookshelf, a tea service, maps stretched out across the walls, before Charon took his face in both hands.

"Let me see you, rabbit," he said, and Sabre made a soft sound as Charon pulled him down into a frankly enormous couch, settling him over his lap. He ran his hand over Sabre's back, pressing lightly on the marks he'd left, stopping over the healed cut on his shoulder.

"Ah, he removed it," he said.

"Yes, he insisted," Sabre said. He wasn't whining, not really, but Charon patted him sympathetically on his sore shoulder all the same. He moved so Sabre could sit up, but wrapped an arm around Sabre's middle, keeping his back pressed to Charon's chest. The marks of the whip and cane stung, but it was light, pleasant, a comforting reminder.

"Next time, you will keep it longer, eh," Charon said. His voice was warm, still threaded with dominance, but the sort that made Sabre want to sink into his hold and lay there for the rest of the day. "A reward."

"Ah, yes," Sabre said. He was starting to understand what Laurent had meant, before. "Yes, please."

CHAPTER 4

hile Charon petted Sabre and showed off his aftercare skills, Laurent took himself to his office and stared in horror at the assortment of cards on his desk.

"You keep getting mail," Rose said, breezing in. She dumped another handful on his desk. "Is this all about Epee?"

"Sabre," said Laurent.

"Does he get to keep his name?" Rose asked. "Or are you gonna change it?"

Laurent fixed her with a look. "You know there are some aspects of this business I don't want to discuss with you, and this is one of them. But, no. Part of Sabre's...appeal, to the nobles, will be his name. But I've got a few ideas. And none of them are appropriate for you to know about."

Rose stuck her tongue out. "He seems nice."

Only his sister would say that, *he seems nice*, about a noble whose family were put to death as traitors, and who might not have ever noticed Rose enough to stop her from being thrown in front of a cart. But maybe that was wrong of him. "He'll be all right. Run along, little sister. I've got work to do."

When Rose flounced off, he turned his attention to the cards awaiting his perusal. They weren't *all* for Sabre; There were the usual requests for Charon, for Yves, and for the rest of the house. Laurent went through all of them, consulted his ledger so he could make the appropriate notes, and then sent the replies with appointments to the nobles who'd requested them.

And then he looked at the requests for Sabre.

One was from Adrien de Guillory, the crown prince of Staria.

Lord Laurent de Rue,

Please accept my request to host Sabre de Valois for his first night. I will pay whatever will be of most use to him, in satisfying the debt to the House of Onyx. You may be assured I will treat him with the utmost respect and—

Laurent groaned and put his head in his hands.

"My lord."

"Charon," Laurent said, recognizing the voice and leaving his head exactly where it was. "How is Sabre?"

"Asleep. I took the liberty of carrying him to your bed."

"Not yours?" Laurent glanced up. Charon looked as imperturbable as always, with his eyes that marked him as a descendant of the First Citizens of Katoikos, and the neatly-trimmed beard that said he was from Arktos. "I thought you might keep him busy, the rest of the day."

Charon shrugged. "I would, if you asked it of me. He is drifting, asleep. Could use it, probably, without the dreams that will come."

Laurent was so curious about Charon, but he pushed the past aside for the present and waved Prince Adrien's missive. "The prince has requested Sabre's First Night."

"Hmm," said Charon.

"Yeah." Laurent leaned back in his chair and steepled his fingers.

"A boon, for the House, yes?" Charon asked. "But it seems like you do not think so."

"The king did not send Sabre here for his son to become his patron." Just the thought of what it might mean, calling Emile's displeasure down on the house like a storm, made him want to break out into a cold sweat.

"I forget, sometimes, that Prince Adrien is his son," said Charon, with a faint air of distaste. He'd never said anything about the rulership of Arktos, but it was clear he didn't much approve of the capricious whims of a monarch who was not answerable to anyone.

"So does the king," Laurent muttered. He was only one of two courtesans that had ever had the dubious honor of serving a night with the king, and the less Laurent thought about that, the better. He imagined Absolon felt about the same. "I'm touched the prince cares enough to reach out, but it's not going to make anything easier for Sabre, if he does."

"Sabre will not want easy," Charon said. "Once the cruelty of those pleased to see his family fall has run its course, he will work less and earn more. True sadists are rare and true masochists, rarer still."

"You know I want to ask you a million questions about how you even came here and know this," Laurent said.

Charon smiled briefly. "Yes. And I appreciate it that you never have. One day, maybe. My story, you might see me differently."

"I doubt that, but at least you have one. I still don't remember anything about my life before I was ten."

"When I was...before. There was a man, his job was to, ah." He tapped the side of his head. "Find things, control them, here?"

"A brainwasher?" Laurent stared at him. "I just picture Arktos full of hot men who look like you marching in formation, carrying pretty men like Absolon around on your shoulders and women who could beat me up."

"You are not entirely wrong, especially about the women. But perhaps sometime you could visit a man like that, to find what you have lost." Charon was quiet. "Or you could let it stay behind the wall, and not seek it out."

"I could. At the moment, it's about my only choice, since I don't think I'd trust anyone in Staria who'd try to *help* me with brainwashing. No offense to your country."

Charon waved a hand. He looked too big for the chair. "There is another problem, yes, with the prince. Even if he was not the son of the king who caused Sabre's family's downfall, he is a submissive. Our Sabre will be in knots again, the prince will be upset."

"Yes. And I can't protect Sabre from being hurt, that's part of why he's here. I should have, maybe, let him just...go. Take the herbs."

"Maybe," Charon said, who never minced his words. "But you did not, so you must make it work. And I think, if you would know the truth of it, that you have done right by him." He paused. "Is it true, what they say of his family?"

"That they were traitors? I have no idea. King Emile is paranoid enough that they might not have been. But I...well, I'm not going to say this to Sabre, but it's not like I could blame his mother and sister, if they were. The king's always been...like he is, but with Adrien clearly a submissive I know the sharks are circling, so to speak. Not that I want any poor woman to marry him, but without an heir, it'll probably get worse before it gets better." Laurent steepled his fingers under his chin. "How do I turn down the prince, though?"

"You are a house that works under different rules, with, ah, specialty courtesans, yes?" Charon tripped over the word *courtesan*, which was not a word he knew in his language. "I think it would be best if you reached out to someone, asked if they were interested. Made it seem like an honor. Find someone more suited to his needs."

Laurent thought about that. "Sabre said he took fencing from the Duke de Mortain. I know he's the king's closest advisor, but I have suspicions he might be the reason Sabre didn't hang with the rest of his family, and if anyone could handle Emile, it's him."

"Lord Laurent," a voice called out, loudly. "I have a report for you about the—oh. Sorry." Yves appeared in his doorway and gave the most longing look at Charon before he chased it off with his usual bright grin. "I can come back."

"I was just leaving. I will let Sabre sleep, bring him back to you when he's awake." Charon rose and gave Laurent a small nod, like he was a noble and hell, for all Laurent knew about the actual hierarchy in Arktos, he was.

"Yes, good. Thank you again. You should rest, too. You've got a full schedule. Lord Mayburn booked two hours."

"Ah. Then I will nap for an hour and forty five minutes, after he comes too quick and falls asleep."

Yves snorted, and Laurent flashed a grin at him, watching with amusement as Yves stared after Charon like a starving man looking at a buffet. "Sabre is, right now, asleep in your *bed*. Ugh. Can *I* learn to like someone putting a gun in *my* mouth that much?"

"You?" Laurent studied him. "Sure. You're not a masochist and fear isn't your thing, but you're fairly opportunistic and you look pretty with your mouth stretched around something hard."

Yves grinned at him. "I love it here."

Laurent was glad to hear that. He tried to run a house with rules and also make it a safe haven for people who both enjoyed their job and wanted to be there, though Staria was a mess of inequalities and it was impossible to know for sure that his courtesans were motivated purely by the enjoyment of their nighttime activities. Yves, especially, was like a hothouse flower—beautiful and young enough to be courted by starry-eyed nobles, but that sort of beauty faded, and hopefully Yves was putting away something for the future. One of Laurent's rules that differed from other houses was how he did not require tips be turned over toward debt unless that was what the person wanted to do with them. No point in paying off your debt to the house and ending up penniless and broke, which happened to plenty of courtesans who didn't think hard enough about their future.

The whole system was broken, but it was what it was, and Laurent was doing his best. "You could just ask Charon if he wanted to fuck, you know."

"Who says I haven't?" Yves threw himself into the chair, sprawling in it like a brat who needed to be corrected, which was his specialty. "Do you want to know about Sabre? He can't kneel to save his life and he's like a kitten, really."

"His protocol can be addressed, but I think part of his initial appeal will be his, let's say, uncertainty with how to act now," Laurent assured him.

"Hmm. You say that, but one thing I've learned about nobles? They take it as an insult if you're not showing enough respect, and I'm not sure it'll go well, for Sabre, if he's seen as being challenging."

"I don't think that's possible," Laurent said dryly, remembering

Sabre asking how to *ask* to come. "His clients at first are going to be very...let's say, aroused by his being a mess."

"At first, sure. But you don't last in this business if you don't adapt, m'lord. Which you should know better than anyone, yeah?"

Laurent considered this. "You're not wrong. All right, you can keep working with him, but let's wait until the initial interest surges."

"Poor unlucky bastard. I can't imagine being all right with that many people wanting to fuck me up and getting off on my misery."

"That's the nobility for you," Laurent said.

"You *are* the nobility, m'lord," Yves pointed out.

"I know." Laurent picked up some of his hand-stamped *House of Onyx* stationary. "Speaking of taking advantage, you've also got a full schedule. Lots of nobles wanting to spoil you and spank your cute ass in those shorts, so you'd best go get ready."

"I'm always ready for that," Yves said, but blew him a kiss on the way out of the door.

Laurent smiled after him, shook his head, and hoped that Yves wouldn't burn out too fast. When Laurent had explained that Yves was pretty enough, and popular enough, to matriculate to the House of Gold and transfer his debt...he'd grinned and pointed out that being popular there for wanting to call noblemen *daddy* was like a cow eating grass back home. Here, he was popular and one of the few who tempered his brattiness with seduction, and stood out amid the house's more unique personalities. It wasn't a bad thought, really. Laurent hadn't been lying when he'd called Yves opportunistic, but it wasn't a bad thing, not at all.

Laurent finished his letter to the Duke de Mortain, then caught Rose when she tried to sneak by his office and ignore work in favor of her theater friends for the day. He gave her the missive to take to the palace, and then decided *he*, too, should get ready for the evening. Sabre would need some direction to observe as part of his training, and Laurent figured it wasn't too early to get a jump on the laundry.

* * *

SABRE WOKE with his legs tangled in Laurent's sheets, fingers clutching at the warm gold of his collar. There were faint scratch marks at his neck, as though he were trying to claw the damned thing off in his sleep, and his heart was beating rapidly, the taste of copper sharp in his mouth.

He'd been under the king's boot again, screaming into the marble to drown out the sound of the crowd, gasping into the unsettled silence as ropes creaked and nobles murmured overhead. Except Sabre hadn't been naked when it happened, he was only stripped afterwards, when the king latched the collar around his throat and threw him to the lords of the pleasure houses.

He stared up at the ceiling of Laurent's bedroom and touched the collar, running his fingers over the etched scales. He didn't know how long he lay there, tangled and panting, eyes wild, but it felt like only a moment before the door opened and Laurent came striding in.

"Oh, yes," Laurent said. "*That's* healthy."

"What." Sabre caught his breath. "I'm sorry, my lord, I didn't catch that?"

Laurent glanced at the ceiling. "Get up and fix the sheets. You're in training, Sabre. You can sleep when the night is done."

Sabre kicked his way out of the sheets and tucked them into a semblance of order, and Laurent tossed a bundle of clothes on the bed. He picked up a soft white cotton shirt, dark brown trousers, and a tie for his hair. No shoes.

"Put them on. I had to guess at your size. We'll have better ones made for you, before your first night."

Sabre pulled on the shirt. It was a little tight around the chest, but it was functional, and the trousers fit perfectly. He started to tie his hair back in the style he preferred, froze, and pulled it loose again. This time, he tied it simply, just a low tail hanging down his back, the way he wore it during lessons.

"You'll do," Laurent said, when Sabre was done. His gaze raked over Sabre, assessing him, likely weighing him up against all the professional courtesans who made a living being charming to distraction. Sabre looked away. "Let's go."

Sabre followed him down the stairs. There were more courtesans out and about, now, running half-dressed between rooms, pinning on false eyelashes, whispering in corners. Simone was in a full evening gown that would have looked at home in his mother's closet, studded with embroidered stars at the hem. When Sabre passed, he spotted her *unzipping* it from the side, revealing the silky cloth to just be cotton, with a pocket of cloves hidden next to the bust. She took one out and handed it to Nanette, who lit it.

"No," Laurent said, snatching it out of Nanette's hand. "Outside."

"You're a beast, my lord," Nanette said, without any heat to it.

"An absolute tyrant, darling," Simone said. She took out another clove. "Tell me, Nan, are we playing a dashing pirate today? Or the kitten?"

"I've lost a tentacle," said a woman with long sheets of dark hair and the most aggressively pushed-up bosom Sabre had seen in his life. She ducked into the bath. "If someone's taken the blue tentacle, I need it for You Know Who."

"Margritte," Laurent said, softly, as they took another turn down the stairs. "They aren't actually tentacles. They're phalluses *shaped* like tentacles."

"Is that…better?" Sabre asked.

"Yes, she tried making ones that moved, before, but it was…" Laurent frowned. "Well, it was eventful. She has casts, if you'd ever like one made."

"I'll be fine," Sabre said. Laurent pulled him out of the way as Yves came running up the stairs, eyes lined with kohl and his chest bare, nipple rings flashing for all to see. "It wasn't this busy last night."

"We were open," Laurent said. "That's when we keep the chaos on the *inside*. Here we are, the laundry."

He opened a plain wooden door, which led to a small patch of open air just behind the main house. They were fenced in on all sides by empty buildings, and the gravel rolled under Sabre's feet as Laurent led him to a shed with a single open window. They ducked inside, and when Laurent lit the lamp by the door, Sabre stared at the vats of water warming over low, grated fires.

"Get used to this room," Laurent said. He tapped a chalkboard on the wall, which had a list of names, times, and marks. "We have a maid who does some of the work on busy nights—Dot, you'll know her, she's a terror—but otherwise, whoever isn't working, or whoever is in training, goes to the chute there to collect soiled bedding or clothes. You'll be receiving them throughout the night. Soiled bedding goes in the first vat, colors in the second, prod them with a stick—You never did laundry, I assume."

"No. We had servants for that." Sabre grimaced. "Sorry."

"Yes, how dare you." Laurent walked him through the next steps, pointed out the lines where laundry dried in the morning, and gave Sabre a stack of sheets to carry up to the hidden closets along the upper halls.

"Do you do this, as well?" Sabre asked. Laurent gave him a dry look.

"That's what you're here for," he said. "Go on, we don't have long."

Sabre spent the better part of an hour running up and down the stairs, hastily shoving sheets and towels into panels in the walls while Laurent watched, stopping occasionally to speak to one of the courtesans. The two lookalikes were at the host table, dressed smartly in black and going over the ledger, and Rose burst in at the last minute to hold them up, talking excitedly about wherever she'd been on her errand.

"Oh, it was so glamorous," she said, leaning on the ledger with both her elbows on the pages. "You should get the uniforms some time, pretend to be guards."

"Rose," Laurent said. "Book."

"You'd think this place was on *fire*," Rose said.

She took over the laundry after that, which left Sabre trying to pretend like he wasn't panting from running up and down the stairs. Laurent looked at him keenly, seeing right through him as usual, and straightened the collar of his shirt. A bell rang from the first floor, and doors shut throughout the house, the chaos of chattering voices dying down to a respectful hush.

"They're lighting the lamps on the street," Laurent said, and gestured for Sabre to follow him down the hall where Charon was only just stepping into his room, the door clicking shut behind him. He stopped between Charon's door and one draped with a violet curtain, and pulled a key from his pocket.

"This is another aspect of our work, here," he said. He slipped the key into a crack between the wood paneling and turned. Something clicked inside the wall. "It's unique to the House—I had these installed when I took over."

He pushed, and the wall slid aside, revealing a narrow, pitch black alcove. He stepped inside, and Sabre had to brace himself before he could follow, shoulders tense in the sudden darkness.

"Close the door," Laurent whispered.

Sabre pushed the door shut, leaving them in the dark. Only two lights shone in the crowded alcove, small holes on either side of the wall.

"Clients at the House of Onyx come here for services the other Houses are reluctant to provide," Laurent said. "While this allows us to be selective in our clients, it also comes with certain risks. If a courtesan isn't with a client, they can come here, to make sure no one crosses a line they'll regret, in the morning."

Sabre pressed close to the wall, peering through the hole on the far side. Yves stretched in the middle of his room, dressed in tight shorts and nothing else, surrounded by silks and jewels and little baubles hanging from the wall.

"I remember hearing once, when I was young," Sabre whispered, pulling away. "That someone in the House of Iron was…strangled."

He couldn't see Laurent's face in the dark. "Yes. Don't mention that to Nanette. She was in training there, at the time."

Sabre leaned against the wall. "So when I receive clients?"

"Someone will be there," Laurent said. "Behind the wall, just in case."

Sabre took a breath, ragged in the dark, and Laurent placed a hand over his mouth. There was the sound of a door opening in Yves' room, a soft gasp of delight.

"Oh, daddy," Yves said, his voice muffled through the wall. "You came."

Sabre pulled a face under Laurent's hand, and Laurent huffed out a breath that could have been a laugh.

They didn't have to watch Yves, really. He played coy, teasing the poor, hapless merchant who followed him around the room, stealing kisses and fleeting touches until—as Yves expected, probably—he threw Yves over his knee and spanked him until he was sobbing, begging him to stop.

Sabre glanced at Laurent, who leaned in so close Sabre could feel his lips brush Sabre's ear.

"He likes to put on a show before he gets what he wants," he whispered.

Sabre suppressed a shiver.

Yves ended up bouncing in his client's lap, still crying softly, breath hitching pitifully as the client stroked his hair and called him his *beautiful, sweet boy.*

"Oh, yes, daddy, I'll be so good for you, I'll—"

There was a crack of a hand striking flesh behind Sabre, and Yves stiffened, scrambling to hold onto his client's arms.

"Please, daddy, please let me come—"

"Charon," Laurent whispered.

Yves came messily all over himself the moment the client grabbed his cock, and whimpered as he was pushed onto the floor, pliant and gasping and still begging even as the client came over his back.

"He's convincing enough," Laurent whispered, as Yves reached for his client, gazing up at him like he hung the stars. "When his client is done, we'll go to Simone. She's in the stocks, tonight."

Sabre couldn't hide the way his breath caught, not so close, and he could almost *feel* Laurent smiling.

"Duly noted," he whispered. "But not yet. First, you'll master laundry. Then we'll see what you look like in the stockades, mm?"

Sabre was grateful, at least, that the darkness hid the way his cock reacted to *that.* "Yes, my lord," he whispered back. "I think laundry's fine."

Laurent chuckled, low and bemused, and Sabre closed his eyes. "Good to know."

* * *

THE REPLY from the Duke de Mortain came the next morning, delivered by a messenger dressed in the duke's livery. Laurent could count on one hand the number of nobles who would so brazenly send someone to the House of Onyx and not give a whit at having anyone see.

Lord de Rue,

I would be interested in speaking with you about the matter you proposed. Please attend me in my suite in the royal palace at your convenience. I am certain you recall the location, but if not, I've included it here.

Yrs,

Isiodore de Mortain

Bold of him, too, just to sign his name like that.

Laurent dressed with care before he left the House of Onyx. He knew what his former clients thought, with him sauntering in the palace as if he belonged there in the daytime. And it delighted him, more than he'd admit, that they had to treat him like an equal *and* a dominant. Meaning he always tended toward more extravagance than strictly necessary, with shined boots and a purple cape fastened with an onyx set in silver.

Most of the house was still sleeping after a relatively busy night, but a few were up and about. Sabre was busy doing various chores under the instruction of Dot, who would make sure he was kept too busy to get lost in his thoughts. Charon was sipping his tea on the balcony, and Laurent endured Yves fawning over himself in delight at his clothing, bowing and calling him *m'lord fancy pants* until Laurent threatened *not* to spank him, *or* let Charon do it for him.

Rose also laughed at him, but then pouted when Laurent refused to allow her to accompany him. Running messages was one thing, but sauntering into the vipers' den that was the Starian court was another. He'd save her from that as long as he could.

He did, however, pick up a trinket from one of the market stalls for her; a colorful sash to add to her costume collection, and a pinwheel made of red and purple and yellow just because he thought it might make her smile. He hired a hackney for the rest of the trip, just because he could, and tugged the brim of his tophat down when they passed the palace gates. Laurent had no idea if they strung up nobles like they did commoners to serve as a warning, but he'd rather not see the decaying bodies of Sabre's sister and mother hanging there in the bright, warm afternoon sun.

The Starian royal palace was set up like a spiral, the center of the sundial that was the city of Duciel. Duke Isiodore de Mortain, as the second-highest ranking noble at Court, had rooms nearest the royal suite itself. His were said to mirror those once used by the de Valois family, as the late Duke de Valois had been almost his equal in court. The walls along the corridor to the royal suites were lined with frescoes of ancient Starian myth, which mostly seemed to feature women standing in fields of wheat with a single goat off to the side for flair. It wasn't the pinnacle of artistic genius, but it was old, and in Staria, that usually balanced itself out.

Laurent tipped his hat to a man who used to dress up like a pirate and chase him around his rooms at the House of Gold, who was, all things considered, a fairly amusing client. He passed a woman who used to feed him truly excellent chocolates and equally excellent gossip while he lay between her thighs, and another who mumbled something and wouldn't look Laurent in the eye, likely embarrassed that he'd always wanted to suck on Laurent's toes and have him recite *you are a worthless scoundrel* while he jerked himself off.

De Mortain's rooms were bright and airy, and looked just as they did the last time Laurent was there, though admittedly this was the first time he was received in the duke's drawing room. De Mortain had always preferred his entertainment be brought to him, and Laurent hadn't minded. He had a hell of a bathing room, and while Laurent was no submissive, de Mortain was dominant enough to make the evening enjoyable, if not slightly terrifying.

Noble he may be, but Laurent still rose and bowed when the duke came striding in, precisely as the clock struck the hour. He was a striking man, tall and lean with thick, long dark hair he wore almost unfashionably long, tied in a neat queue with a black silk ribbon, and cold, clear gray eyes. His clothing was perfectly tailored, and as much as Laurent liked his colorful ensemble and silks, he felt a bit like a carnival barker compared the austere, crisp perfection of de Mortain's somber black.

De Mortain arched a dark brow, and Laurent realized he was staring.

He smiled wryly and bowed. "My apologies. I was just thinking that old adage was true, about how you can't turn a sow's ear into a silk purse. I don't know if there are enough hours in a day for me to learn to wear a suit as effortlessly as you."

De Mortain didn't smile, but there was a hint of amusement in his voice when he said, "Perhaps, but if you've the money, my tailor will find enough hours in *his* to make sure you don't need to. I'll make the introduction, if you like."

Laurent laughed. "Thank you. And thank you for seeing me. I—"

"M'lord! Oh! Oh, no!"

A brief look crossed de Mortain's features before he schooled them into impassivity and turned, facing a young house maid with a mass of red hair and huge aquamarine eyes. She looked perhaps to be Rose's age, and while Laurent watched in something like amused horror, she bowed to de Mortain, then Laurent, then de Mortain again.

"The, the tea!"

"Yes," de Mortain said. "That would be lovely, Moira, thank you."

"Is it—oh, no," she whispered. "I don't. I'll be just a—" she said something in a language Laurent didn't know, but was vaguely musical and, oddly, vaguely familiar. She seemed to realize she hadn't spoken in their shared language and went even paler. "I'm so—"

"Please do bring the tea, Moira," de Mortain said, so much dominance in his voice that *Laurent* might have gone to fetch the tea, maybe.

"My apologies," de Mortain said, after she'd dashed off again.

"She's new. For the first week, she ran out of every room I entered, which is quite distressing."

Laurent snorted. "What language was she speaking? It sounded familiar."

"Is that so?" De Mortain studied him. "Morrey, I believe. You've been to Kallistos?"

"Ah," said Laurent. "No, I've never been to the eastern continent. Have you?"

"Once, when I was younger. Brace yourself," de Mortain muttered, and Laurent was slightly charmed by seeing the notoriously put-together duke even a tad bit ruffled.

Moira came in with a death grip on the sides of the silver tea service, which jingled dangerously. He and de Mortain both let out a relieved breath when she got it to the table without dropping it.

"Thank you," de Mortain said, to her, and sighed as she dropped to her knees and started sniffling. "Moira, we've discussed this."

"Yes, m'lord. Your Grace! I know."

De Mortain poured his own tea with a sigh, while Moira composed herself. When she climbed to her feet, she poured some— rather ungraciously—for Laurent, and then handed it over with a bob of her head while tea sloshed over the side. "Beggin' your pardon, m'lord, I get a bit—It's always a bit much, when you do well. You understand."

"Yes," Laurent said, amused. "I do."

She peeked at him and smiled, then said something in her sing-song language to him. When he stared blanky at her, she flushed and said, "Oh, I'm so sorry, m'lord! I thought you was. Were, I mean. I thought you were from where the mages live."

"What," Laurent said.

"Mislia, you've the look of them."

"Thank you, Moira, for bringing the tea," de Mortain said, carefully enough that she didn't wail at the censure or burst into tears at the praise.

"You should send her to my house for a few days," Laurent said, idly, still thinking about what the girl had said.

"Are you suggesting a Kallistoi maid who talks to herself and can't pour tea would make a good courtesan, de Rue? I suppose maybe she could fail at service and please the sadists among the nobility. Though being one, I cannot say I find it all that worth paying for." He sipped his tea.

Laurent had no idea if he was kidding or not. "I meant during the day, when we have training for things like that." He waved a hand. "I'm only amused I looked like a Mislian. Don't they go about in cloaks summoning demons?"

"You do have a cape," de Mortain said, and Laurent had no idea how to process that he'd just made a *joke.* "And while I appreciate your offer, I have my hopes she'll calm down after a bit. I believe most of it is still nerves."

"Well, I do have some experience with that, and yes, it usually does work itself out." The tea was good, nowhere near as strong as the brew Charon preferred, but decent enough. "Thank you for seeing me, Your Grace."

"You're welcome. And I must extend my thanks to you, as well, Lord de Rue, for taking in Sabre. A dreadful business with his mother and sister, of course." De Mortain's cold eyes did not warm when he smiled, not a bit.

"I confess I don't know anything about that," Laurent said, which was truthful enough. "I've enough to attend to in my own house."

De Mortain's eyes were still cold as diamonds when he said, "Treason against our king concerns all of us, de Rue. Nobility more than most. But as goes the crown, so goes the city, and your pleasure houses depend on stability, you realize. No one has time for indulgence in chaos."

No one but the rich has time for indulgence, ever. "Of course," Laurent demurred, though it rankled a bit that he had to, now that he had a title. But even a man noble-born who didn't earn his title on his back would have to defer to de Mortain.

"You've always been clever, de Rue, I know an intelligent man when I see one. I signed the writ of execution for Sabre's mother and sister, because I assure you, they *were* traitors. Any longer, and they would have used Sabre for their own ends. And as I'm sure you learned by now, he has no stomach for subterfuge. He would have been found out in a week, maybe less. And then I would have had to sign his warrant, too. I felt I owed something to his father, who I counted as a friend."

Laurent put his teacup down. "I wanted you to take Sabre's First Night, but I'm...not sure that I'm that—" he caught himself with effort, cursing inwardly. He hated the palace simply because he'd gotten used to speaking far more freely in his house than the king's. "I'm not sure how to say this."

"I'll say it for you." De Mortain put his teacup down, leaned back in his high-backed chair and laced his still-gloved fingers over his knee. "You don't think that you're cruel enough to make him fuck the man who sent his family to the gallows?"

"Ah," said Laurent. "Yes. I mean, no, I don't think I am."

"They were traitors, and they knew the risks inherent in undertaking such a plot. It was poorly thought out, at that. They wouldn't have succeeded."

"If you say you didn't sign Sabre's writ of execution, why was he on the gallows at all?"

De Mortain's mouth tightened, so minutely that only someone trained to pay close attention to the reactions of others for a living would notice it. "That was not my doing, nor my idea. And I suppose it is fair to say the king might have hanged him regardless; He *is* the king. But I will show you the order myself, if you wish to see it."

"I would rather not," Laurent said, as the idea of it made him queasy, men and women's lives signed out of existence to keep an unstable man on his equally unstable throne. "And perhaps don't mention it to Sabre. He has nightmares."

If he expected to see something close to empathy on Isiodore de Mortain's face, he was sorely mistaken, because there was none to be found. "Of course. I instructed him in fencing; He was easily distracted, a bit sloppy, but eager. I assume he's much the same under your tutelage."

Laurent gave an elegant, meaningless shrug. "He's settling in. I know what the nobles who will want him are going to do to him, and I don't think they'll care much if he's any of those things when they get their hands on him."

"I doubt they will, either. We're not known at Court for our appreciation of subtlety. You realize that even if I take his First Night, I cannot take them all?"

"Yes, of course."

"Then I'm curious why you asked me. And spare me the flattery—you were never required to do it as my whore, so please don't as my fellow noble and guest."

"You're sort of terrible," Laurent said, staring at him. "Your Grace."

Isiodore's smile flashed, and for a moment, his eyes looked less like cut glass and more like rainclouds before a storm. "I know. Answer the question."

"Well. He knows you, and trusts you, and you're a sadist, so you'll at least be able to put him under. And while I believe that you signed his family's order of execution, I also find it interesting that when he was brought to the nobles of the pleasure district, it was only the Houses of Gold, Silver, Bronze and mine that were there. The House of Gold would never touch the son of a traitor, the lady of the House of Silver would have hanged him herself, and the House of Bronze has no idea what to do with men like Sabre. But there are others. They might have taken him without knowing or caring how to see to him, just for the notoriety. Where were they, that day, I wonder?"

"I obviously have very little knowledge of how the lords of the pleasure district spend their days, I would imagine it was some miscommunication."

Or you're still protecting him, and were always going to offer for his First Night, but wanted to see if I was smart enough to come to you and ask. "I imagine that was it, then." Laurent rose. "I should go, I've quite a bit to do but if you're amenable, I'll make sure it's settled. He should be ready in a month's time, I'd imagine."

"And here I thought you were good at your job, de Rue."

Laurent grinned at him, and bowed. "He'd be ready for you now, if you want the truth. But the nobles that will come after, no. After all you've done to protect him, surely you can do just a bit more."

De Mortain's stare was chilly, but his voice was not quite as cold when he said, "Proper nobles don't speak of such things in their drawing rooms, de Rue. Thank me for the instruction, and then I shall pass along my tailor and have Moira show you out."

Laurent gave a theatrical bow and said, "Thank you, but I'm fond of mine and I can see myself out. Spare you the waterworks, or your lovely divan covered in lukewarm, mediocre tea."

De Mortain laughed, and it seemed genuine enough. "I'll have you know I signed your titular decree, you scamp. And I always knew you were no submissive."

"They say you're a master tactician indeed, Your Grace." With a wink, Laurent settled his tophat back on his head. "I'll be in touch."

CHAPTER 5

Sabre was elbow deep in dish suds when Laurent delivered the news.

"We have a client for your first night," Laurent said, breezy as anything, waltzing through the kitchen like an actor in one of the open-air plays in the park. Rose walked like that, too, Sabre realized. Confident, yes, but calculated, every step designed for show. "Isiodore de Mortain will expect you in his suites at the palace in a month."

Sabre dropped a plate in the sink with a clunk of ceramic. Rose, who had given him helpful advice while he fumbled in search of taps and soap and drain plugs, smiled and flipped a page in her script book. "De Mortain? I thought...I thought maybe it might be the king."

Laurent raised his brows. "I don't believe you're his type."

"Does that matter?" Sabre asked. He thought of Isiodore, barking commands as Sabre wrapped his fists in gauze to hide cracked knuckles from his mother, a hand on his back to guide him into the proper form. He'd always been so...impersonal, with Sabre. Like he didn't know what it did to him, to be ordered around all afternoon.

"The king *might* request you, eventually," Laurent said, like he was humoring Sabre. Like Sabre would *want* that, the king's boot on his back again, holding him down.

"Laurent visited him, once," Rose said. "They dressed him all in white, and a carriage came by with *four* horses."

"Rose, a little discretion," Laurent said.

"I can't be discreet if I'm going to run my own opera house one day," Rose said, narrowing her eyes at him.

Something ached in Sabre's chest as Laurent narrowed his eyes back, and Rose smiled.

"I remember that," Sabre said, scrubbing at the plate he dropped. "When the king tried for an heir, with the pleasure houses."

"Do you?" Laurent gave him another one of his thoughtful looks, leaning against the wall.

"He hates them," Adrien had said, fifteen and huddled up in Sabre's bed with a book neither of them were supposed to read. He'd insisted on staying the night when he heard there was going to be a courtesan in the palace again. "He's only doing this because he's humoring his nobles. They say he needs to father a dominant son, and quick." He'd smiled. "Which is why he's making sure none of the courtesans he's seeing can conceive."

"That sounds awful," Sabre had said. "Forcing yourself to be with someone you don't love."

"That's how it is, though," Adrien said, passing Sabre the book. "Nothing good ever comes from royalty who admit they love people. You're lucky, Sabre. You never have to hide anything."

Now, Sabre dried the plate with a cloth and dug through the sink for another.

"I don't see him putting himself through the trouble in your case," Laurent said, and glanced at Rose, who was trying to eat a slice of a cherry tart without scattering crumbs on the script.

"Oh." Sabre nodded. "Right. Of course."

"Hey, Rose," Rose said, without looking up. "Can you kindly give us space so we can talk about sex in hushed voices, because gods forbid you learn that *sex* might happen in a *pleasure house.*"

"This is far worse," Laurent said. "We might even cross the line into hand-holding."

"Disgusting," Rose said, shoving the rest of the tart in her mouth.

She grabbed the script. "Immoral. I can't bear to think of it. My own brother."

She flounced off, and Sabre looked down at his hands rather than linger on the look Laurent gave her, fond and exasperated all at once.

"You won't have much time," Laurent said, after a minute of silence. He crossed to the sink, leaning against the counter. "I don't need to tell you that de Mortain is not known for pity."

"I know." Sabre pulled the plug, watching dark water swirl down the drain. "He isn't known for cruelty, either. I don't think he would have done it, the way it happened."

"Maybe not, but he won't make it easy."

Sabre nodded. "I don't think he knows how. But thank you, for not accepting one of the others."

Laurent kept his gaze on the door, and lowered his voice so that Sabre had to lean in, hands slippery on the edge of the sink.

"Is there a reason, then, that Prince Adrien would be one of the others?"

Sabre slipped, banging his arm on the sink, and hissed out a curse as Laurent grabbed him. "He wouldn't. You're lying."

"Careful with your tone," Laurent said.

"Sorry, my lord, he just, surely he knows what that looks like?"

"That did cross my mind," Laurent said, still in a low voice. "You're close, then?"

"Not as close as anyone else…" Sabre caught Laurent's eyes, the hard dominance there, a warning. "Yes. Close enough."

"Will he stop, then, if it's known you've already found a client for your first night?"

Sabre sighed. "No. He's too much like his father."

Laurent stared at him, brows lowered. "Like his *father?* The court's always saying he's the spitting image of the late queen."

"Yes, but he's loyal. He feels very strongly, when he cares for someone. He can be a little reckless."

"Prince Adrien," Laurent said. "The crown prince, Adrien. That is who you mean."

"Yes, I said he was like his father, didn't I?" Sabre winced at the sharpness in his voice. "Sorry, my lord, but the king, he doesn't show his true feelings to anyone. You know that."

Laurent was oddly silent for a moment, arms crossing slowly over his chest. "He felt powerfully enough to kill his own wife for treason," he said. "His cousin. Her daughter."

"His wife was different," Sabre said. Laurent's eyes widened.

"He was found with her blood on his hands," Laurent said. "There have been *ballads* about it. And you don't deny that he's killed others. Friends. Courtiers. An entire squad of guards."

"Yes," Sabre said, before Laurent could bring up the queen again. "But he had reason—oh, I'm defending him. I used to *defend* him."

"And he held you down," Laurent said. His voice was soft, relentless. Impossible to escape. "While your family was hanged."

"Because he thought they betrayed him. It's all loyalty again," Sabre said. He could feel the bile in his throat. "And Adrien, he's the same. He *knows* I'm loyal. I've always been loyal."

"And now?" Laurent tightened his grip on Sabre's arm.

"Adrien can trust me," Sabre said. "If he thinks he can't, tell him nothing's changed, but he can't come here."

"Do you love him?"

Sabre frowned. "What?"

"It's a valid question," Laurent said. "Are you lovers? Tell me now, so I know what I've signed up for, bringing you here."

"No," Sabre said. "No, we're not lovers."

Laurent released him. "But you're loyal to him, you said. Not to the king," he added, when Sabre looked away. "This isn't about the king. Does anyone else know this?"

"No," Sabre said. "My mother and sister are dead."

"And the king? Does he know?"

"He doesn't even know what the prince looks like, these days," Sabre said.

Laurent flapped a hand, like a father ignoring his own son for ten years was nothing of import. "But does he know."

"No," Sabre said, carefully. "But if Adrien keeps trying to find me, he probably will."

* * *

THE STORM HIT A WEEK LATER, low and heavy with rain that flooded the lower circles of the city and washed the upper streets clean. It was a cool rain, so thick no one could see more than a few inches in the dim of twilight, and it took only half a minute for it to soak into Sabre's skin.

"You're mad," he said, as Yves, also drenched but far more fashionable about it than Sabre's brand of wet cat chic, ran a length of leather from Sabre's cuffed hands and under the back door to the House. "We can't do this inside?"

"No," Yves said. "Because you're not desperate enough."

"There has to be a better way than—" Sabre groaned as Yves slammed the door shut between them. "Yves!"

"Beg like you *mean* it and I'll let you *in!*" Yves shouted back.

Sabre groaned. Lessons with Yves we're continuing to be an unmitigated disaster. He could kneel well enough, but he couldn't pretend not to be bored when Yves asked him to moan and whine like he was writhing in someone's lap. Even *actually* writhing on one of Margritte's far too inventive phalluses wasn't enough. He was just a terrible liar, and there was no getting around it.

"Yves," Sabre said. "Let me in."

"That doesn't sound like, *Please, my lord, let me come,*" Yves said. "Or *I'm a dirty slut who needs your cock.* Either or."

"But I'm *not* one," Sabre said. "And I don't want to come, I want to come *in.*"

"Not unless you're a dirty slut who wants to come!" Yves shouted.

"Oh, no," Sabre heard someone say on the other side of the door. "I do *not* want to know."

Sabre tugged at the leash. It was attached to something on the other side of the door, possibly the handle. "Please," he said, as rain rolled down his back. "Please, let me come."

"Please, my *lord,*" Yves called out. "And I don't believe you!"

"Are you sure you aren't a sadist in disguise?" Sabre asked.

Yves *laughed.*

Sabre spent almost ten minutes trying, with wildly varying degrees of enthusiasm, to convince Yves that he was, actually, about to die if he didn't come. After a long period of silence, though, Sabre tugged at the leash and realized no one had answered him for at least five minutes.

"You left me," he said to the door. "You *bastard.*"

Rain pummeled the gravel at his feet, making the stones rattle, and Sabre sighed and sat down. Above him, lights flickered on in the House as the dark set in, and shadows crossed the windows, tugging at curtains and sealing gaps.

"Oh, please," Sabre said, kicking at the door. "Let me come."

"Sabre?"

Sabre froze. The rain obscured the buildings around him, darkening the narrow alleys and surrounding the House with a gray curtain.

A darker shadow appeared through the rain, draped in an oiled black cloak. They were a little taller than Sabre, with the fine boots of a noble and expensive leather gloves, and Sabre stood, dragging at the cuffs. The door rattled dangerously.

Whoever it was had come from one of the alleys. There wasn't another exit out of the House so far as Sabre knew, and every inch of them screamed *noble.* A noble who knew Sabre's name. And Sabre, left outside while Yves fucked off to prove a point about *applying himself,* was cuffed to a fucking door.

Sabre placed a foot on the door and dragged at the lead. Leather ripped at the seams. The door groaned alarmingly, and Sabre pulled away with about a foot of lead still hanging from his cuffs, just in time to swing his fists into the stranger's stomach.

The man went down like a sack of bricks, and Sabre pushed him over with a foot, revealing a wheezing, wide-eyed Prince Adrien.

"Shit." Sabre fell clumsily to his knees as Adrien clutched his side with both hands. "What were you *doing?* Why are you *here?*"

"I'm fine, thank you," Adrien said, in his soft, cultured voice. "And I forgive you, of course."

"You came out of the rain like a ghost," Sabre said. He tried to peel back Adrien's cloak to get a look at his ribs, but it was difficult with his hands cuffed. "You shouldn't be here."

"Neither should you," Adrien said. He grabbed Sabre's wrists. "Look at you. They tied you up here in the *rain?* Do you *sleep* here? Is this why you're dressed so terribly?"

Sabre sighed as Adrien gingerly got to his knees, fumbling with the latches on his cuffs. "Adrien. It's good to know that you don't hate me, but this is a little excessive."

"Why on *earth* would I hate you?" Adrien asked. "I know you wouldn't lay a hand against me. Well, you did, but you didn't know it was me. You would never betray us." He took Sabre's face in his hands. Adrien had his mother's red hair and dark eyes, and if Sabre hadn't seen him drinking out of a horse trough at age eight on a dare, he would have found him achingly beautiful.

"I'm sorry I couldn't save them, Sabre," Adrien said. Sabre took a shivery breath. "Father locked me in my room when it happened. But I can save *you.*"

"Adrien."

"I'm your prince, and you're not even a lord, now, so you have no choice," Adrien said, in a quavering voice. The door opened, spilling light over the yard, and he tried to drag Sabre behind him. It wouldn't have done much good—Adrien always was a little too willowy for a proper Starian prince.

"The fuck did you do to the door?" Yves asked. "The fuck is *he?*"

"You'll turn around if you know what's best for you," Adrien said. Yves looked at Sabre and mouthed, *What?*

"Can my friend come in?" Sabre asked, and Adrien looked at him in open alarm. "It's really coming down, at the moment."

Storms always unsettled Adrien. He used to cry and lock himself away when he was young, and only his mother could coax him out long enough to close the curtains and light a lamp.

"I see things, sometimes," Adrien had told him, once, when the queen was still alive and Sabre was staying the night in the royal suites, making blanket forts while the storm thundered outside. "Flashes. Little things. I saw you break your arm on the window."

"How do you break an *arm* on a *window?*" Sabre had asked. Adrien just shrugged.

"No, I saw it in the rain, when it hit the window," he said. "It was sunny, and your father was on a horse, and you broke your arm."

It wasn't until months later, when Sabre was lying in bed with a splint and his father was telling funny stories about falling off a horse, that Sabre remembered what Adrien had said.

He'd been sworn to secrecy, later, when the Misli, whose magic was inherent rather than infused in everyday crafts like Starian magic, were pushed out of the city limits and chased to the sea. It wasn't safe, Sabre decided, for a Starian prince to see the future in patches of rainwater, so he cut his thumb to swear, and Adrien had burst into soft, gasping tears and bandaged him up again. The only thing that upset Adrien more than rain, it seemed, was blood.

The fact that he chose to stage his daring rescue during a storm made Sabre unsure if he wanted to hug him or punch him *again.*

"Don't tell them who you are," Sabre whispered, guiding Adrien through the door.

"One of them, um...one of them might know already," Adrien whispered back. Sabre raised his brows, and Adrien blushed furiously. "I can't tell you everything I get up to, you know."

"A little warning this time would have been nice," Sabre said. He took off Adrien's cloak while Yves ran off down the hall, probably to fetch half the House. "You know if I run, that will look like an admission of guilt."

"Yes, but I'm the prince," Adrien said, tugging off his gloves. "And you're, you know, like Isiodore is to my father. I can't very well be king without you."

"Adrien, we are *not* in *private,*" Sabre hissed.

Adrien frowned slightly. "You're trembling."

"What?" Sabre pushed wet hair out of Adrien's face, an old habit. He was always playing the older brother, even if Adrien was only younger by a few months. It came with the territory. Adrien was so quiet, most of the time, so strange, that it was Sabre's first instinct. "It's cold, of course I'm trembling."

"I'm not," Adrien said. He narrowed his eyes. "You're scared. I thought you might be, when I saw you."

Sabre met Adrien's dark gaze. "How."

"We aren't in private," Adrien whispered. He clutched at Sabre's hand. "I wish…Sabre, I wish I could have—"

"I know," Sabre said.

"Oh, for fuck's sake," said Laurent, turning the corner at the end of the hall. Yves hovered behind him, hands shoved in his pockets, staring from Adrien to Sabre and back again.

"My lord," Sabre said, keeping a hand placed firmly on Adrien's shoulder. "If I could introduce my cousin."

* * *

Laurent briefly considered screaming.

It wasn't dignified, it wasn't even all that necessary and still, it was so very tempting. The house was always somewhat less crowded when it rained, but it was still a *pleasure house*, and the man standing in the back hallway was the *crown prince.* "You—yes. Of course." He bowed. "Your Highness. What a surprise, to see you in the hallway."

"Oh, wow," Yves said, from behind him. "You're so *hot,* Prince Adrien. I've only ever seen you from a distance, and wow. Look at you. And you two are friends?"

The Crown Prince of Staria did look like his late mother, and he had none of his father's dominance, but he was *still* the heir to the throne. He drew himself up to his full height, which was considerable, and said with a polite bow, "Sabre is my cousin, and yes, a dear friend."

"I need to go lie down," Yves whispered.

"Yes, you *do,*" Laurent said, threading his voice with dominance. "On your bed. For the noble who will be here in forty-five minutes to fuck you on it."

"Oh, no, it's Lord Lafleur. He likes to fuck me over the—"

"Yves," Laurent said. "I will put you on laundry duty for a week and gag you for longer if you don't stop talking."

"As my lord commands. But, Prince Adrien, I'm available for—"

Laurent turned, gave him a *look* and said, "Two weeks. *Go.*"

"This is where you are, now," Adrien said, and god help him, but Laurent heard a thread of something wistful in the prince's soft voice.

"Yes," Sabre said. "And I heard you offered for me, for my First Night."

He stared up at the ceiling. "Neither of you have the sense given a bedbug, so go to my office, *now*. Sabre, practice your service and fetch His Highness some tea and a blanket, and get yourself in dry clothes before you kneel."

"Oh," Adrien interrupted. "That's not necessary. Sabre doesn't need to. He's—"

"He is in training to serve this house, Your Highness," Laurent said, wondering if *he* was going to end up in the gallows, now, for interrupting a prince. "It would be the best for everyone if you allowed me to do that."

"Of course, I didn't intend to disrupt your—anything," Adrien said, wet and dripping on the floor, his eyes wide and locked on his friend. There was something there, maybe, despite what Sabre said. Maybe unrequited, and how *tragic*, there were Katoikos melodramas with less plot twists than this situation.

"Come with me," Laurent said, and tried not to sigh as he heard the Crown Prince of Staria's boots squelch on the tile floor as they walked to Laurent's office.

"I do promise, Lord de Rue, that my intention coming here is not to put Sabre in danger, or your house," Adrien assured him. He was so earnest, their future king, even though Laurent would eat his top hat and Yves' sparkly shorts if he really believed Adrien would take the throne of Staria.

"I understand, Your Highness, but you must understand that I am, actually, trying to keep Sabre safe."

"Yes. And it's Adrien, please," he said, wringing his hands. He wouldn't sit down in the chair, though perhaps it was because he was still wet from the rain. Even de Mortain hadn't told Laurent to use his given name, and here the *crown prince* was standing in front of his desk, allowing a former pleasure slave to use his name. "Thank you for what you did for him. I know you took a risk."

"Your Highness," Laurent said, settling behind his desk. "Please have a seat. Before Sabre returns, I want you to understand why I decided to, ah…decline your offer, to take Sabre's First Night."

Prince Adrien did sit, eventually, but he said, "I do understand, Lord de Rue." There was an odd smile on his face that Laurent couldn't quite place. "You are trying to keep him safe. But are you sure my father's closest friend is the best choice?"

"You're aware Sabre is a submissive, and a masochist?"

Prince Adrien blushed hot, and Laurent, who didn't often think about the night he spent in the king's bed for many reasons, could not find any shade of Adrien's father in his awkward sincerity. "Of course, being friends, we've discussed such things. May I, before he comes back, ask you something of a personal nature?"

Adrien could, if he wanted, murder him right here with a vase and nothing would happen to him. "If you wish."

"You are not, are you, a submissive? Or a masochist." Adrien whispered it to the floor.

For a horrible moment, Laurent wondered where this was going. If the prince wanted to hire *him*—

No. Laurent was no longer for hire. It was fucking with his equilibrium to be around the royal family, apparently. "No, I'm not."

"You were lying, before? With your…past clients?"

"I was surviving, Your Highness. May I ask why this is relevant?" If Adrien asked about Laurent's night with the king, he was going to lie and tell him they'd read a book or taken a bath or something.

Adrien shook his head. "Not yet. But sometime, you probably won't have to."

Before he could figure that out, Sabre returned. He was in dry clothes, hair hastily braided with ribbons and his eyes lined—Yves, probably—and had a warm blanket and a tea tray that he carried into the room.

Adrien looked horrified and uncomfortable, but Laurent didn't stop Sabre from draping the blanket around his shoulders or serving the tea. Sabre was not a noble, not anymore, and the sooner these two ridiculous young men got this through their minds, the better.

"If you two promise not to go anywhere, or plot something that will end badly," Laurent said, voice heavy with command. "I will let you speak alone, for a time."

"You have my word, Lord de Rue," Adrien promised.

Laurent walked over to where Sabre was kneeling with at least a modicum of grace—his posture was still too lax, he was going to have to have a word with Yves—and grabbed Sabre by the hair, pulling his head back. "You are representing this house. Your First Night belongs to someone, and you belong to me, and this House, until your debt is paid."

"As for his debt, I could—"

"Prince Adrien," Laurent said, again interrupting him. "Your father would simply raise it and you know it. Sabre, tell me you understand what I am saying to you." He pulled Sabre's hair, harder, and saw the flash in his eyes, something hot and desperate.

He should, maybe, have Charon see to him after Adrien took his leave. But Charon was busy that evening, and the thought of doing it himself made Laurent's blood heat. He shouldn't. But he wanted to.

"I understand, m-my lord," Sabre murmured.

"And please see to it that the Crown Prince understands why he might want to think a bit more, before *visiting unannounced*." He pulled harder, and then smacked Sabre across the face. "Well?"

"Yes, my lord," Sabre said, swaying, and he didn't need to look down to know his cock was probably growing hard.

Good. That got the point across well enough; both who Sabre was, and who he belonged to, now. Laurent bowed. "Your Highness. If you've a mind to hire any of my courtesans, we would welcome your patronage, as always."

"Yes, all right, thank you, Lord de Rue, I shall keep that in mind."

Laurent gave Sabre another hard look, then went into the hallway. Where he immediately turned, slid open a panel, and ducked into a hidden area cleverly built behind his office. Laurent hadn't built it, but this wasn't the first time he'd found it useful, and he doubted it would be the last.

"He's, ah...quite something. Does he do that often, strike you like that? Would you like me to see if I can have you moved to the House of Gold, Sab?"

Laurent rolled his eyes. He was certain that if that smack bothered Sabre, it was only because Laurent hadn't done it hard enough.

"No, Asa, it's fine."

Gods help him, but Sabre was *domming the crown prince.*

"I saw you with him," Adrien said. "Izzy. He was hurting you, Sab, so much, and you were sobbing."

For a moment, Laurent didn't understand what he was hearing. Who was Izzy? He knew Sabre had been with others, of course, but— Izzy? That wasn't. There was no way—

"Asa, you know that's what I like," Sabre said, soothing. "It's going to be okay. Is that why you didn't press it, when Lord de Rue said he'd be my first?"

For the—was Izzy *Isiodore de Mortain*? But that hadn't happened yet. Or—was this some kind of trick?

"I could still talk to him, you know. Maybe I could—"

"Asa, no, you can't," Sabre said, and what a horrifying realization to know that *Sabre was the voice of reason* here. "It's all right. I know him, and he'll tell me the truth about my family."

"And you'll sob for it," Adrien said. "I saw it."

But how?

"I cried for Charon, and it was...oh, Asa. It was like it's supposed to be. What we're told it would be."

"Maybe what you were told," Adrien said. "I'm not supposed to be a submissive. And what about Lord de Rue?"

"What? What is that look, Asa, what."

"I saw you when he smacked you," the prince said. "Here, I mean. Not in my...you know."

Wait, his *what?* Laurent was still not over the fact Prince Adrien called Isiodore de Mortain *Izzy*.

"It's fine, really, you need to not worry about me."

"I'm just glad you're all right," said Adrien, softly. "I don't under-stand why I can see so many things, and I missed this. I missed *them*. Maybe you shouldn't ask him, Sabre. Maybe it's better not to know."

"If I'm ever going to get over it, I have to," Sabre said.

Laurent figured he'd heard enough. He sighed, left the hallway, and went to find Charon. He knew he had a gap in his schedule, and maybe he could do the Prince a good turn—and give himself a decent excuse if the crown prince was caught visiting that had nothing to do with Sabre. "Have time to entertain the Crown Prince tonight?"

Charon smiled. "I think so, yes."

"Good," said Laurent. "Let's go get the subs out of my office, then."

"Where is Sabre to go, if you wish me to take care of the prince?"

"I'll take care of Sabre," Laurent said, and ignored Charon's low chuckle as they headed toward the office.

CHAPTER 6

The crown prince left with Charon, looking a bit dazed, and Laurent took a moment to make a note in his ledger book —luckily Charon had a sizeable amount of time in his schedule for Laurent to record Adrien's visit, with the same name he'd given before.

"Are you angry," Sabre asked, when Laurent turned to him.

"Should I be angry?" Laurent asked. He walked over and closed the door, locking it. "Are you planning on running off with the prince?" He doubted it, since it sounded like, somehow, Sabre was the one with the common sense between them.

Adrien, with his flights of fancy, was perhaps more like his father than anyone realized. Except, it seemed, for Sabre.

"I wouldn't let him, even if I wanted to, which I, I don't." Sabre's eyes were wide, and he swayed forward a bit on his knees.

Laurent said, "Do you want me to be angry? You won't need it, pet, if you want me to put you in your place you can just ask me."

"Oh," Sabre whispered. "Do you want me to?"

"I would enjoy feeling as if I have *some* modicum of control in this situation, as elusive as it may be." Laurent snapped his fingers. "Come here."

Sabre blinked. He went to stand up, and Laurent said, "No."

"But you want—"

"I want you," Laurent said, in a hard voice, "to come here. Not like a noble, because you're not one, anymore. Like a courtesan in training in my house. I said I'd put you in your place, and it's my decision what that place is, so. *Crawl.*"

He didn't miss what that did to Sabre, the flash of heat and embarrassment, the sweet burn of humiliation that Laurent was sure Sabre wanted even *before* his nobility was forcibly ripped away from him.

Sabre dragged in a harsh breath, then slid to his hands and knees— and crawled.

He was graceless, of course, with none of the style of the house's other submissives but the desperate, aching want couldn't be faked and it did go a bit soothing Laurent's dominance, which was roused by his feeling completely out of control.

When Sabre knelt at his side at last, he reached down and grabbed him by the hair, pulling him bodily to his feet.

"I, my lord—"

"Don't speak," Laurent said, then shoved him against the closed door, leaned in and kissed him.

Sabre went still, but he kissed Laurent back, almost shyly. He was trembling, but Laurent could tell he was hard, and when Laurent pushed against him, Sabre groaned into his mouth and gasped softly.

Laurent reached down and palmed Sabre's cock, squeezing it through his pants. "Do you want to come, pet?"

"If my lord wishes," Sabre said, and ah, that was good.

Laurent sucked at his neck above his collar, biting down and leaving a mark. He gave Sabre's cock another squeeze. "Your lord wants you to beg for it. I want to hear how much you want my hand on you."

"Please, my lord, I do."

"Use your words, pet." Laurent pulled back, tipped Sabre's chin up. "Your job is to do what you're told."

"I want your hand on me, please, my lord," Sabre said. "I want to be good for you."

"Should I frighten you, like Charon? I have no gun to put in your mouth, pretty thing. Will you still go under for me?"

"Ah," Sabre said, looking down. "Yes. If you want me to, I will."

"I want you to." He deftly worked open Sabre's pants, kept another hand wrapped in his still-damp hair. "They will take you, put you on your knees. Frighten you, make you come. Put you under like you want. You'll be so good for them, won't you?"

"Yes," Sabre gasped, when Laurent got his hand around his cock.

"Yes, what?" Laurent pulled harder.

"Yes, my lord," Sabre responded, his hips pushing.

"Stay still and take what I give you," Laurent ordered. "Put your hands behind your back." He moved back enough to let Sabre get his hands behind him, then kissed him again, rough and bruising. "And tell me, pet, tell me who you'll belong to. Even when they give you what they want."

He stroked Sabre's cock with the perfect pressure, his technique as impeccably perfect as ever, even if he no longer did this for anyone unless he wanted to.

"Yours," Sabre whispered. He dragged his lip between his teeth, trying hard not to move and thrust into Laurent's hand. "Yours, my lord. Yours."

"Good. That's good. Don't forget. The king put that collar on your neck but you belong to me, and I don't care how good it will feel to kneel for anyone else, you won't forget that."

"I won't, oh, my lord, I—" Sabre was almost in tears, just from this, being pinned against a wall and *owned*. "Please, please let me come, let me show you—"

"Go ahead," Laurent allowed, and stroked him until Sabre came over his fist. He stroked him until the last tremor was wrung out of him, then shoved his fingers in Sabre's gasping, wet mouth. "Clean them off like a good whore."

Sabre did, moaning around his fingers while Laurent shoved them deep enough to make him choke.

"Do you want my cock, my pretty whore? Want to kneel, show me how grateful you are to be mine?" It'd been some time since Laurent felt his dominance this roused, reminding him of how it was after he was no longer in debt and forcing himself to be the submissive he wasn't for his noble clients.

"Yes, I—take my mouth, please, my lord," Sabre said, and the eagerness to please in his voice wasn't what the nobles who hired him would want, maybe, but it was exactly what *Laurent* wanted.

Laurent shoved him to his knees, drew his cock out and held Sabre by his hair while he thrust hard into his mouth. He gave him his cock with sharp, deep thrusts, not going slow, thrilling as Sabre choked and shook there, on his knees before him. He was dangerously close in seconds, and this wasn't just about training, it was about *claiming*, and he didn't stop or slow.

"You'll cry for me," Laurent ordered, holding himself deep with his grip in Sabre's hair. He kept it up, watched Sabre's feet kick on the floor and noted with a hazy sense of satisfaction that Sabre's hands were still clenched behind his back.

He wasn't sure if it was the choking—an understandable fear given what had almost happened to him—or his dominance that had Sabre crying, but either way, it was putting Sabre under and satisfying Laurent's urge to control him, so he didn't much care either way.

"I will keep you safe, make sure you get what you need. Not the crown, not the prince, *me*," he snarled, holding Sabre's head back and baring his throat while he stroked himself off over Sabre's lovely, upturned, tear-streaked face. "Thank me for it, whore."

"Thank you," Sabre moaned. "Thank you, thank you, my lord."

Laurent's own moan was loud as he came all over Sabre's face, slumping forward in his release as the pleasure washed over him. When it ran its course, he blinked and saw Sabre's messy face, the way he was breathing easier, his posture at long last perfect.

Laurent stroked a hand over Sabre's hair while he drifted, under and quiet, and wondered for the first time if he was in trouble.

* * *

IT WAS STILL RAINING the next morning, a light, dull rain that made the city beyond the windows seem hazy, and Sabre was serving tea. It wasn't *technically* on his list of duties, but he'd learned quickly enough that half of the house tended to wake up at noon, grab what they could from the kitchen, and have a haphazard midday tea in Simone's sitting room. Simone was one of the only ones to have more than a single room to herself, and her sitting room was stuffed full with chaises, footstools, curtains and cushions.

"I can't believe you saw the prince and didn't *tell* me," Simone said, holding out her teacup for Sabre to refill. She was dressed in a cotton gown in the Gerakian style, all severe lines and a high waist, and her hair tumbled artfully over her shoulder, glittering with strings of colored glass.

"I was a little distracted," Yves said. He grabbed the teapot before Sabre could reach him and poured himself a cup. As a courtesan in training, Sabre had been unanimously voted to serve the tea, but Yves kept forgetting. "He's so hot, Simone. Like, what's that story Percival told, about the guy who fell in love with his own statue? That kind of hot."

"Oh, my," Simone said, smiling into her cup. She glanced at Sabre. "Tell us, Sabre, is he right, or is he thinking with his moneybags again?"

Sabre took the teapot from Yves and put it back on the warmer. "I don't know. He looks like his mother."

"Poor thing," Percival said, lying upside down on a chaise. His hair was in curlers, dropping slightly as he slid towards the floor. "Must be a shit job, being a prince when you look like the woman the king hated enough to execute himself."

Sabre grimaced. "No one said he killed her."

"They didn't have to, love," Simone said.

"Yeah, fuck." Nanette, sitting at Simone's feet, pulled a face. "That's depressing. Let's go back to the shit about Yves having a crush on the prince."

"I'm just saying, I admire his whole...look," Yves said. "Sabre, back me up, here. You two had to've…you know. Don't tell me you grew up next door to *that* and didn't try once."

"We kissed when we were eleven," Sabre said, and Yves choked on his tea. Percival laughed. "He was terrible at it. So was I. We decided not to repeat the experience."

"Are you *mad?* That's what practice is for." Yves sighed. "I told Ma I should've been born a noble. This proves it."

Simone stretched out, laying her head in Yves' lap. "Clearly. But that's all right. He just has different tastes, our Sabre."

Sabre startled, slightly, rattling the tray of cobbled-together breakfast leftovers. No one had called him *our Sabre* since before the execution. His mother used to say it, when she was feeling uncharacteristically soft, running her hands through his hair. *Our Sabre.*

"He seemed happy enough with Charon, anyways," Nanette said. "Margritte saw him limping down the stairs. It was a good limp, though," she added, glancing at Sabre.

"Didn't see *you* after that little debacle," Percival said. Sabre could feel the blush rising on his cheeks. He could still hear Laurent's voice in the back of his mind, feel the heat of his gaze. The relief that washed over him when he yielded, on his knees with Laurent standing over him, hands in his hair.

"You didn't see him because what's-his-name was watching you fuck Gwydion with that glowing pink dick of yours," Yves said.

Percival gave him a bored look. "It was the blue one, and they don't *glow*, they glitter. Why buy your own if they aren't going to be interesting?"

"Hey, mine's interesting," Yves said.

"Yes, precious, all four inches of it."

"Sabre, hit him," Yves said. He grabbed at one of Simone's limitless supply of pillows. "You're in training, so you have to listen to me."

"Says *who?*" Percival asked. An edge of dominance crept into his voice. "Sabre, ignore him, he's just a pampered sugar-baby with a god complex."

"Not while I'm *lying* here!" Simone cried, as Yves threw a beaded pillow at Percival. "You *beasts.*"

"Children," Nanette said, leaning over to grab the rest of the muffin on Percival's plate.

"Are all of the houses like this?" Sabre asked, as Yves snarled, scrambling over to Percival like an irate housecat.

"Gods, no," Nanette said. "The House of Iron would've never let us out of assigned spaces during off hours. Don't want courtesans finding out if they're being paid differently for servicing the same noble, right?"

"Or forbid you step outside without permission," Simone said. "Lord de Rue is soft in that way."

Nanette handed over a piece of Percival's muffin. "Only you would call him *soft.*"

"Because he is. I worked here before it was the House of Onyx, you know." Simone pushed a lamp out of the way as Yves pinned Percival down, reaching for his curlers. "He came in here dressed like a country noble with last season's styles, bought out the House from under the old lord, and started rattling about like a hornet in a cup. Talking about tips and security measures and an open ledger. I was sure the other lords would eat him alive by now."

Sabre searched Simone's face. It was hard to believe that she was as old as she claimed to be—as old as Sabre's mother, at least—with her carefully-applied face and elegant gowns. It was harder still to know what she was thinking, and when she cast Sabre a soft smile, he wasn't sure if he wanted to smile back.

"Then he took *you* in out of the proverbial cold," she said. "None of the other lords would have taken such pains to keep you alive. The nobles are restless, now. I'm sure the others have noticed."

"*My* nobles are too distracted to be restless," Yves said, from where Percival was sitting on his chest in apparent triumph. He didn't seem all too put out by it.

"One of mine asked about it," Nanette said. She glanced at Sabre. "Apparently, the king hinted that you wouldn't have to be trained. Nobles aren't really used to having to wait. No offense."

Sabre shrugged. It was true. He had an army of servants at home— He hadn't even thought of where they'd gone, after his house fell.

Laurent would have thought of it, if he were in Sabre's place. Sabre doubted Adrien even gave them a second thought. He had a bad habit of avoiding servants, since it made him uncomfortable to be waited on.

"I'm sure if Laurent had his way, you wouldn't serve anyone at all," Simone said, pouring herself a new cup of tea.

"But. I've served *him*, though," Sabre said, carefully. "When I needed it."

There was a short silence.

"Fuck," Nanette said, and dug in her pants pocket for a crumpled bank note. She tossed it in Simone's lap.

"I told you, like a stray puppy taken in out of the rain," Simone said, smoothing out the note. She smiled at Sabre. "We had a bet, you see. How long before dear Lord Laurent gave in to those sad eyes of yours."

"Who's giving in to what, exactly?"

Sabre, who was already sitting on the floor next to Simone, sank down another inch as Laurent leaned against the doorway. He was beautiful in a white shirt with belled sleeves and black trousers that could have been stolen from Nanette, and when he looked at Sabre, Sabre tried to suppress a full-body shiver.

"Tea," Simone said, smoothly. "Would you like some? Sabre's serving. It's good practice."

"I had tea at the theater," Laurent said. "Rose invited all of you to her production, by the way. She'll be Maiden Number Three, in Act One."

"That's a step up from being a tree, though," Percival said.

"Yeah, well done," Nanette said. "Is she remembering to project from the diaphragm?"

"Constantly," Laurent said. "Sabre, time to leave the layabouts behind and go to work."

"Yes, my lord." Sabre paused, unsure if he was expected to crawl this time, and Simone gave him an arch, knowing look that made his face heat like a flame. He stood.

He half expected to be on laundry duty again, but Laurent led him downstairs, to the common room where Gwydion was stitching feathers on a mask. A whole tray of them lay on a rolling table next to the couches, glittering with colored glass and wire. Gwydion waved without looking up, trailing strings on his free hand.

"You'll be hosting tonight," Laurent said, opening the gate to a protected, screened room where nobles were supposed to put on masks to hide their identities from other guests. "It's simple enough. You greet them, mark them down in the ledger, and offer them a mask. Tea and coffee is served in the common room."

Sabre looked down at the black ledger chained to the podium by the door. "Will *I* be masked?"

Laurent's sigh was only just audible. "No."

"Oh."

"You haven't had your first night, though," Laurent said. "They won't risk making enemies of the noble who's claimed it, so they'll have to try to get under your skin in other ways. It will give you an idea of what to expect."

"I can't..." Sabre ran a hand over the ledger. "I can't fall sick, suddenly, or..."

"You don't have the luxury of avoiding this," Laurent said, and Sabre watched him, searching for the softness Simone said was there. His violet eyes gave away nothing. "Only clients hide their faces, here."

Not just clients, Sabre thought, breaking Laurent's impassive gaze.

Sabre was kept busy for most of the afternoon, cleaning the common room and foyer while Gwydion made an elaborate mask shaped like a bird of prey. Gwydion was quieter than Percival, more inclined towards comfortable silence, but he did stop every now and then to ask Sabre what he thought of a mask, holding them up to his angular face. He looked like one of the year-end dancers, lithe and wiry and a little severe, and only his soft blond hair smoothed his sharp edges.

Then he was gone, and Sabre found himself wheeling the cart of masks into the foyer while the lamps were lit on the street outside.

Someone knocked on the other side of the partition, and Sabre jumped. Laurent stood there, dressed all in black, jet earrings dangling in his hair.

"I'll be here to greet the guests, for a time," he said. "Since it's your first night as a host."

"Y-yes, my lord," Sabre said. "Thank you."

"Don't thank me just yet," Laurent said. "It's a full night."

Sabre's fingers curled on the ledger.

The first knock on the door felt like the pounding of boots on the ballroom floor. Sabre opened the door for a tall, light-haired Lord Chastain, the minister of the Hunt. Lord Chastain had given Elise a mare for her birthday just last year, but their invitations to the hunt on his estates dried up a few months ago. Now, he gave Sabre a long, steady look and handed him his cloak.

"Has becoming a whore robbed you of your tongue?" Lord Chastain asked. "Greet me properly."

"Yes, my lord," Sabre said. He took a steadying breath that did nothing while he hung up the cloak. "Welcome to the House of Onyx. If you would please choose a mask."

Lord Chastain chose a mask shaped with wings on either side, black as a raven. It didn't do much to hide him, not with his distinctive trim beard and silver-tipped boots, but the masks were probably just there for drama more than for real secrecy. Sabre opened the door of the partition and pulled on the string that would notify Nanette that her first client was waiting, making a bell chime somewhere upstairs.

"My lord, welcome." Laurent lounged on a couch near the far corner of the room, next to the coffee service. "Sit with me while our dear Nanette puts her face on."

Lord Chastain sat stiffly, and Sabre only just managed to fill his cup without spilling it over the edge. He felt like a shadow, scuttling under Lord Chastain's notice while Laurent laughed and spoke of hunting dogs and city nobles like he'd been born to the title, and almost breathed a sigh of relief when there was another knock on the door.

The woman who entered this time didn't recognize Sabre. She was a merchant, possibly, wealthy enough but without a title to ingratiate herself into the court. She even flashed Sabre a smile as he handed her a mask with gold lining. Percival and Gwydion greeted her almost immediately, kissing her on the cheek one after the other and guiding her up the stairs by the hand.

The third client was Roland Garnier, the second son of Lord Garnier, the minister in charge of the treasury. They'd been friends of a sort, even if Sabre's mother and Lord Garnier didn't exactly get along, and Sabre's breath caught as Roland stared at him from the doorway. Roland broke into a slow smile.

"Well," he said. "I *thought* you were sent here."

"Roland," Sabre said.

"That's my lord now, isn't it?" Roland said, taking off his coat. "Here you go. What am I supposed to call you? Courtesan? Mister? Slut, maybe, people in your profession like that, don't they?"

Sabre blinked. Roland had always been so pleasant to him, before. Maybe in a dull sort of way, sure, but he'd gone along whenever Sabre suggested they go for a ride, and he'd danced with Sabre at more than one ball, then ignored their dance cards to drink stolen wine in the back with other second sons like Roland. Now, Roland's voice had a harder edge.

Roland snapped his fingers. "Pay attention, Sab. Maybe they did strangle you with that rope, after all. I asked you a question."

"I...don't have a preference, my lord," Sabre said.

"Then I'll call you whore, because that's what you are, right? Easier that way. All right, whore, summon the pretty one and get on with it." Sabre moved towards the partition, and Roland snapped his fingers again. "Is there something you forgot to say, traitor?"

Sabre closed his eyes for a moment. "Yes, my lord. I apologize."

"I'm sure there's a lot you're sorry for," Roland said, picking out a mask as Sabre pulled on Simone's cord. "You know, me and Devon and Olivier, maybe we should all hire you for a night. It'll be like old times, except your bitch of a mother won't be around to stop us from wiping our boots with you."

Sabre had to force his hand not to shake as he opened the door to the partition. "My first night is already reserved, my lord."

"We'll take the second, then. It'll be fun, I bet. You'll like it," Roland said, collapsing on a couch, "serving us the way you're supposed to. Devon's wanted to gag that mouth of yours for years. Maybe we'll take you all at once, make you work for it. You'd like that, wouldn't you?"

It was harder, this time, to pour the tea. When Sabre knelt to serve it, Roland leaned forward, grabbing him by the side of the head. Sabre glanced at Laurent, who was watching them, eyes dark.

"This is the collar he gave you," Roland said, and he touched the scales of the king's collar at his neck. "It's prettier than you deserve."

"My lord!" Sabre tensed at the sound of Simone's voice behind him. "How lovely to see you again so soon."

"Next time, then," Roland said to Sabre. He stood. "Simone, don't you look divine."

"I'm pleased my lord thinks so. If you'll follow me?"

"Sure. Let me get rid of this tea, first," Roland said, and, before Sabre could even rise from his knees, tipped the contents of his teacup over Sabre's back.

* * *

It went about how Laurent thought it would.

The men and women who were of the merchant class did not recognize Sabre, for the most part. One or two stared at him a bit overlong, and he had a discreet inquiry by way of the silk merchant on his way out, but nothing overtly rude. Proving, Laurent thought, that nobles were in fact *not* the pinnacle of nobility, but rather the moss-strewn rocks on the bottom.

Which, he'd always known that, hadn't he? There was a difference, they said, between nobles who earned their title through so-called *service to the crown* and those who inherited them. That without the generations of noblesse oblige to guide you, you'd be as uncouth as a merchant newly swimming in gold. And Laurent, who had a title, thought the difference was how those who inherited their titles didn't have to earn them, and therefore did not comprehend what it might be like to lose them.

He'd known this would be unpleasant for Sabre, of course, which was why he wanted to get it over with before Sabre's First Night. Lord Chastain had been a previous client of Laurent's, a man who liked edging more than was sensible and was one of the few who could make Laurent say *please, my lord, let me come* and actually mean it. His tone toward Sabre wasn't kind, but it was about what you'd expect from a man in charge of hunting small, defenseless animals and killing them for sport. He wouldn't be surprised if his name showed up sooner rather than later in Sabre's ledger. Nanette reported he liked to dress her as a boy and hunt her before fucking her. Sabre likely wouldn't give chase as elegantly as Nanette, but the novelty would get Sabre a few ticks against his debt all the same.

Roland, though. The pleasure he took in his cruelty toward Sabre was simply the other side of what he enjoyed with Simone, but there'd been real antagonism there when he'd spilled the tea on Sabre's back. And even though Laurent expected this, had in fact banked on this very thing making his House a tidy profit, it still took all his training not to grab the little pissant by his too-coiffed hair and snarl something about taking sadist lessons from an expert before trying to dom the help. But he'd done nothing, merely watched Sabre's face when the scalding tea soaked through his shirt, saw the miserable expression at war with something entirely different, some other, darker desire coming so easily to the surface.

His first thought at Roland's smirking promise to hire Sabre with his former friends had been an emphatic *over my dead body,* but then he remembered, again, why Sabre was there. Laurent was mildly disconcerted at how it seemed to be *him* that needed the reminder, not Sabre.

He'd asked Sabre to change his shirt, then got himself together and waited for the rest of them.

The next noble who sailed into the house that night was Lord Verre, who stared with hunger and barely-concealed hostility when he saw Sabre there.

"Well, the rumors are true, then," he drawled. "And here I was hoping the king let you hang. Disgusting, but I suppose he wanted your traitor of a mother's last thought to worry at what would become of you." He looked pleased with himself, for that.

Thought of that on your way here, did you.

"Yes, my lord," Sabre whispered.

"You know, if the king really wanted to have made an example of you, he should have used your mouth and come down your throat the moment he told them to let your family hang," Lord de Verre said. "I was there that morning. You looked lovely under his boot while they choked to death. A pity how long it took your poor sister to die."

Laurent cast his eyes heavenward, wondering if he really thought that was some original taunt and also a bit surprised King Emile *hadn't* done that. It seemed like something the king would do, which did perhaps suggest he believed Sabre wasn't involved in the de Valois plot. Whatever it was, Laurent didn't know the particulars and didn't want to.

"Would you, a mask, my lord," Sabre managed, trembling on his knees, his eyes bright.

Lord de Verre smiled, reached out and took one from the table, crimson red, and honestly, it did very little for his coloring. "Maybe I'll have an evening with you myself, whore. Do what the king should have done, make you take my cock while I tell an executioner to *let them hang.*"

He wouldn't, Laurent thought, be the first.

Sabre spilled the tea, his hands shaking, and Lord de Verre just laughed until Margritte came to greet him. De Verre was, according to Margritte, *a sadist, but an uninspired one,* and that seemed to track.

Laurent watched Sabre clean up the tea service, kneeling and breathing too hard. "This is why they won't want you to have lessons with Yves. They like seeing you serve, and fail, and bow beneath their cruelty."

"Yes, my lord," Sabre said, softly, and Laurent wondered if he even knew it was Laurent who was speaking to him.

One noble asked if he could strike Sabre, which Laurent played off with a laugh and a *not without an appointment,* and settled for having his tea with his boots on Sabre's back, while Sabre braced himself on all fours as the lord's heeled boots dug in hard enough to ensure he'd have to change his shirt, *again.*

It was after Laurent sent him off once more that Delauney de Mazet sailed in, beaming at Laurent and sweeping him a valiant bow. "Lord de Rue, your infamy continues to grow by leaps and bounds. You're an inspiration to us all."

Laurent took Delauney's coat himself, and smiled as he accepted a kiss on each cheek. De Mazet was one of the rare nobles who didn't seem to take himself quite so seriously, and whose primary mission in life as a second son seemed to be having fun and spending as much time away from Staria as possible. He was a commissioned officer in the royal navy, and had always been one of Laurent's favorite clients. He was a submissive who liked Charon to work him over after long bouts at sea, where he was required to subdue his urges in favor of his command.

Delauney had been a frequent client at the House of Gold, one of the few who *wanted* Laurent to be dominant and who'd offered to marry him on no more than four occasions, or to bring him along as his personal valet while at sea. He was as far from cruel as a man could be, and Laurent had always been pleased to see him, even if he knew Delauney's wild declarations of adoration were merely post-sex bliss and the relief of being put under. Laurent would not have done well, at sea. The saltwater did not agree with his hair.

"That's the key to success in any endeavor, isn't it, Lord de Mazet? Adaptability?"

"Is it? I rather thought it was audacity, myself." Delauney grinned and took his favorite mask, one with a variety of rainbow feathers that made Laurent think of some rare tropical bird. "I've been away for ages and am in dire need of the back of Charon's hand, do tell Yves and the twins it's nothing personal, won't you?"

"They won't hold it against you, I assure you, de Mazet. If they were the type, they'd be working elsewhere."

"You can call me Delauney, you know. We're peers, now."

De Mazet used to insist on it, back when he was paying Laurent for the evening. Laurent smiled at him, perhaps a tad warmer than most. "Normally I'd disagree, you're the son of a Marquis. But if you're ever looking to retire from His Majesty's Navy, you'd be a formidable House lord indeed."

Delauney laughed, but then his eyes widened as the door opened and Sabre walked in. "Sabre. It's been some time."

"Lord de Mazet," Sabre said, eyes lowered. "It has."

"I'm pleased, I really am, to see you alive. And I'm so sorry about what happened to your mother, and your sweet sister." Delauney said, and it sounded sincere.

"They were traitors to the crown," Sabre whispered, still to the floor, as he knelt once more before the tea service. It was probably cold, but Laurent doubted Delauney cared.

Delauney, who was seated at the couch, leaned forward and placed a careful hand on Sabre's arm. "Be that as it may, they were your family, and it doesn't make me any less sorry for your loss, or how you lost them."

Sabre gave one soft, hiccuping sound and said, "Thank you, my lord. My sister, she always said that she wanted to—to horrify mother at her coming out ball, and dance first with you."

Delauney said, "I would have been happy to, I'm a terrible dancer really, but much better at a little low-level scandal."

"Ring for Charon, pet," Laurent said, dominance threading his words.

Sabre drew in a shaky breath, and did as asked. Somehow, Laurent knew, Delauney's well-meaning condolences were worse than all those other nobles' casual cruelty could ever hope to be. That, he could get lost in, suffer so he went under. This was too raw, a different kind of pain entirely.

Charon appeared a few moments later, while Sabre composed himself and Laurent wondered if Delauney would be a good client for Sabre, or just leave him frustrated *and* miserable. Probably.

"Ah, there you are, you gorgeous beast of a man," Delauney said, hopping to his feet when Charon entered. "Do you know I met a man from Arktos on my last trip? I'll tell you all about it while you ravish me like a stolen Katoikos war prize."

"As you wish, my lord," Charon said, but perhaps there was something of a fondness there, too. Delauney wouldn't have been the first to roleplay that with Charon, but he would probably laugh a lot more, until Charon had him under.

"Sabre, I...you're in good hands, here. Remember everyone has secrets, and they all talk in their sleep." Delauney reached down and ran his fingers through Sabre's hair, which Laurent knew was doing Sabre no favors, before he left with Charon.

"My lord," Sabre managed, white-faced and trembling. "Would you please...may I ask."

Laurent sighed, grabbed a fistfull of his hair and pulled it, hard. "I didn't allow for the possibility that a Starian noble would be capable of sincerity. That was worse than the taunts, wasn't it."

It wasn't a question, but Sabre nodded. Or maybe he was just trying to make Laurent pull harder on his hair.

"He isn't like the others, no," said Sabre. "Please don't send me to him. I don't know if I could."

"You don't make the rules here, pet. I do. If he offers enough, you'll go to him." Laurent's voice was firm but not unkind. "I know what you need and I know de Mazet isn't it. You were almost under before his regard dragged you back up, weren't you?"

"Yes," Sabre said.

Laurent sighed. "Go warm up the tea and come back. The night is far from over."

No one else exhibited any surprising amount of concern for Sabre's well being, though, and there were certainly no more expressions of *sorrow* about Sabre's family as people who lost their lives in the gruesome display of King Emile's power. But Sabre was either outright ignored, stared at, mocked or belittled—and once, kicked, though Laurent did add a surcharge to the woman's bill, for that—for the rest of the night, until Laurent stopped making him freshen his clothes and just let him be a mess. It went over well with the nobles, and when the last of the evening's clients disappeared up the stairs—Lord de Baux, one of Yves' favorites because "he comes in three minutes then brushes my hair for an hour and feeds me chocolate, it's barely any effort"—Laurent considered telling Sabre to put the tea things away, but he was shaking so hard they'd end up with broken glass on the floor instead of cups.

Which Sabre would like kneeling on, probably. Considering he'd been doing the equivalent, mentally, for the last few hours.

"I'll see to it, my lord. Take the fawn upstairs." Simone stood in the doorway, makeup removed and dressed simply in her linen shift and a silk robe, her hair unbound. She looked smaller like this, without the armor of silks and satins, paint and perfumes they all donned to keep the softer parts of them safe. Courtesans like Simone were not the usual. She, like Laurent, long ago chose to hide her dominance in favor of sheer survival.

"Thank you, Simone," Laurent said. "I'll make a note for you on the ledger."

She waved a hand. "It isn't necessary."

"Yes," Laurent said quietly. "It is. I promised everyone who came here that you'd be paid fair for your work and I meant it."

She shook her head. "You were a whore long enough, you should know that there are some things worth more to one than money. Like safety. Someone who understands." Her eyes flickered to Sabre, swaying on his knees, his head pressed to Laurent's thigh. "I hope you are right about what he can handle, my lord. There's a difference between going under and drowning."

Laurent inclined his head. "There is. And you'll have to trust me."

"I do. With my life. All of us here do, my lord. That's what I meant, when I said some things matter more than money."

"Come with me," Laurent said, to Sabre. This time, he didn't even have to tell him to crawl—Sabre did it, out of the front room and over floors stained muddy from the boots of nobles eager to see him break, shatter apart like glass.

* * *

THERE WERE voices in the communal baths when Sabre passed them, and while Sabre had joined the others once or twice at the end of the night to bathe quietly while courtesans laughed and tossed scented soaps across the tile, Laurent led him on. It was a relief not to have to see anyone, and Sabre wondered if it would be like that every time, drifting uncomfortably on his own. Only Laurent's hand on his hair grounded him.

"My mother would call this a lesson," Sabre said, quietly, as he was led into Laurent's private baths. "I think she would have taught me, eventually."

"Would she." Laurent's tone of casual disinterest sounded affected, there in the dim light of the bath. "Prepare the bath, pet."

"Yes, my lord," Sabre said. He turned on the taps and knelt there for a moment, watching the sunken tub fill with steam. "It's a fault of mine."

"Running a bath? Awkward for you. Strip for me. Fold your clothes when you're done."

Sabre moved slowly, fumbling with the buttons of his shirt. "Not that. I was inclined to think I was apart, from politics. Too close to the throne to worry, too far to be trouble. I was going to go into the military, did you know?"

"Can't say I was aware."

"I swore myself to the king," Sabre said. "When his wife died."

"I suppose you'd have to, to prove your loyalty."

"Oh, no. I just felt sorry for him," Sabre said. "Maybe that's why he's doing this. Maybe it hurt him the same way, being pitied. Maybe that's what broke him."

"The man killed his own wife, Sabre." Laurent was already undressed, beautiful in the hazy air of the baths. "Even if she was a traitor. You might be overthinking it. That's enough, I think. Don't speak when you enter the bath."

"He didn't kill her," Sabre said.

Laurent went still.

"That is." Sabre's stomach lurched, terror stirring below. "No. I could tell. It was a guess."

It wasn't, though. He knew because Adrien had told him.

Adrien, gangly for a young teenager, had pounded at the door of their royal suites in the dead of night, and sobbed brokenly in the hall as Sabre's father opened the door. Sabre had come with Adrien and his father to the throne room, with Adrien clinging to his hand, pale and wild-eyed.

She saw something when she cut herself on a knife, tonight, Adrien had said, as they ran. *She tried to, tried to change it. Change the future, with a spell. But she—she cut too deep—*

Enough, Sabre's father had said. *Tell no one of this, Sabre. Adrien. Even your mother, or your sister, or the king.*

They'd sworn, there on the way to the throne room, where the queen lay dying. They'd stayed silent as Sabre's father dragged the king away from her body, as the court whispered around them in the days to come, as the king started the first string of executions, searching for the one who taught his wife the magic that killed her.

Then Sabre's father had died, and there was only Sabre and Adrien left to remember.

"He killed his cousin, though," Sabre said. "Her daughter." He slipped into the bath. "Maybe it's because I take after my father. Ah. Sorry, my lord. I'll be quiet."

It was better, that way. He sank into the heat of the bath, and wondered if the king thought of him, hidden away in the pleasure district. If it was a more satisfying end than a death in the quarries. If there was any part of him, the part that belonged to the man who didn't have to watch his wife die by her own hand, that thought he was worth saving.

Laurent watched him carefully as Sabre followed his instructions to wash Laurent's hair and knead product through his own until it was silk-soft. He was still drifting, but it was easier to be quiet, to follow simple orders. He wasn't trembling by the time he stepped out of the bath, at least.

"My lord," Sabre said, when he was dry, setting his towel aside to be laundered in the morning. "What will I do, to come down, when I start taking clients?"

"The other courtesans usually get together in the baths, afterwards," Laurent said. "Or they go to Charon."

"Does anyone..." Sabre tilted his head so he could rest against Laurent's thigh. Laurent touched his hair, still damp from the baths, and Sabre held back a sigh. "Does anyone go to you?"

Laurent was silent.

"Would you let me," Sabre said, quietly. "If I asked?"

"It isn't a common practice," Laurent said, which wasn't a no. Not exactly. "Come."

Laurent lit a lamp by the bed while Sabre knelt there, watching the light slide over Laurent's body as he moved. He couldn't imagine daring to hire him, if Sabre were still a noble. Sabre wouldn't have known how to speak around him, even how to *look* at him, without making an utter fool of himself. That it took his title being stripped away to be able to speak to him at all wasn't lost on Sabre.

When Laurent returned with the cuffs, Sabre shifted uneasily, looking down. "My lord." He dragged his lower lip between his teeth, steadying himself. "Could I sleep on the floor, tonight?"

Laurent's gaze was dark, shadowed by the light at his back. "Fetch a blanket from the closet and kneel at the foot of the bed. No cushion tonight, I think."

"Thank you, my lord," Sabre said. He didn't think he could manage a soft bed. Not just yet. He took down a blanket from the closet and knelt for Laurent, sighing when the cuffs were slipped on and the lead tied to the end of the bed.

For a moment, he thought Laurent would ask more of him, standing there with Sabre kneeling at his feet, but then he just tugged at Sabre's hair in farewell and climbed into bed, leaving Sabre feeling strangely hollow.

It took a while for Sabre to sleep. He wasn't sure when it happened. He slid into dreams so smoothly, rising from bed with his hands bound behind him rather than before him, climbing the rickety steps to a wooden platform under the open sky.

His sister was hanging beside him, thrashing on the end of her rope. Her feet kicked at the air, and the sounds she made were unnatural, inhuman, low and guttural.

"Poor thing," said a woman at Sabre's feet. He looked down. The queen sat on the edge of the platform. Blood ran down her hands as she stitched at an embroidery hoop, her dark hair spilling over one shoulder. "Poor thing."

She'd called Sabre that, before. When he was young, running about with Adrien while the queen watched them with her odd, distant gaze. *Poor thing.*

Maybe she'd seen him on the platform, long ago, when she pricked her finger on a needle or stared down at a gash in her leg from a fall. Maybe that's why she never invited Elise, when she was born, or Sabre's mother, to the rare outings she and Adrien and Sabre used to go on, when the queen wasn't wrapped up in her husband's embrace.

In the dream, the queen stabbed the needle through her arm and tugged it through.

"Poor thing," she said.

The platform fell under Sabre's feet, and he fell. The rope jerked at his throat, then gave, ripping apart as he tumbled alone in the dark. He scrabbled at nothing, scraped his fingers against a wall he couldn't see, before he was flung into the open, the empty, where there was nothing to meet his grasping hands.

He woke sobbing, his hands clenched tight around the lead, curled up at the foot of the bed with the sheets kicked off in a tangle behind him. He gasped for air, shaking violently, and flinched when Laurent's shadow passed over him.

"Do you know who I am?" Laurent asked. He didn't touch Sabre, just sat there, a hand on the mattress, leaning over him.

"Yes," Sabre said, in a terrible, harsh voice. "Yes, my lord."

"Will you let me release you?"

"Not from the..." Sabre could barely get the words out. "Not my hands."

"I'll leave them bound. I'm just removing them from the bed."

Sabre flinched again when Laurent came close, but allowed him to guide him to his knees. "I'm. I'm sorry I woke you."

"I doubt you could help it," Laurent said, dryly. He tugged at Sabre's hair, which helped somewhat, dragged him farther from the brink. "Remember to breathe."

His heart was still hammering too hard in his chest, but it was easier to breathe with Laurent there at the end of the bed.

"My lord," he said, still a little breathless, still half frozen with terror, closing his eyes to the pull of Laurent's hand in his hair. "My lord, if I asked, would you help me."

"Is this not helping?" Laurent asked.

"Please." Sabre raised his bound hands, bowed his head. "I can't bow the way you're supposed to, anymore, and I know it's asking, asking so much of you, but please, if you could…help me feel something else." He took a shivering breath. "I'll try to make it up for you. To be good. Please, my lord." He didn't think he could bow all the way, not after being held down by the king, but he did bend over his knees, fingers clenched before him.

"Please."

CHAPTER 7

*I*f Laurent had half the sense he liked to think, he'd call for Charon. Charon would handle Sabre with his calm indifference, hurt him to the point where Sabre lost that sheen of terror in his eyes and then gentle him into sleep. He wouldn't mind it, either. He'd done it for everyone in the house, a time or two. Even Laurent, once or twice.

But he knew he wasn't going to. Sabre looked too beautiful like this, sobbing and broken, begging in his noble's voice for Laurent —*Laurent,* an orphan from some unknown land who couldn't remember a day before his tenth birthday, who didn't even know what his real name was—to settle him, to be good.

He could tell himself he was going to do it for the House, hell, he could say he was going to do it for Sabre—because of course he was going to do it—but he was honest enough to admit that he wanted to give Sabre what he was asking for so prettily, and it had nothing to do with anything other than the simple fact that he wanted to.

"Come up here." Laurent sat up. The truth was he himself had yet to fall asleep, sensitive to every twitch and soft sound of misery coming from the floor. "The lead is long enough."

Sabre said, "I can't move. *I can't move.*"

108

Laurent got out of bed. He walked over and knelt by Sabre, and he couldn't deny he was affected by the sight. He'd seen a lot, in his time at the House of Gold. Courtesans ill-suited to the job, terrified what might await them if they didn't take to it anyway. Courtesans who were no longer in demand and who hadn't yet made their house debt, frantic at the thought of their debt being sold to some lower-tier house, or worse, to the quarries. He'd seen children as young as six, dropped off by desperate parents who thought their children had no future beyond growing up in a pleasure house, learning how to one day be a whore. It was equally as awful when the children were accepted, as when they weren't.

There were other houses, the ones the minnow-catchers worked for, that weren't quite so picky. And they didn't always follow the rules of age of majority, either.

He'd seen miserable courtesans, plenty of times. Even ones that were doing well. The House of Gold had been a hotbed of competitiveness and underhanded dealings, with all of them vying for attention that would pay out their debt faster, get them noticed by a noble who might want to sponsor them, install them in some side-chamber in one of their estates and at least remove them from the constant competition and fear of being surpassed by someone else.

The smart ones knew it was temporary, in the House of Gold. Laurent knew it, the House's former top earner before him knew it, and the one after Laurent probably did, too. Being installed as some aging noble's plaything in a country estate sounded like a fate worse than death to Laurent, but for some, it was the only reasonable goal they had. Of course, even then, you could be returned. It happened sometimes, a sobbing courtesan brought back, a whole new debt added to the old. Out of the limelight long enough that no one remembered who you were. The sound of the quarry cart trundling up to the House at dawn, the pleading that never once managed to change the house lord's mind.

But he was almost certain he'd never seen anyone as miserable as Sabre de Valois, sobbing his fear and loneliness out on Laurent's floor. Plagued by nightmares from almost being hanged and hearing the king give the command to have his family die. Everything torn from him, ripped away, and Laurent using it for his own means, his own house's infamy. At least that was the litany singing through his head as he looked at Sabre there, on the floor. Undone by cruelty and kindness both.

Laurent went down on his heels. He tipped Sabre's face up to his, and wondered if he should ask him about the herbs, again. Or just bring them anyway, let him feel safe for a bit, slip into better dreams and not be torn out of them.

He sighed. "You have no idea how you look right now. I've never seen anyone so broken look as beautiful as you do. And I should, if I were a better man, do something for you. Something more than teach you how to take their cruelty and disdain and drink it like fine wine. But other than deliver you sweetly into death, all I can do is this."

"They'd know," Sabre said, as Laurent drew him close. "If it was peaceful. It would be your house that suffered and I don't want that."

Laurent thought of him, then, as the noble he might have been. At what an evening would be like, if Sabre had hired him, begged to be taken and hurt. "That you would think of that, first, shows you are a good man. But ah, I am not, my Sabre. I'm ruthless and I'm using you, and I'd like to tell you that it's because I know it will help you, but it might just be because I like seeing you hurt."

"That's." Sabre drew in a breath, pushing against Laurent's hand on his head. "Fine."

Laurent almost laughed. "Come up with me, to bed. I'll settle you. But I don't want you to think I'm something I'm not."

Sabre blinked at him, and Laurent decided this wasn't the time to assuage his own guilt at what he was doing. So he drew Sabre up to the bed, kept his hands cuffed in front of him and unclicked the lead, just to wrap it firmly around his own wrist. "Did you like it when they called you a whore, a slut?"

"Yes," Sabre said, staring as Laurent unbound his hair, letting it fall in soft, red-gold waves around his face.

"They'll call you that a lot. They'll say those terrible things, and most of them will hurt at first, deliciously, you'll feel like you're kneeling on glass, like every snide word is a whip, fire-tipped." He pushed Sabre to his back, leaned over them. "They won't know that you like the way it feels. They want to hurt you."

"Yes," Sabre said, again, starting to writhe.

"Focus on that, when it gets mixed up with what really happened. Everyone here hides behind something, you'll need to find it, too." Laurent kissed him, took his time with it, overwhelmed him. Bit his lip, hard enough to get Sabre moaning.

"It will grow dull. You'll hear those things, terrible words about your family, about the king, about their pleasure in watching the worst thing that ever happened to you. You will playact, as all of us do, even Yves who seems content to be nothing but a noble's plaything. Don't ever let them know, your clients, that it stopped hurting like you want it to. That you're bored. Earn your debt and have a life somewhere else, where your nightmares are your own and your pain isn't fodder for some bored nobleman's lust." Laurent caught himself, recognizing the impending dominant-drop after years of suffering it post-assignation, when he wasn't allowed to be what his nature had already decided he was. "What hurt you more, pet? Your old friend threatening to hire you for an evening and making it clear he never liked you, or de Mazet's sincerity when he apologized for what happened to your family?"

Sabre twisted on the bed beneath him. "That—that did."

"That's why you won't go the prince, or de Mazet, or anyone who meant you well." Laurent shifted on top of him. "You used to fence with de Mortain. He's a cold man. Exacting. Not known for his empathy. I chose well for you. You'll thank me, when you come back, and he's hurt you, fucked you under."

"Yes, I—I will, I'll be good for you, I just want to be *enough*."

"You are what I say you are," Laurent said. He smacked Sabre across his pretty, miserable face. "And I am not going to tell you that again. You'll be good because I say you are." He rolled on top of Sabre, let him feel how hard Laurent was, knowing it was overwhelming, the full press of his naked body where before he'd always been dressed. "You have me hard for you, do you think that isn't enough?"

"Ah, my lord—" Sabre pushed his hips against him, his cock as hard as rock, more even than Laurent's.

"Shh. I'll hear you moan and beg when I'm ready for it, but you'll let me settle you. You'll stop fighting." Laurent bit him on the shoulder, the neck. Forced his mouth open, spit it into it, smacked him over and over until Sabre swallowed and tears spilled prettily from his bright gold eyes.

There was really only so much Laurent could do, as turned on as he was, as Sabre was, with his first night promised to someone else. He thought about straddling Sabre while he lay there beneath him, choking him with his cock, but what he wanted to do was *fuck him.*

So instead, he grabbed his hair and choked him a little above his collar and thought how it was all wrong, should be sleek and black, something that was *his*, not the king's. And that way lay danger, the same kind that sent Sabre's mother and sister to the gallows. Laurent pinned him down and rutted his cock against Sabre's, and the room was thick with the sounds of their breathing. Laurent did not fuck his courtesans. But he wanted to fuck this one.

Sabre was undone there on the bed, lost in being put under by casual cruelty and Laurent's firm dominance. He was gasping and arching, trying almost shyly to rub himself against Laurent, give him pleasure, let himself be used, useful.

Laurent groaned. "Gods, how I want to fuck you."

"Yes, oh, yes, please, my lord, I—please, please," Sabre begged, and there was no artifice, nothing in it but want.

He pushed his face into Sabre's neck and shoulder. "That doesn't— belong to me."

"I belong to you," Sabre said, as if it was scripted, so perfect that it seemed almost as if he'd always been born to be a whore, not a useless noble no one took the time to settle properly.

Laurent fumbled for the oil by his bedside, kneeling up on the mattress as he opened the bottle. Sabre panted up at him and spread his legs, and Laurent threw his head back and groaned, grabbing the base of his cock to keep from coming all over himself and Sabre.

He backhanded Sabre. It split his lip, and Sabre—trapped on his back with his hands bound before him—cried out and begged, "Please let me come, my lord."

If he'd had one less ounce of self-control, Laurent would have done it. Fucked him hard, right then and there and damn all the consequences. But instead, he spilled the oil on Sabre's firm, pale thighs, ruining the sheets, and fell almost gracelessly on top of him. "Not yet, no, tighten your legs for me."

Sabre did it, head thrashing on the pillow, and Laurent fucked himself to a blinding, shuddering orgasm there between his slicked up thighs. It took no time at all, and when he growled out, "Beg me to let you come, now," Sabre tightened his legs even more and did it, begged desperately and without hesitation.

"Please, please, my lord, oh, please—*Laurent*—"

And that he shouldn't allow, but instead he bit Sabre hard enough above his collar to break the skin and snarled, "Do it," and felt Sabre go tense beneath him, shuddering in pleasure as he came, rubbing himself desperately against Laurent's stomach and spilling warm and wet between them.

By the time Laurent moved away, Sabre was a mess—his face flushed and tear-streaked, panting, his hair everywhere, covered in oil and their combined release. But his eyes were soft and unfocused, clear, and there was a little smile on his face, and a smear of blood above the bright gold of his collar, like a sunset.

Laurent stroked his hair and waited for his heart to stop pounding. It took a long time. When he could finally rouse himself and stand on legs that were also unsteady, Sabre was asleep. His breathing was deep and even, and if he had nightmares, they did not wake him.

Laurent could tell, because he lay there, unable to sleep, until dawn.

* * *

"Honey, you can't keep doing this."

Sabre grimly washed his mouth out with some of Gwydion's tooth-cleaning solution, which was bright green and vaguely suspicious, but made his mouth taste like he *hadn't* just thrown up his lunch for the second time that day. Gwydion himself stood in the back, fixing loose threads on a mask, while the entirety of the House crowded up between him and Sabre.

"I'm fine," Sabre said.

"Of course you are," Simone said, running a comb through his hair. "We were all nervous before our First Night, weren't we?"

"Mine wasn't even special," Nanette said. She was sitting on the sink, a pot of black face paint in one hand, brush in the other. "Just the House lord, believe it or not. He claimed every courtesan's First Night, and he didn't even pay us for it."

"I feel like that should be illegal," Simone said. Nanette snorted.

"Yeah. Well. You wonder why I moved here?"

"Because Lord de Rue doesn't force you to wear dresses," Yves said, hauling in a bag full of clothes.

"That's just a perk," Nanette said. "Open your eyes wide, Sabre-baby. Do you want this guy to see you cry, or do you want to look, what's the word…"

"Dishabille," Simone said.

"Yeah. That."

Sabre felt a little lightheaded. "I don't think he's ever seen me in makeup."

"Ohh, then let's be dramatic," Nanette said, swooping in with the brush.

It had been like that all day. The dread of the First Night had faded in the chaos of cooking breakfast for the regular gossip crowd, cleaning the baths, scrubbing out couches, hanging up clothes to dry, and the countless other chores necessary to keep the House running. He'd almost forgotten it until that morning, when he woke up, stared at himself in the mirror of Laurent's baths, and retched water and bile into the sink.

In only a few hours, he was going to be kneeling for Isiodore. He almost wished that the House of Onyx *was* like the House of Iron, and Laurent could claim his First Night. He'd know what to do. What to say. How to make Sabre feel like he didn't want to crawl out of his own skin.

"What," said Percival, in a horrified tone, "is *that*."

Margritte, who Sabre had only seen in passing a handful of times, held up a pile of gray rags with a slightly bewildered look.

"But he's trying *not* to be a noble," she said.

Yves sighed. "This is why you leave the clothes to me."

"The man who wears skin tight shorts with the words *Daddy's Boy* embroidered in silver," Percival drawled. "No. I'm supervising."

"Shouldn't I get a say in what I wear, though?" Sabre asked.

They all stared at him for a moment.

"Right," Yves said, like he hadn't spoken. "So I was thinking gold."

"Let them fuss," Simone whispered, braiding small silver bells in Sabre's hair. "It's their way of showing they care."

"I can't imagine why," Sabre whispered back.

Simone smiled at him through the mirror. "This is one of the only Houses in the district that isn't full of people trying to cut each other out of a noble's favor. We're all…unusual, here. Too old." She winked. "Too strange. Too dominant, for some. The only person you might want to watch out for is Yves, and there's still too much of the farmboy in him for him to be *truly* ruthless in his ambition. So perhaps we have a fondness for hopeless cases."

"I don't know if I should be insulted or not," Sabre said.

"That's how it always is with Simone," Nanette said. "Hold still, I need to fix your eye."

When they were done with him at last, Sabre almost didn't recognize himself. His hair jingled softly when he moved. His eyes were lined, his freckles made more prominent by the small amount of powder Nanette had used to draw attention to them, and he was wearing one of Yves' robes, silver and soft as silk, tied just so that his chest kept slipping in and out of view.

"Oh," he said, quietly.

"What do you think?" Simone asked. "Will he ruin it properly?"

"I think so," Sabre said.

"Good, because that's the point. It's like knocking over a sandcastle. Deeply satisfying, however brief."

"You," Percival said, narrowing his eyes. "You're one of *those* people."

"Of course I am, darling."

"Uh." Sabre ran a finger under his collar, which was the only thing that didn't match, stark gold against all the silver. "Thank you, for doing this."

"Oh, I'll cry," Yves said, utterly dry-eyed. He reached out and squeezed Sabre's hand. "You'll tell us how it went, right?"

"And I have time, after," Charon said, from the corner where he'd been reading through the entire afternoon. "Should you need it."

Sabre opened his mouth to say he'd probably ask Laurent, actually, and closed it again. He couldn't keep depending on Laurent for everything. It wasn't fair to Laurent, who likely had better things to do with his time, even though Sabre could have sworn he'd been looking at him, when Sabre wasn't paying attention. There was hunger there, just for a moment, but every time Sabre thought of asking, it disappeared behind Laurent's careful mask.

Laurent met him downstairs, dressed in a slightly subdued suit of the latest fashion, shades of black and deep violet that brought out the strange color of his eyes and the pallor of his skin. He raised his brows when Sabre headed down the stairs, and Rose, who was doing sums from a large book on the couch, whistled.

"You look like the moon prince," she said. "Doesn't he, Laurent?"

"Yes," Laurent said, with a flash of that hunger again, hastily snuffed out. "Close. We'll have to leave now if we're to make it to the palace in time."

"We?" Sabre asked. There was a little too much hope in his voice, he knew, but he couldn't help it. "You're coming?"

"You've been asked to come to the palace, away from any security measures we have in place at the House. Of course I'm coming—I need to protect my investments."

Rose snorted, and Laurent glared at her. "And that's why *I* can't come, I guess," she said.

"You wouldn't want to," Sabre said.

"You're both so boring," Rose muttered, marking something on her notes. "Off to the palace while *I* do math."

"Truly, yours is a life of suffering," Laurent said, taking Sabre by the shoulder. "I'll light a candle in your honor."

Rose flipped him a rude gesture, and Laurent laughed softly as Sabre followed him through the foyer. He kept his hand on Sabre's back, and Sabre only hesitated for a breath before he stepped outside and into the carriage waiting for them. It had the royal crest on the side, outlined in gold as bright as Sabre's collar, and Sabre lifted his braided hair over his shoulder as he sank onto the bench.

He would find out tonight. Isiodore had no reason to lie about Sabre's family—He'd been friends with Sabre's father, and saw Sabre make his fumbling vow to the king at thirteen. He wouldn't couch it behind compassion, either. Just the truth. *Your mother and sister were innocent, and the king killed them anyway.*

"I'd probably be in the military, by now," Sabre said. "I was planning to wait until after Elise's birthday to give them the news."

"I don't see you killing anyone," Laurent said, crossing his legs. He propped his chin on his knuckles, looking Sabre over.

"I don't know if I could, either," Sabre admitted. "I can fight well enough if I have to, but seeing one dead body in my lifetime is more than I need." Laurent raised his brows. "Not my sister, or mother. I never actually saw them, after."

"Ah. Your father, then."

Sabre almost said no, that he hadn't been there when his father died, but that would have meant admitting that he'd seen the queen in the throne room, her blood staining the marble. He shrugged, and his voice came out oddly hollow, false. "He died on a hunt. Something caught his saddle. It happens."

He'd been almost inconsolable when his mother gave him the news. Sabre and his father were always close. Sabre's father had practically grown up with the king, and Sabre, with Adrien clinging to him like a post in a storm, followed his father in the vain hope that they would end up the same. That if he could be enough of a bulwark, he could protect Adrien from the centuries of tradition he had to contend with between him and the throne.

Now, he was cast out to sea himself, and anyone foolish enough to reach for him would drown.

"I don't know how much of myself I can hold in reserve, tonight," he said. The sun was starting to set over the city, slashes of violet and red flickering between buildings.

"He'll know if you are, I suppose," Laurent said. "He knows you well enough."

"Maybe. Only through training. He knows what it takes to fell me. Oh." The palace rose above them, framed by the high walls where traitors were displayed. There was nothing there, just a stained and empty patch of stone, but that didn't mean his mother and sister *hadn't* been hanged from the edge. The king always took down bodies when nobles complained of the smell.

"Careful," Laurent said. The carriage was almost entirely dark.

"They weren't up there," Sabre said. "It's fine. It's all right."

"Remember to breathe."

Sabre took a long, shaky breath. The carriage rolled to a halt, and Laurent stepped out first, looking utterly at home in his fine suit and cloak. Sabre followed after him, dressed like a painted whore, and looked down, breath catching in his throat.

They had to walk through the main hall to reach the residential branch of the palace, and Sabre kept his eyes lowered, following at Laurent's heels. He could hear whispering as he passed, and his hands locked behind his back despite himself, an old habit that brought more fear than comfort, now that he couldn't shake the feel of rope around his wrists. His cock stirred, and he knew they could see it, the nobles watching him, following the traitor's son as he was delivered to Isiodore.

"Is he here, my lord," Sabre whispered.

"No," Laurent said. "Or I'd be obligated to bow."

Sabre could already feel the pressure to slip under before he'd even crossed the hall. The residential wing wound up a stair on the right side of the gates, but Sabre kept his hands behind his back, his gaze lowered, following the path more through muscle memory than by sight. Laurent stopped him at Isiodore's suites, and tipped his head up by the chin.

"You won't leave?" Sabre asked.

Laurent brushed his mouth with a thumb, almost gently. "No."

"Thank you," Sabre said, so soft he couldn't tell if Laurent could even hear. "My lord."

Laurent held his gaze for a moment longer, then turned to knock on the door of Isiodore de Mortain's suites.

Isiodore didn't open the door for them, of course. They were greeted by a terrified maid, who took one look at Sabre, fumbled over what honorific to use, and settled for not addressing him at all. Which was fine, really. Sabre felt half in a daze already, pulled along after Laurent by an invisible tether, and when he was led to the training room and left there, Sabre went calmly to the center of the room and glanced back at Laurent.

"He usually has me stand, when we spar," he said.

"Then kneel," Laurent said.

Sabre went to his knees as clumsily as ever, more painful than with any grace. There wasn't any doubt, when he risked a look at Laurent, that Laurent knew he hadn't knelt for Isiodore. Not exactly.

The door opened, and Sabre looked down at his knees. Heavy footfalls made the ground tremble, slightly, and Sabre saw the familiar leather of Isiodore's boots, smartly polished and buckled.

"Hm." Isiodore took Sabre by the hair and pulled his head back. He was dressed simply, his hair pulled back, just as he would during any of their sparring lessons. "You did this for me, did you? Dressed yourself like a whore?"

Sabre had to take a moment to gather the breath to speak. "Yes, sir. Ah, I mean—"

Isiodore backhanded him so hard that only his grip on Sabre's hair kept him upright.

"Yes," Sabre said.

"And is that what you are?" Isiodore leaned down to tug the sash holding Sabre's robes closed, revealing his half-hard cock. Isiodore nudged it with a boot, and Sabre hissed out a breath. "A whore?"

Sabre glanced at Laurent, sitting on the bench at the edge of the training circle, and Isiodore jerked his head to the side.

"Don't answer him. He isn't the one who asked you a question. Are you a whore?"

"Yes, sir."

Isiodore slapped him again, and Sabre tasted blood on his tongue. "No. You aren't one. Not yet. Stand up."

"Ah, yes m—" Sabre gasped as he was hauled up by the neck, scrambling for purchase. For a terrifying moment, he dangled from Isiodore's hand, then he was set down and left staring wildly as Isiodore took out a length of rope.

"Ask me to put it on you," Isiodore said.

Sabre's tongue felt like it was made of lead. "Please. The rope..."

"Where do you think I'll tie it?" Isiodore asked. "Your hands? You're keeping them too still. Your neck?" He stepped behind Sabre, and smacked him on the thigh. "What did I tell you? Hold still."

"Yes, sir, sorry, sir," Sabre said, automatically.

"Can't have you falling to your knees at a little pain," Isiodore said, which was laughable, because he knew *exactly* how much Sabre could take. He tugged at Sabre's hair, and it wasn't until the bells started to jingle and the pain became just short of too sharp that Sabre realized he was being held up by it, the rope wound in with the ribbons and bells and tied firmly to a hook in the ceiling. If Sabre stood on his toes, the pain lessened, but he didn't know how long he could manage before he started to shake.

"These, you'll remember," Isiodore said, and Sabre only just stopped himself from twisting on the rope to look. He waited for Isiodore to walk around him, and couldn't hide the way his cock hardened at the sight of the knife Sabre had given him for a years-end gift not long before. It was part of a set—they were expensive, functional, and were said to keep their edge long after other knives went dull. The blade shone wickedly in the lamplight, and Sabre tensed, rising on his toes.

"Hold position," Isiodore said, and Sabre clenched and flexed his hands as he stood on his toes, watching Isiodore bring the edge of the blade to Sabre's throat, just below the collar.

He was trembling with the effort of holding himself up by the time the blade slid over his belly, curving towards his inner thigh. Isiodore only just pressed the edge of the knife to Sabre's thigh, so close to his flushed, hard cock, and Sabre made a soft sound in the back of his throat.

"Your Grace, please."

Isiodore brought the knife closer, letting the flat of it rest under Sabre's cock. "Vague questions get unpleasant answers," he said. "What is it you want of me? Answers? Release?"

Sabre shook on his toes as the knife was withdrawn. "I don't know."

"Why don't I give you the question, first," Isiodore said, lifting Sabre's chin. "Why did the king set your debt at fifteen hundred crowns?"

Sabre blinked, slowly. "What?"

"You aren't ready for the answer, yet. I'll have to break you for that. But you want it, don't you? You want it so badly, it burns at you. To be broken. To be made a whore. Don't you agree, Lord de Rue?"

hy did the king set your debt at fifteen hundred crowns?

It took Laurent a moment to understand the question—to say he was distracted was an understatement. Sabre was tied up by his *hair*, and if he only knew how beautiful he looked like this, one of the old stories about sacrifices left for the gods of the sea, beautifully dressed and presented in due reverence for the old ones to drag down into the dark and devour.

Even if he couldn't quite remember that story, or why he knew it. The capital of Staria was at least a day's hard ride to the coast, more if you were going north, and their stories were more about noble knights than sea gods. Maybe he'd heard it from Rose, in one of her books. Either way, it didn't change that Sabre looked like an offering, displayed and adorned as he was.

Sabre's debt *was* astronomical. It was one reason why Laurent thought his house would be the only one to help him achieve it, but he'd thought that was the point. Not that there was an actual reasoning behind Emile setting it at that exact number. Laurent was having a difficult time thinking about that, though, because he was only thinking about Sabre as the sacrifice and he, Laurent, as the monster.

But he wasn't, not now. This was Isiodore's night, bought and paid for, and from the look of it, Sabre was going under even despite his clear distress...or perhaps because of it. And that's how it should be. Laurent had chosen well, and they were gorgeous together. Sabre, trembling in his delicious fear with his cock rising from between his legs, and Isiodore, as put together as ever, his sharp features composed, his commands falling nearly with the same weight as the king's.

"Oh, I do, Your Grace," Laurent said, shaking himself for a moment. "They did him a disservice, didn't they, not sending him to the houses sooner? Think how easier it would have been, for him. No weight of expectations, just the weight of a man's cock in his mouth."

"He would have taken to the training with a bit more grace, I think, than he did to nobility. A pity no one saw to him, he could have been married off to some adoring noble, kept safe from the perfidy and machinations of the Court." Isiodore did something with his hand holding the knife that made Sabre gasp and *twitch*, hanging there, and Laurent was momentarily impressed at Isiodore's ability to hold a conversation with a knife under an attractive man's cock, who was panting and so close to begging already. "But that's always been the way they failed you, hasn't it, Sabre? They never did want to take you as you were. Sent you to me, thought perhaps your innate desire to serve would impress me."

"My father," Sabre whispered. "He...he always said that..."

"What's that?" Isiodore pulled the knife back, traced it up Sabre's chest, the silver flashing against his skin. "Finish your sentences, I've no use for whores who can't carry a conversation."

Laurent wondered if, perhaps, he could hire Isiodore to give lessons. Probably not possible, given the man was a duke, but gods, if he could bottle that dom energy and present it alongside Charon's? Laurent would be richer than the king. Though perhaps that would be far too dangerous to his continued health, even though Emile, for all his paranoia and the way he wielded his dominance and absolute power like a cudgel, was not known for being ostentatious—almost the opposite. Laurent had heard more than once that the king, who favored simple attire and wore his reddish-brown hair tied back, was most recognizable by his cold blue eyes and tendency not to blink.

"My father called you his friend," Sabre said.

"Your father *was* my friend," Isiodore replied. "And I do not say that easily about anyone. And he would have said the same, that you belonged in lessons with the prince, learning to kneel for the ones who would take you, keep you safe. But your father trusted the wrong people and paid the price for it, and you paid the price for other things, and there is little to be done about it now." He stroked the blade of the knife against Sabre's throat. "Show me your throat, then. Your father never learned to be sensible enough to do the same for a dominant that deserved it, not the first bitch who let him mount her. Does that make you angry? Hearing me speak of your dead mother like that? I was there, that day. I saw her neck break. I was sorry for your sister but I knew her a lost cause. Your mother was a viper and your sister would have been the same."

"Stop," Sabre gasped. "Please. They were my *family*."

"They did not know the meaning of the word, Bumblebee," Isiodore said, with an odd little smile on his face. "Ask me what you want to know. Give up what ties you here, this pit where you have never belonged."

Sabre sobbed; something about the nickname was making him thrash, unheeding of the delicate way he was bound. "I can't." He tried to look at Laurent.

Isiodore used nothing but the press of the tip of the knife on Sabre's cheek and the quiet dominance in his voice to bring his focus back. "I'll tell him to leave, Bumblebee. Your lord might be a lord, but I am a duke and he will not put the safety of his house at risk to disobey me. Lord de Rue, do I lie?"

"No, Your Grace. I am aware of the balance of power, here," said Laurent, which was true.

"I fucked him, a time or two," Isiodore said, to Sabre. He was tracing Sabre's mouth with the knife, and Sabre was panting, his cock so hard it looked painful. "Your lord. Do you remember, Lord de Rue, what I told you, that first time?"

Laurent did remember. "You told me that playacting would get me escorted home, Your Grace."

"I did. I knew you were no submissive, and I liked that you knew that I knew, and putting you in your place was still very satisfying because you fought it, and yet I knew you weren't lying when you moaned under me. I am surrounded by enough liars in the court, I don't want it in my bedroom. Did you know I took him, your lord, did he tell you?"

"I," Sabre said. "I figured. You always liked sharp, elegant things. Like, like my lord."

Laurent smiled, pleased at the compliment.

"Indeed," said Isiodore. "Do you think you are either?"

"No, my lord," Sabre said. "I am not a dominant. And I am not, not elegant, like Lord de Rue."

"Neither was your father," Isiodre said, in a soft voice. He flipped the hilt of the knife around, and pressed it into Sabre's mouth. "And I fucked him. Did you know that, Bumblebee? I fucked him, and I told him not to marry your scheming bitch of a mother, and he did not listen and thought it a good match. And he was so very, very wrong."

"Mmph." Sabre started to struggle, as Isiodore pressed the hilt in a little more.

"I will speak of this once, and only once, Sabre. You swore your oath to Emile, and the worst of it is, that you meant it. Just like your father's wedding vows. You don't know how to lie that way. With your whole body. If Emile had let you swing with your mother and sister, you would have been the only true noble to die that morning."

He pulled the hilt out of Sabre's mouth, and dragged it wet over his cheek, smearing the tears that have spilled over Sabre's eyes. "Ask me if they were traitors, Sabre. Ask me how your father died. If you want the truth, you may have it. It will break you, Bumblebee. Let it."

Sabre raised his head. Tears dripped from his chin, but Laurent saw it, then. The power all submissives had, inherent in their nature, to bend and break but never shatter, not completely. To withstand the cruelty, the sadism, the control and take it all, twist it into something lovely, make a dominant kiss them sweetly and thank them when it was over. Submissives were not weak, and the ones who understood that were worth their weight in gold.

"Why," Sabre asked, misery in every lovely line of his body, shaking his head and making the bells jingle in his hair. He arched his back and went up on his toes, and Laurent's breath caught at how he so effortlessly made it look beautiful. "Why is my debt fifteen hundred crowns?"

Isiodore smacked him, hard, across the face. Then he smacked Sabre's cock, too, then used the blade to tease the head of his cock, which took an astounding amount of precision and control. "It's the amount your traitorous bitch of a mother paid assassins to see the king dead.It includes the amount she paid to have a footman undo the straps of your father's saddle so he'd fall during a hunt. It includes the dowry for your sister, who she intended would marry Adrien after his father was killed. The only thing it doesn't include, Sabre, is the money she would have paid to see you and Adrien dead in the north sea, if you didn't *behave*. That, your sister promised, but she didn't have the time to see it done."

* * *

For a long, agonizing moment, Sabre could only hear the ragged inhale of his own breath.

When he was still young, Sabre was caught brawling with the oldest son of Lord Chastain. He'd flown at him for making a snide remark about the late queen in front of Adrien, who just stood there with his chin raised and his eyes glittering, fighting back tears. They were both a mess by the end of it, but Sabre had broken the little weasel's nose, and he had to be dragged before the king for brawling on the palace grounds.

"You can't fight everyone who offends you, Sabre," his father said, later, still trying not to look like he was laughing. "You're loyal to Adrien, and that's good, but you have to think it through, first. Be *practical.* All you did today was make a potential enemy."

"Not like I wanted him to be my *friend*," Sabre said, and his father had laughed at that, pulled him into a one-armed hug and kissed his forehead. "I just don't know why everyone thinks the king killed her."

"Because the truth is harder," his father said, lowering his voice. "Because when we learn of a terrible thing, our minds try to patch it up. The queen is dead, and the king is...behaving strangely, so the king must have killed her. The king killed her, so she must have betrayed him. We try to justify what sickens us, Bumblebee. It's better than admitting that sometimes, terrible things just happen."

His father died a few weeks later, while Sabre was staying in the residential wing of the palace. He could still remember the look on Isiodore's face when the message runner interrupted their lesson, the fleeting look of pain, the slow, deliberate way he moved.

Had he known, then? Sabre always knew Isiodore kept an eye on most of the comings and goings of the noble classes. It was like he was an invisible man at a card game, passing behind the other players, always aware of what they held. Had he known that Sabre's father— Had he suspected that—

He could feel his thoughts trying to fill in the gaps. His mother didn't kill his father. She loved him. She mourned him. Except— except she'd worn her mourning colors as briefly as possible, when other widows and widowers kept colored bands on for years to mourn the dead. And she'd never spoken of him, except to say how much Sabre was like him, when he'd talk back at tea or ask to stay with Adrien for a week in his house in the country.

She'd always despised the king. She and Sabre's father used to fight over it at night, their voices whisper-soft but sharp as a nail boring through the walls, with Sabre trying to distract Elise in the nursery. There was a reason, Sabre realized, that his father made Sabre swear not to tell his mother about the queen, or Adrien. There was a reason Sabre never broke that vow, even if he didn't have the words for it at the time.

And Isiodore de Mortain never lied.

"I always thought." Sabre's hands were limp behind his back, sliding out of their perfect form. "After he died, someone petitioned for me to move to the palace. I thought it was Adrien, because mother was..."

Starving him, he didn't say. He didn't have to. After a few days of locking himself in his room, Sabre's mother ordered the servants to stop leaving food at his door. It took Adrien, turned away at the front gate for three days in a row, sneaking into the garden to see Sabre lying dead-eyed in his bed, barely rousing to glance at whoever was trying to wrench the window open, for anything to be done.

"Yes, I can see how you'd think that," Isiodore said. "But you told the king it wasn't necessary. In your mother's words, I think. Am I right?"

Sabre wanted to cover his face. He wanted to crawl under the benches, disappear, tear out the bells that still shivered and sang in his hair.

He could still remember the look on his mother's face when he asked to leave. It was like a door closing, a window shuttering. The light stamped out forever.

"Yes," he said, in a broken voice.

"You could have seen her for what she was," Isiodore said. He grabbed Sabre's face as he tried to look away, held it in place. Sabre's breath quickened. "You had years to learn what we knew when that snake killed your father, and you closed yourself to the truth. Lived in that house with a murderer and her little protege."

"You knew," Sabre said.

"I suspected, first. You were given the opportunity to learn. And now you're here."

He cut through the rope tying Sabre in place, and Sabre dropped to his hands and knees. His hands crept towards his face, but Isiodore kicked them away.

"The king should have sent you away years ago," Isiodore said, and Sabre let out a cry that felt like it was wrenched from his stomach as Isiodore lay a boot on his shoulder, pressing him down. He held himself up by the arms, and when he finally sobbed, it came out low and anguished, the cry of a boy who'd lost his father.

"Now you know," Isiodore said, and there was no cruelty there, no pity, just the truth, hard and terrible as it was. This must have been what Adrien saw in his vision, the pain that made him march across the city in the middle of a storm. "And you don't even hate them, do you? Not yet."

Sabre swallowed tears. "Your Grace." The boot shifted on his back, and the pressure lifted enough for Sabre to breathe again. "Thank…" It was hard, harder even than kneeling for the king with his sister and mother on the gallows. "Thank you, for telling me the truth, when I asked. I would like to." He sat up on his knees, tears still hot on his cheeks, shivering from the touch of the knife. "I would like to be someone who…isn't Sabre de Valois, right now. Please."

"You haven't been de Valois since your mother paid assassins to kill the king."

"Yes, but Your Grace, I need to be something…else."

"And this is it," Isiodore said. He ran a thumb through the mess of Sabre's makeup, smearing it over his cheek.

"Please," Sabre whispered.

* * *

THE WAY SABE LOOKED, begging—ah, well, that's what he saw, wasn't it, when he took Sabre home to the House of Onyx? This was going exactly like it should, and Laurent could tell it wasn't just Sabre who was affected. He knew what a dominant who was edging into top space looked like—he knew what *Isiodore* looked like, heading into top space—and Isiodore's usually cool gray eyes were burning bright like starfire.

"You sound much better begging like a whore than calling me *sir* and trying to match me with a blade. Come with me, Sabre. When you leave in the morning, you won't remember the shape you used to be, when you were here before." He tugged Sabre's hair, nodded once, and stood up. Then he kicked Sabre over onto his side, and his eyebrows went up when Sabre *moaned*.

He turned to Laurent. "I knew he was a submissive, but what a delight that he's such a slut for pain."

"He's one of the few I've ever seen handle Charon," Laurent said, rising from the bench. He gave a cursory glance around the room—only the highest-ranking noble in the Starian court would have a full sparring ring in his suite in the palace.

"Is that so?" Isiodore kicked Sabre again, like he was an errant piece of laundry. "I've heard tell of him, your Arkoudai whore. They're not much given to the arts of pleasure, are they?"

"I wouldn't say that," Laurent demurred. "It's just a certain kind of pleasure. Sabre enjoyed it."

"Hmm," said Isiodore, and there was a smile there, brief and fleeting, so much so that Laurent thought perhaps he imagined it. "Heel, little whore, and follow."

Sabre struggled in all his messy glory to his hands and feet, and Laurent noticed that as unpracticed as he was at it, it still looked gorgeous. He took note of how artfully his makeup was smeared from his tears, the tangle of his hair in the braids and bells, the sounds he made as he carefully made his way along the polished wood and cold tile to the plush carpet of Isiodore's bedchamber.

Laurent remembered it well. It had a large bed with cotton sheets so soft they felt like silk, and an adjoining bathing suite with a deep-water pool made of marble. He'd taken Laurent there, after, let him ease the soreness and gave him sweet wine and chocolate, watched him with a little satisfied smile before his eyes went sharp and his tone polite, distant. The way he fucked Laurent made him think the duke was under quite a bit of stress, perhaps more than the king.

Sabre stopped near the bed, kneeling with the sort of poor form that would have had Laurent punished at the House of Gold—shoulders hunched, hands on his thighs, breathing uneven.

Isiodore pulled him up by the hair. "Lord de Rue, if you'd like to sit there, on the chair. I know the custom of First Night involves a witness, yes?"

"Yes," Laurent said. He settled in the chair, a comfortable chaise, and it was sort of hard to imagine *Isiodore de Mortain* sprawled out in it, dressed in pajamas and reading some kind of torrid novel.

Laurent, though. He might get one. He settled back and watched as

Isiodore pulled Sabre up and pushed him on the bed. Sabre was naked, hard, and when he tossed his messy hair back out of his face the gesture was both unpracticed and incredibly arousing, enough that Isiodore stared at him for a long minute, then glanced at Laurent.

Laurent shrugged. "He's a natural, isn't he? A better whore than a noble submissive."

"It would appear so," Isiodore said. He slipped off his coat and climbed on the bed, kneeling in front of Sabre, and kissed him. "Don't touch me unless I tell you that you may."

He'd given Laurent the same instructions, and he'd never undressed fully until they went to the baths, after.

Sabre went pliant in Isiodore's firm grip, and Laurent watched them, pushing aside the simple enjoyment of seeing a dominant handling a submissive—always arousing—and the vague stirrings of something possessive that he absolutely couldn't indulge in, with Sabre, who was just starting out and would be taking many more clients before his astronomical debt to the crown was satisfied. Instead, he tried to remain impartial and take notes for later, which was part of why the House Lord served as witness for these assignations. Sabre would be a unique asset to the house, and while his performance didn't need to be perfect, there were always things clients liked.

He choked when Isiodore fucked his mouth, his head tipped back and his hands clasped behind his back without the need for restraints —that, Laurent knew, wasn't done to spare Sabre the trauma of remembering his moments on the gallows, but because Isiodore liked to be obeyed without them. Sabre didn't fight being used roughly, and Isidore's harsh breathing and occasional murmur, along with Sabre's choking sounds, were the only noises in the room.

Laurent could feel his cock grow hard as he watched them, remembering how it felt to take Sabre's mouth like that. He knew he shouldn't have done that, really—given how Sabre's inexperience was supposed to be part of his appeal—but he couldn't regret it, even as he told himself he needed to not let it happen again. Sabre would need to find his comfort with those in the house who could give it to him, not with Laurent. Maybe if he repeated enough, he'd believe it and actually be strong enough to refuse, if Sabre came to him again, seeking to be settled.

"There you go, pretty thing, look at you," Isiodore murmured, only the slight huskiness in his voice belying how affected he was to have his cock thrusting in and out of Sabre's mouth. "Did you used to think about this, hmm, when I had you kneel after training?"

Sabre tried to nod, and Isiodore laughed softly, ran his fingers through Sabre's hair a moment in an oddly fond gesture before pulling, hard. Sabre moaned, and Laurent shifted on the chair.

"I thought perhaps you might have," Isiodore said, still so proper. "Did you go home, lock yourself in your room, touch yourself while you thought about me putting you in your place?"

"Didn't—ah. Make it home, my lord. Your Grace. My family had a suite in the palace, I...went there, sometimes, to do that."

"How flattering," Isiodore said, and pushed him away. "Get the oil, then, and I'll take you like you wanted me to."

According to a conversation they'd had shortly after Sabre arrived, this was not the first time he'd been taken. Most courtesans trained for that with glass toys and oil and lessons, and more often than not they indulged with one of their fellow courtesans long before the negotiations for their First Night were complete. You put that many attractive people in one small space and had them practice and think about nothing but sex for the majority of their waking hours, and it was bound to happen. For most, the additional practice wasn't seen as anything but a bonus, but Sabre was, of course, a bit different.

Despite having had some experience, Sabre was clearly overwhelmed by having a man he'd fantasized about take him; he was on his hands and knees at Isiodore's instruction after he'd fetched the oil, shaking, staring down at the covers of Isiodore's bed. Isiodore had him facing Laurent, kneeling behind him, and grabbed his hair again to pull his head up so that Laurent wouldn't miss the exact moment he pushed himself inside Sabre, because apparently Isiodore had some talent with theatrics that Laurent had missed, before.

Sabre was grasping the coverlet in his hands, tight and white knuckled, and wasn't breathing. But the look on his face had Laurent inhaling slowly, counting, trying to keep his hand from pressing on his cock, which was uncomfortably hard now in his pants.

"You may attend to yourself if you wish, Lord de Rue," Isiodore said, only a little breathless as he eased himself in, slow and steady. "I certainly won't mind."

Of course he wouldn't. Starian nobles were, as a rule, full of themselves. Even Isiodore, who wasn't nearly as ostentatious or obnoxious about his status as most, hadn't entirely escaped that ingrained arrogance. Laurent had a title, but he wasn't sure he'd ever manage to sound like he was *born* to one, quite like Isiodore.

It did rankle, a bit, to have Isiodore treating him like a submissive. Laurent gave an easy shrug, reminding himself firmly that Isiodore treated everyone that way, possibly even the king, and said, "Thank you, but I'm here as a witness. It does speak to your prowess, Your Grace, that you've managed to rouse us both."

Isiodore outright snorted. "A flatterer to the end, aren't you. Very well. Sabre." He smacked Sabre hard on the flank. "I'm going to fuck you and you're going to take it. You're also going to be loud for me, just like a good whore should when he's being fucked like he deserves. And if you come without permission, I'll be *very* disappointed in you, do you understand me?"

"Yes, sir," Sabre whispered, and Isiodore didn't even correct him for the address.

Isiodore looked mostly in control, though his hair did escape his queue and lend him a bit of an attractively disheveled look while he started fucking Sabre there, one hand around the back of his neck above the collar, the other holding Sabre's hip. Fucking was fucking, and most people looked the same when they were doing it, but Laurent noticed that there was something...remote, about Isiodore, almost distracted. He clearly enjoyed it, but while Sabre was moaning and pushing back and gasping, Isiodore reminded Laurent of one of the machines in the training room—methodical, impersonal, even as it certainly got the job done.

I don't think he really wanted to fuck him, Laurent realized. *What he wanted was to tell Sabre about his family, so that when the nobles tried to use them against him, Sabre would have something to guard against it. Anger, maybe, that his family really were guilty of treason. That his mother had his father killed.*

"Does that feel good, pretty little whore?" Isiodore asked, and Sabre moaned his assent and nodded, but Laurent had checked out of enough sexual encounters of his own to recognize when someone else was doing it.

He wondered idly what really would do it for Isiodore, get him to lose his cool, calm and collected facade. He'd been more turned on, Laurent thought, by putting Sabre in the hair rope bondage, by using the knife. Breaking him, not fucking him.

Sabre, though. He was clearly having a teenage fantasy come to life, and Laurent couldn't blame him for enjoying it. "Please, my lord," he begged, shifting, hands fisting in the bedding.

"You won't come yet, but by all means, keep begging," Isiodore said, slamming his hips forward and pushing Sabre forward on the slick silk coverlet.

But as Isiodore increased his pace and fucked Sabre harder, pulling his hair—Sabre lifted his head, opened his wide, glassy copper-bright eyes and stared right at Laurent. "Please, fuck me, harder, please—"

Laurent grabbed the sides of his chair, fingers curled around the upholstered edges as tightly as Sabre was grabbing the bedding. He should have looked away, but he didn't.

"Please," Sabre whispered, and Laurent's equilibrium shifted, dangerously. "My lord."

Isiodore shoved him down on his stomach, held his hips in both hands and fucked him with sharp, hard thrusts. Sabre was whimpering, and Laurent had to give in and rub his hand over himself a few times because Sabre was still trying to lift his head, to look at *Laurent* while he begged Isiodore to let him come.

Which Isiodore didn't. He eventually pulled out and shoved Sabre on his back, knelt over him and came all over his face. His head tipped back and he gasped, softly, but other than that he remained as restrained and in control even in the throes of his release as he had during the whole thing.

He stayed kneeling on the bed and dragged Sabre to his knees again, turned him to face Laurent and then whispered something Laurent couldn't hear while his hand expertly stroked Sabre's cock.

What he did hear, though, was Isiodore saying in a wicked purr, "Ask your lord if you performed well enough to come." His other hand rested right above Sabre's collar, squeezing gently. "Ask him if you've proven yourself a better whore than a noble."

Sabre, who was clearly already under and was, probably, the second Isiodore told him the truth of his family, said, "Yes, sir," and then blinked his hazy eyes open and focused on Laurent. "My lord, please may I come?"

Laurent almost told him *no*, just because this really wasn't supposed to be how it worked, a First Night with a witness. But Sabre was different, this whole situation was different, and Laurent was perhaps trying to justify it but he wanted to see it, to see Sabre come apart and know that maybe there was a small part of it that was for him.

This is dangerous and you need to stop it, Laurent said, firmly, to himself. But the voice of reason was overcome by the voice of lust, and Laurent said, "Yes, you've done well, go on," and watched with rapt attention as Sabre shook and shuddered out his release with a loud, gasping cry.

Isiodore de Mortain's eyes were on Laurent the whole time, a little smile on his face that said, quite clearly, that Laurent hadn't fooled him one little bit.

* * *

FOR THE SECOND time in his life, Sabre was well and truly under. He knew that grief was threatening to creep its way through like an oncoming tide, but Sabre was too far down to notice, yet, drifting on a different current.

Laurent was watching him. He could feel Laurent's gaze even as

Isiodore rolled him onto his back again, and tipped his head back to make sure he was still there.

"Yes, I know," Isiodore said, so softly only Sabre could hear. He kissed Sabre long enough that Sabre had to gasp for breath when he pulled away, and passed him a cloth for his face. "I would offer you the use of my bath, but I suspect you'd prefer to be otherwise engaged."

Sabre couldn't hide the way his face heated at that. He glanced over his shoulder to where Laurent sat, deliberately relaxed like an actor in a play, waiting for his cue, and raised a hand as though to touch Isiodore's chest. He stopped only an inch away, and lowered his hand to his side.

"Your Grace," Sabre said, and ah, he was too close, he could feel the way Isiodore hesitated at the sound of the title, this time. "Has anyone ever told you that you're too perceptive, before?"

"Your father," Isiodore said. "All the time."

Sabre looked up at him, narrowing his eyes. He knew men fucked each other in the military. It was practically expected. But Isiodore had never taken a partner afterwards, as was custom. Sabre and Adrien used to whisper about it when they were young, coming up with dramatic tragedies with Isiodore at the heart of them, watching his star-crossed lover die on the battlefield or be eaten by sirens on the distant sea.

Perhaps it wasn't quite so distant, though.

"None of that," Isiodore said, smacking Sabre lightly on the cheek. He rose from the bed, adjusting his clothes, and Sabre sprawled there for a minute, his silver robes a rumpled mess beneath him.

He was the son of a traitor. He rolled that thought around in his mind, testing it the way he would have prodded at a sore tooth as a child. Elise, that was still too painful, a dark shadow he couldn't yet grasp, but his mother had always been...hard. Cold, holding herself apart, bearing stiffly through court as though her noble heritage was a second skin she couldn't wait to rip off. Maybe she, too, didn't belong there. Maybe none of them did.

"I'm his son, too," Sabre said. He didn't realize he'd said it out loud until Isiodore turned to look down at him, dark eyes impassive. "Whatever else I am."

"It takes going under for you to do more than stammer at me, does it?" Isiodore said. He tugged at his cuffs. "Off my bed, whore."

He didn't say it with any derision. It was just the truth. Sabre tumbled inelegantly to his knees and started trying to slip on his robes again. Laurent was still sitting on the chaise, watching him, and Sabre risked a quick glance up, settling on the dark earrings in his hair. He couldn't possibly hide himself as cleverly as Laurent or Isiodore. He was just open. Everywhere, like a flame without a candle, too quick to burn.

He wondered if Laurent saw it, then. When Isiodore was fucking him, when Sabre was in the throes of it, grabbing at the sheets and rocking back on Isiodore's cock, he'd looked at Laurent and wondered what it would have felt like to have those firm hands on his neck, silver-violet hair brushing his skin as Laurent took him. Isiodore knew—He had to, there was no way he missed the way Sabre choked on Laurent's name under his breath—and Laurent, too, was a perceptive man. More perceptive than Sabre.

"It's customary," Isiodore said, crossing the rug to a chest of drawers, "to give a member of the Houses a gift when they've served well. That, at least, I remember. It was the same for you, was it not, Lord de Rue?"

"It varies," Laurent said.

Isiodore lifted something out of the top drawer. "I found this on a trip to the country. Useless, now, just a relic of a fallen house, but you might find a purpose for it."

He tipped Sabre's head up and pressed something cold and hard into his palm. "Don't look at it until you've left the palace," he said.

Sabre closed his hands over it. It was probably the only bauble he was likely to get—the nobles who hated his family, or who wanted to show to the king how loyal they were, weren't going to give him anything that could lessen his debt more than necessary.

"Thank you, Your Grace," Sabre said.

"Go with your lord, then," said Isiodore. "You aren't meant for this place."

"If I knew that sooner—"

"Your family would still be dead," Isiodore said. "But you are not. Go on."

Sabre didn't bother getting to his feet. He knelt before Laurent, slowly meeting his gaze, and let out a soft sigh on pleasure when Laurent laid a hand on his shoulder to rise from the chaise. He kept his hand there, teasing the messy strands of Sabre's hair, and the bells rang faintly.

He barely registered Laurent and Isiodore's exchange of pleasantries at the door. He crawled at Laurent's side through the dark corridor and into the main hall, even though no one asked him to, and grimaced when he had to stand to cross the carriage yards.

"You'd crawl through the streets if I asked you to, wouldn't you?" Laurent said, holding Sabre up by the collar. Sabre blinked slowly.

"If you asked, my lord," he said.

Laurent's gaze flashed with heat, and his fingers tightened around Sabre's collar. But he didn't kiss him, even though Sabre could tell he wanted it, could feel himself leaning towards him, and Sabre had to stumble after Laurent into the carriage.

"My lord," Sabre said, carefully, as the horses were urged to a trot and the carriage started to roll over the smooth path leading down from the palace, past the square where Sabre was nearly hanged. Where Laurent claimed him. "Did I not do well?"

Laurent cut him a sharp look. "You left de Mortain satisfied, didn't you?"

"In a way," Sabre said. "I think as much as he can be. But you haven't been, yet."

"That wasn't *about* me," Laurent said. Sabre started undoing the sash holding his robes together, and Laurent's voice rang so sharp with dominance that Sabre tried to get to his knees on the carriage floor. "What are you *doing?*"

"My lord," Sabre said. "You've been careful. But you shouldn't have to be, anymore."

"I'm the lord of your House, Sabre."

Sabre let the robes fall. "Other lords take their courtesan's First Night."

"Other lords aren't—"

"You, I *know*." Sabre climbed up onto the bench, naked, with Laurent staring at him like he was a wild spirit drawn in from the woods. "They would have let me die in the quarries. They wouldn't have cared about the truth. I wouldn't want them to take my First Night."

"De Mortain already took that," Laurent said, but he held Sabre by the waist, his fingers gripping him tight enough to send a small thrill through Sabre's skin.

"The night isn't over yet, my lord," Sabre said. "Please, I want…I want to be good for you. Let me be good for you."

Laurent stared at him for another endless second, then snarled something under his breath and pulled him into a crushing kiss. Sabre fell into it, jostled slightly by the carriage, and moaned when Laurent raked his nails up his sensitive back.

"Thought I was yours." Sabre's breath hitched as Laurent bit down hard on his neck, just above the collar.

"You are," Laurent said, in that dark, possessive voice Sabre had been dreaming of, in the dark hours when he lay at Laurent's feet. "Not de Mortain's. Not theirs."

"Yes," Sabre said, fumbling with Laurent's trousers. He could feel his cock pressing up against the fabric, painfully hard. "Please, my lord, may I serve you, will you take me—"

Laurent bit on Sabre's lip hard enough that he gasped. "Show me how well you take my cock, pet," he said.

It was difficult, at first, to maneuver on the bench, but Sabre finally settled over Laurent, bracing himself so close his bare chest slid against Laurent's shirtfront, and lowered himself over his cock. It felt right, even as he started to slip under again, the fullness of him, the slight discomfort as he adjusted, rocked by the movement of the carriage. He rolled his hips, desperate to give Laurent the pleasure he deserved, riding him hard as they passed the first lights of the pleasure district.

It was impossible for Laurent to hide, this close. Sabre could feel his desire in the way he left lines down Sabre's back with his nails, the blown-out pupils in his gorgeous eyes, the way his lips parted, just slightly, as Sabre shivered and moaned and Laurent's cock drove into him. Laurent gripped Sabre's thighs and fucked up into him as the carriage slowed, and Sabre braced himself over him, closing his eyes.

"Look at me," Laurent ordered, fiercely, quietly. He took Sabre's cock in hand, already hard again, and Sabre grabbed onto the side of the carriage for support. "Look at me when you come."

"Yes, my lord," Sabre gasped, and met his gaze as Laurent came inside him, bouncing him on his cock in short, heavy thrusts. Sabre tipped over the edge with Laurent's hand on him, spilling over his own chest.

The carriage was halted a few paces from the door to the House of Onyx when Sabre slid back to the carriage floor, breathing hard. He barely bothered to put his robes on all the way, and only just remembered to stand when he tumbled out of the carriage. Laurent stepped out a minute later looking barely the worse for wear, his hair impeccable, only the slightest wrinkle of his shirt a sign that Sabre was a hair's breadth from ripping it off. He jerked his head, and Sabre followed at his heels without a word.

Nanette met them at the door.

"Wow, was makeup a good idea," she said, and held a hand to her chest when Sabre flashed her a small smile. "Hold on, warn me when you're about to look human, kid. Looks like you had a good First Night, yeah?"

"It's...better," Sabre said, and glanced at Laurent, who was back to his polite, professional mask.

"Well, good for you. We're preparing a room for you, but we're also *working*, so tell us how grateful you are first and then we'll show you in the morning."

"I'm exceedingly grateful," Sabre said.

Nanette snorted. "I like this one, my lord. You should keep him."

"Please," Sabre said, and Nanette *pushed* him, which he was only just starting to realize was supposed to be a sign of affection.

"I'll keep your suggestion in mind," Laurent said. "No fires tonight?"

"Simone's second client got, uh, *pissy* when we charged him extra for laundering her dress," Nanette said, "but she's the only one who can handle him after the House of Iron banned him for the same problem."

"Charge him double," Laurent said. "I've seen that dress, it's actual silk."

"No, it's not, it's—" Nanette paused. "I mean, right. Yes. The silk one."

"Good night, Nanette," Laurent said. He took Sabre by the collar again, just a finger slipped between the gold scales and his skin, and led him up the stairs to his room at the highest floor of the House.

Laurent brought down scented sachets for the bath, and Sabre was permitted to attend to him, leaning back against the side of the bath while he ran his fingers through his silvery hair.

"I bet you've heard people say how lovely your hair is too much already," Sabre said, kneading a scented soap through his hair.

"You *are* bolder when you're under," Laurent drawled. "And yes. More times than you know."

"It's still true," Sabre said. "My father told me a story about people with silver hair, who came down to the sky on dragons to teach people magic. His nursemaid used to tell him stories like that. She was from…I don't remember. It's probably terrible, that I don't remember. She was with us her whole life."

"You were a noble," Laurent said. "Nobles don't pay attention to details."

"They should," Sabre said. "I should have. But maybe she didn't want to say. She always called it *back home*, like she was only in Staria on a holiday."

"Well, she was wrong in any case," Laurent said. "The dragons we have in Staria eat *stone* and sound like a flock of hawks. You couldn't pay me nearly enough to ride one, let alone pretend I know magic."

"That's an image," Sabre said, and he could just see the edge of Laurent's smile. "Rose could do it, though."

"Rose could tame a fleet of them," Laurent said. "And you'll never, *ever* suggest it."

"On my honor as a whore, my lord."

Laurent half turned, brows raised. "You'll find there's more of that here than there ever was at court."

"I wouldn't argue, my lord," Sabre said. "Not tonight."

Laurent kissed him, then, not nearly hard or long enough, and drew away.

It wasn't until Sabre was lying at the foot of Laurent's bed again, comfortably curled on his side, that he remembered what Isiodore had given him. He slipped to the edge of the bed and carefully walked to the place where he'd left his robes, and fished into their pockets for the cold lump of metal.

Alone, in the dark, Sabre opened his hands.

His father's signet ring gleamed in his palm, white gold twisted like tree branches around a disc engraved with his seal; A golden stag, the same crest on all the banners and tapestries kept locked away in his estate.

His father had been wearing that ring when he left for the hunt with Elise.

Sabre slid the ring over his left forefinger, and for a second, his hand was not his own. His father's hand crossed a sliver of moonlight, and Sabre shivered and fumbled to yank off the ring. He pushed it under Laurent's mattress, and knelt there for a long while, holding his hand to his chest and watching the patch of moonlight glide across Laurent's bedroom floor.

CHAPTER 9

*S*abre was starting to wonder if he shouldn't just greet all his clients naked.

Devon Chastain, whose brother Sabre did punch in the nose before their fathers arranged for them to forgive each other and become "fast friends," barely even permitted Sabre to greet him before he had him laid out on the floor of the common room with blood in his mouth and a jagged tear over his right sleeve. Gwydion and Percival were hosting together that night, and Percival made it two steps across the room before Sabre tightly shook his head.

"Can't imagine what a traitor like you thinks you're doing, wearing fine clothes like you're a person," Devon said, and ripped open the rest of Sabre's shirt, scattering buttons.

It was the fourth time someone had chosen to ruin his clothes, and the gut-wrenching humiliation of it was starting to give way to the very real dread of having to sew it all back together in the morning. Sabre forced himself to look at Devon instead, and something in that must have infuriated him even more, because Devon growled and kicked Sabre across the carpet. Sabre gasped softly, and winced as Devon spat on his back.

"Get up, cur," Devon said. Sabre got to his knees, and Devon kicked him again. "Don't walk. I almost don't want to lower myself to fuck you."

Some didn't. After Sabre's First Night, Sabre was booked through year's end with requests, but several of them didn't have more than a passing interest. Those would just ask him questions, maybe slap him once or twice, flog him if he was lucky, and never call on him again. The rest were like Devon, venting out years of frustration, or nobles who wanted to brag to their peers about how they beat Sabre until he was sobbing and fucked him until he was begging for more.

Devon, Sabre thought, would probably come back.

Sabre had his own room, now, prepared by the other courtesans while he slept through the last of his First Night, but he discreetly returned half the furniture after he spent an entire evening frantically trying to clean up the mess before a new client came to wreck it again. Now, Devon looked at Sabre's simple bed, the chair next to a desk he only used to be fucked over, and the worrying hooks on the walls and floor, and snorted.

"Far cry from your usual palace," he said. As a second son, all Sabre knew Devon could hope for was the name Chastain and a pittance from his father, or a life spent in the military. "Fetch a chain, and shackles. You *have* those, don't you?"

"Yes, my lord," Sabre said.

"Bet it galls you, having to call me a lord. I know what you think of me. You and the prince were so close, looking down on the rest of us while you, what? Tried to fuck your way to the throne? I bet that's what your mother wanted. You were too busy sucking Adrien's cock to care."

Sabre brought the chain, attached to heavy, impractical cuffs that would have been hard to lift if Sabre hadn't spent most of his afternoons training with Isiodore, and grunted as Devon dragged him to the wall.

Devon caned him until his skin split and he started to shake with the effort of staying upright, then put clamps on his tongue and made him kneel in the middle of the room, desperately apologizing while Devon prowled around him like a furious hunting cat, stopping only to flog his shoulders in sharp bursts that did no more than leave Sabre wanting, his cock hard between his bare legs.

"You're sick," Devon said, not even stroking himself while Sabre rutted against his boot, eyes closed, face burning with mortification. "I don't think I *can* bring myself to fuck you. Maybe next time, when you've earned it. Apologize for ruining my night, cur."

"Ahh," Sabre was down to one clamp, but it blocked his tongue, making his words slurred and incomprehensible. Devon took it off and tossed it in the corner with a snarl of frustration. It was strange, Sabre thought, as Devon stared at him with overbright eyes, that Devon hadn't used the natural dominance in his voice even once. Perhaps he didn't have enough to notice.

"Stop looking at me," Devon said, tightly. "Stop looking at me like you're *sorry* for me."

When Devon slammed the door after him, Sabre lay in the middle of the floor, naked, his clothes shredded, his cock still hard.

"Look sharp, kiddo," said a voice through the wall, and Sabre jumped. Nanette laughed. "You've got Lord…oh, this is one of Simone's. Lord Beaufort."

"Was he the one who wanted the stocks?"

"Yeah, he's, uh. Look, wear clothes you're okay with laundering really well, okay?"

Sabre looked down at the scraps of his last outfit and sighed.

Later that night, when the last of Sabre's clients were gone, Sabre limped naked into the communal baths, climbed down between an alarmed Percival and Simone, ducked his head underwater, and screamed.

"That's comforting," Simone said, as Sabre came up for air.

"The last one broke the mirror," Sabre said. It had been enough to startle him out of the pleasant haze he tended to fall into at the end of the night, and Yves, watching through the alcove, had almost gotten up to fetch Laurent.

"They do pay for damages," Percival said, which wasn't the point, really. "Do you want to hear about the *Dear Brothers Woman*?"

"Oh, no, what's she up to this time?" Nanette asked. She was still wearing a pair of cat ears as she slipped into the bath next to Simone, who gingerly unpinned them from her hair.

"Wants us to live with her in her country estate," Percival said. "As *friends.*"

Nanette groaned.

"At least she isn't writing us poetry!" Gwydion called, from the bath where he was letting Margritte do his hair.

"Or crying," Margritte said. "I hate when they cry. I never know what to say."

"You don't say anything," Charon said. "Unless it's how pretty they are when they do it."

"Crying isn't pretty, it's embarrassing."

"I am *very* charming when I cry," Yves said, sneaking a sidelong look at Charon.

"No, you aren't." Margritte's voice was inflectionless, matter-of-fact. "You screw your face and hiccup."

Yves gasped in horror.

Simone gestured to Sabre, who swam to her side. She liked to wash his hair—It was strange, as a man grown, to let people do those things for him, but he found it comforting after a night spent being hissed at and spat on.

"You seem to be holding up well enough," she said, threading his hair through her fingers.

"It's easier, some nights," Sabre admitted. "Harder, when they mention my father, or cousin Adrien."

"Really? But your father died so long ago. I listen to gossip, love," she said, when Sabre turned to look at her.

"Old wounds, I guess," Sabre said. The truth made it hurt less, when he could bring himself to look at it that way. People telling him that his mother was a traitor didn't sting so much now that he wasn't fumbling in the dark. But he still wept for them, at night, in dreams where his father rode a horse through a forest of gallows, his mother and sister dangling from the ropes, Sabre staggering after as his father's saddle started to slip.

"Old wounds always ache," Simone said, softly. "When the storms come. There. Yves and Percival are arguing again. You can sneak out without unnecessary questions."

Sabre gave Simone a curious look, and she smiled.

He had half a mind to wrap himself up in a towel and head back to his room for once, just to show that he could, but as Sabre slipped out of the baths and into the main stairwell, his gaze automatically turned upward, to Laurent's door.

He shouldn't. He knew it wasn't right, taking advantage of Laurent's kindness, stretching out what welcome he had, but Sabre couldn't stop himself from climbing the steps to Laurent's room. It settled him, in a way he couldn't place, to lie there while Laurent slept or to sit by the desk and watch him go through the night's numbers, to work on his endless sewing while he told Laurent stories his father's nursemaid used to tell, ones full of strange creatures living in the stars and women falling from the heavens to distribute things like math and philosophy.

Sometimes he would just sit there, watching Laurent sitting in the lamplight, until Laurent inevitably glanced his way again.

Laurent could, and did, settle him properly when he asked for it, but Sabre was starting to look forward to the quiet, too, when Laurent's hard edges seemed to soften.

He knocked on the door and went to his knees on the soft rug, waiting patiently for Laurent to answer.

* * *

LAURENT STARED at the numbers he'd recorded, wondering why he didn't feel happier about what he was seeing.

Sabre had been an enormous asset to the House. He was always booked, and while most of his clients visited once or maybe twice, there were already a few who were going to be regulars. One of them was Lord Chastain's son, Devon, who'd marched out of the house when his time was up like a man going to war against a hated enemy, trembling with rage and a wild, dangerously unstable look about him.

There were others eager to see the former noble of House Valois, and Laurent knew that when the shine was off the coin—a crude but apt phrase—it would ease up, for Sabre. He knew what the nobles did to him, the kicking, the tearing of clothes, the stocks. Two had choked him with a rope and been angry when they'd come too fast from Sabre's terror. Yves, who'd been assigned to watch that night through the wall, had fled and begged Charon to take his place.

It was Nanette, Charon and Simone, mostly, now. Laurent would not allow himself to do it, because the second he saw someone put a rope around Sabre's neck and get so aroused they came in their pants...well. He would not be responsible for what happened, except he would be, and then the whole house would suffer for someone doing exactly what Laurent had known they would do.

Finally he'd gone to Charon for tea that morning, sick with himself for how Sabre looked when he came to him at dawn after a night full of clients; not shaking and wreathed in horrific bruises, trembling and sobbing from fear...but quiet and calm, eyes red but clear, as if the gauntlet of humiliation and pain had done more for him than any quiet touch ever could.

"It is not one or the other," Charon had explained, pouring him the strong Arkoudai tea. "Sabre is a masochist. It is as natural an urge as submission, and our..urges...are stronger, when we are under stress. When we are kept from having what we need. In Arktos, I met a man, like your Sabre. He was brought to me to break. But I was not a man who broke others for pleasure. Which you have learned, I think, by now."

Laurent just nodded. "Your secrets are your own, Charon. You needn't tell me about them, if you don't want to."

"That I am a sadist is no secret, my lord. That Sabre craves darker things is why he's here, yes? He is getting what he needs, and you should be glad of it. I think they would do these things to him even if he were not inclined to like them, and that would be worse." Charon's dark eyes were steady, even. "Most of the men I broke, they did not like it. The nobles here, they are too...like, what do you call them, the birds, with the feathers? They have them, in the royal menagerie. They show them off, the feathers, and scream for a mate."

"Peacocks," Laurent said, trying not to choke on his tea. "Those are peacocks."

"And that is what they are, these nobles. They do not know the difference or care. And just as there are only a few true masochists like Sabre, there are not many who know how to handle him. As he settles, he will see the ones who are true and the ones who posture."

"The peacocks," Laurent had said, lifting his teacup.

"Yes," Charon'd responded, lifting his. "The peacocks."

"I would never think someone would like it, the things they do to him," Nanette said, when she made her report. If she was bothered by what she'd seen, it didn't show. "But I know someone getting hot and bothered when I see it. The only time he looks legitimately uncomfortable—without liking it—is when they tear his clothes."

"He hates the mending," Laurent had said, then thanked Nanette and went back to chastising himself over being too involved when he knew he shouldn't.

And it was lucrative, both for the House and for Sabre himself. His debt was impressive, but he wasn't adding hardly anything to it as the others did—his room remained simple and unadorned, and maybe he thought he *couldn't* do anything but mend his clothes, or maybe he simply didn't see the point of adding to his debt by ordering new ones. It wasn't nearly out of the realm of possibility he would earn it out, if he stayed as frugal as he was and put everything toward it.

And I'll get rich while he suffers, Laurent thought, then reminded himself he'd saved Sabre from a life of toil and hardship in the quarries, and also, Sabre liked what was done to him well enough, on some biological level that made little sense to anyone.

And then, he inevitably flashed back to Sabre's First Night, and how he'd stripped in the carriage, climbed on Laurent's lap. *They wouldn't have cared about the truth.*

Had he? Or had he used Sabre's desire to know to his advantage? Did it matter, anymore? He'd gotten off to the memory of Sabre on his lap more than he wanted to admit, stroking himself in the bath and gasping out his pleasure as he remembered how Sabre felt around him, staring at him, saying *I want to be good for you* while he bounced so eagerly on Laurent's cock.

When the knock came as he knew it would, Laurent threw down the quill and nearly knocked over the ink pot, standing up and taking a slow, deep breath even though it wouldn't matter. The second he saw Sabre, under and lovely, the raging *want* would come back. Laurent wasn't a sadist like the men who wanted to see Sabre humiliated. He liked watching an eager masochist writhe under the lash as much as the next dominant with similar urges, but it was putting them under, settling them, that he craved.

Laurent ran his fingers through his hair. He could ignore the knock, and Sabre would kneel there, pretty and quiet like a gift by his door. "Come in."

Sabre entered, on his feet, and he was naked and freshly bathed. "My lord. If you're busy."

He said that, every time. Laurent shook his head. "I was finishing up. Come in. How was this evening?" Of course he knew, already. And Sabre knew that he knew.

"They're very into breaking things," Sabre said, padding over, sinking to his knees next to Laurent. "My things. I'll need another mirror. Nanette offered one, but it would be on her debt, wouldn't it, if the next one broke it?"

"We'll get you a mirror. Basic furniture isn't your responsibility to replace." It was in the House of Gold, but this was not the House of Gold. Laurent could afford to replace a few broken things. "Devon Chastain wasn't too awful, was he? He will request you again. He had that look about him."

"Yes. He didn't quite get to fuck me. Said he couldn't make himself. I think he doesn't like sadism as much as he thinks he does, or he came too fast, and didn't want me to know."

"They do that," Laurent said, amused. "I had a client, once. Marlow, his name was. Apprenticed in an accounting house, could hardly carry on a conversation, and was...unfortunately put together, let's say."

"Ah," Sabre said, smiling a bit, twisting his damp, red-gold hair into a sloppy braid.

"Come here and let me do that," Laurent said, rolling his eyes as he sat on the edge of his bed and motioned to Sabre. "Anyway, this poor man must have spent his entire savings on a night with me, because he came the second I took my robe off. Then he taught me how to balance a ledger book."

"You're making that up," Sabre said. "I've learned nothing useful but the various ways to kick a man and that I have, I think, a bit of a fondness for a certain type of leather boot."

Laurent laughed. "You're a delight when you're under, you know that?" He set about braiding Sabre's hair. "It's remarkable how different you are, when you're...ah. Not."

"They kept that way, I think. My mother, at least. So I wouldn't notice things. I don't know. It seems like she would have preferred I didn't...or wasn't...fully myself. But please, my lord. Tell me more of your accounting lessons."

Laurent tugged his hair. "Brat. Well, he taught me and he was...an entirely different person. He spoke so confidently, that his, let's say, unfortunate arrangement of physical characteristics—"

"Just call him ugly, my lord," Sabre said, and laughed.

It was, Laurent thought, the first time he'd ever heard Sabre laugh. A real laugh, deep-chested and lovely. "All right, he was ugly, but when he spoke about numbers and ledgers, he had this...power, about him. Dominant, certainly, but not even that. Confidence. Anyway, I asked him some questions about how to cheat at cards, too, and he *also* knew that. I was so turned on by how smart he was, I offered to suck him off even though his time was up."

"Did that go better, then?"

"For me or for him?"

Sabre smiled. "Both, I suppose."

"He came when I breathed on his cock, but I suppose it was easy enough work for me." Laurent finished with his braid, pulling just a bit too tight to hear Sabre gasp.

"Did he come back 'round, afterwards, to try it again, then?"

Laurent almost messed up tying the end of the braid, he was so unaccustomed to Sabre sounding like a young noble, which he did in that moment more than he ever had, before. "No, my prices were suitably unaffordable for the laymen. But I hired him to look over my investments, and once a month he comes too fast for Yves and then teaches everyone else how to manage their own money, when they're done."

"You've the soul of an economic revolutionary," Sabre said, smiling a bit.

"Hardly. I'm a whore who became a lord, unless that's the sort of revolutionary you mean, and Sabre, perhaps that's a poor choice of conversation for us to have."

Sabre's smile faded, but he nodded. "Perhaps so. Would you like me to go back to my room? I am sure the glass is swept up."

"No," Laurent said, because he didn't want him to be anywhere but right here. "It's all right. Your company is hardly a bother, you realize."

"I ask for much of your time," Sabre said, and it was clear he was starting to slip, maybe, come up a bit from the place where a night of humiliating degradation had sent him.

"You do, and if I minded, I would tell you. Remember who's the whore and who's the lord, here, Sabre." He tugged on the braid. "Is there something you need, specifically?"

"I...it always feels better, when I come back up, and you're here."

Something sweet and hot kicked around his chest at that. "Then stay here. Would you like more stories about my time as a whore, then? I had a client who could only get off to the sound of sneezing, that was quite memorable. I had to inhale a variety of things to make myself able to sneeze long enough for him to find his pleasure—regrettably, he did not come as quickly as the accountant—and to this day, I cannot stand the scent of black pepper or ginger in excess."

Sabre's mouth quirked. "Is that story true."

"As I live and breathe," Laurent said, stretching. "You may attend me, if you like."

Sabre had a healthy dose of service submission along with his fondness for pain and humiliation, and he rose easily to his feet and began to attend to Laurent's clothing, which were simple enough as he'd changed after the first of the evening's rush. "May I ask you a question, my lord?"

"You may." Curious, Laurent tilted his head, watched Sabre's long, elegant fingers as they undid the buttons on his shirt.

"How did you come to be in Staria?"

"Well, I would imagine my mother lay with my father and—what?" He laughed. "How does anyone come to be anywhere?"

"But you aren't...my lord, you aren't Starian, are you?" Sabre blinked up at him. "You're taller than most, which I suppose isn't all that rare but...your coloring isn't found here, and sometimes you speak with an accent."

An accent? That was new, no one had mentioned that since his early days in the House of Gold. "Oh. Well, yes, originally, I suppose I wasn't. But I've been here as long as I remember, though I suppose it's possible...you mean to say, the others haven't told you? My harridan of a sister?"

"Told me...what, my lord?"

Yves could pull off coy, Sabre could not. Laurent sighed and let Sabre help him undress, then slipped into a robe and tied back his hair as he went to a small liquor cabinet near the desk. "I don't have any memory of my life before I was at the House of Gold."

"Oh. You were brought there young, then?"

"No, that's the thing. Kneel for me, pet, by the bed, there. Good." He took up a bottle and waved it at Sabre. "This is athenero. It's liquor made from desert wildflowers, they grow only in Arktos and it's impossible to get some. I gave a bottle to Charon after his First Night, and he wept. Actual tears. I think he would give up all his maps, his books *and* his tea to keep it hidden."

"It's that good?" Sabre asked.

Laurent poured some in a glass, two swallows-full. "Gods, no, pet. It's awful. It tastes like—what?"

"You said that once, before." Sabre's eyes went downcast. "*Gods.* Just, um. Just once, when I was in your bed."

Gods, how I want to fuck you.

"Is it that strange?" Laurent asked, walking over, holding the glass out. "Go on, try it. It will help you sleep, if nothing else. It's bitter, which Charon says is because the Arktos are contrary about everything, even flowers and things that should taste good."

"We don't believe in gods, here," Sabre said, and took the glass. He sipped it, and then coughed immediately. "This is foul. Why would anyone, ever drink this."

"Take another sip, wait about two minutes, you'll see. It sends you under without the pain, that might be why."

"What's the fun of that," Sabre coughed, but he took another sip and immediately pulled a face.

"Charon said if you ever go to Arktos and add honey to your tea or your athenero, they'll lose all respect for you. Considering I've lost respect for their palate and think their taste buds must be permanently damaged by all the bitter tea..." he knocked back the rest of the drink, shuddered, and then put the glass on his bedside table. "I came late to the House of Gold, actually. I was—well, I was told somewhere between ten and thirteen, no one was sure, not really. I woke up in a bed, and it was sunny, and I could hear the last lingering bits of a lullaby, just the...edges of one, like someone sang it while I was asleep." He whistled it, just a bit.

Sabre's eyes went vacant. "That's familiar, I...I swear I've heard it before."

Laurent shrugged. "Then you're one up on me, I have no idea what it was. The proprietor said I'd been brought here by a woman who said she'd found me in an alley, wracked by a fever and muttering in a strange language. But I woke up and called myself Laurent, spoke the common tongue with a slight accent that I assumed was just a mark of the lower city, and never remembered how I'd ended up there, or where I was before."

"Did you try and find her, the woman who brought you?"

"There was no reason, really. It was said she covered her face, refused to sign her name and was *adamant* about taking no coin for giving me over, which I assume was because she knew it would go toward my debt if she didn't take it for herself, but...well, it's hard to believe a stranger would be that caring about someone they found feverish in an alley. I assumed it was my mother's way of making sure I didn't know who she was, and the least I could do was honor that wish and not find her."

Laurent climbed into bed, and said, "Go ahead and bring the water carafe, if you want to clear the taste from your mouth."

"I could do that another way, my lord."

The warm, strong liquor made the protests that Laurent already wouldn't have wanted to listen to weak and unsubstantial. He reclined in the sheets of his bed, and said, "All right, then, show me how a good whore pleases his lord."

Sabre was eager, and warm, his hair soft against Laurent's thighs when he took Laurent into his mouth. And maybe it was the alcohol softening the edges of his dominance and Sabre being a little under along with it, but it was...easier, between them, than it had been before. Laurent let Sabre pleasure him and didn't try to grab or choke, just kept a firm hand in his Sabre's hair and sometimes held him for a second or two, just to feel Sabre's throat flutter around his cock. And he came in Sabre's mouth without bothering to pull out and finish on him, as dominants were wont to do with their clients.

Sabre did not, in that moment, feel like a client. Laurent drew him up when he was finished, kissed him and murmured, "Taste better, then?"

"Oh, yes," Sabre said, and kissed him back.

"Do you want to come, tonight, or would you like to lie there and ache for me?" He smiled when Sabre squirmed, clearly aroused by the thought of it, being denied. "My little masochist, I've never met anyone who likes being hurt like you do. Go ahead, curl up there at the bottom of the bed and I'll see to you in the morning, if you're good. I might let you hump *my* boot, mine are far better leather than Devon Chastain's."

"Yes, my lord," Sabre murmured, and moved to lie contentedly at Laurent's feet.

Laurent was nearly asleep when he heard Sabre say, quietly, "My lord, I remember when I heard that song. Before. The one you were humming."

"Oh?" Laurent shifted on the silk, yawned. "When was that?"

"She used to sing it," Sabre answered.

"Who? Your mother?"

"No," Sabre said, surprising him. "Not my mother. Adrien's. The queen." He hummed it, again, and it went on and on, and somehow, without knowing exactly why or how, Laurent realized he was humming, too, fingers tapping out a forgotten rhythm on the silk of his pillowcase, over and over, in the dark.

CHAPTER 10

"If this beast you employ as a whore knew better than to *antagonize* a woman with a lash in her hand—"

Sabre lay on the floor of his room, staring up at the ceiling. His face felt like an enormous, throbbing bruise, and when he touched his cheek, his fingers came away red, blood rolling between them and onto his palm. Somewhere above him, just out of sight, Lady Auclair was working herself to a froth against Charon's implacable calm.

"My lady," Charon said. "A scarred courtesan loses the House income."

"Then he can go to the quarries, if he's a burden."

"My lady, come with me to the foyer, and I will put your name on the gray list, with your signature."

"You wouldn't!"

"Well, hello there, my love." Simone's dress appeared before she did, a voluminous gown in olive green, and Sabre idly reached out to run his fingers over the satin. "Don't you look dramatic."

"I'm in a swoon," Sabre said, and winced as the left side of his face burned with pain.

Simone clicked her tongue. "Yes, I'm dying with envy. Don't move.

I *think* we can keep you from scarring. What did she do, roll you on your back and whip you?"

"Yes," Sabre said, and Simone went still above him, a damp cloth held over his face.

"Ah," she said, in a short, quiet voice.

At first, Sabre had thought she'd only grazed him. Sometimes, when he was whipped, the rare few with enough control to do it properly would barely miss him, letting him tense and gasp at the feel of the whip lashing the air, unsure when it was going to connect. But Lady Auclair either didn't have that control or didn't want to, and Sabre didn't realize he'd been struck until Charon pushed open the door, and the shock of it gave way to the stinging pain over his face and chest.

"Even if it does scar," Simone said, rinsing off her cloth in the basin next to Sabre's window, "it's close enough to your jaw that you can hide it."

"Any chance…" Sabre gasped slightly as Simone started cleaning the weal over his chest. "You can tell Lord de Rue *after*, then?"

"Oh, darling, he already knows," Simone said, and Sabre cursed under his breath as a thundering of footsteps rolled down the hall outside. The door slammed open again, and Sabre lifted his head just enough to see Laurent's wild expression before Simone pushed him down again.

"Where is the one who did this," Laurent said.

"I'll be fine," Sabre said.

"Downstairs, being signed onto the gray list," Simone said, covering Sabre's mouth with a hand. Laurent's boots thumped down the stairs, and Sabre winced as his voice rose from the common room, muted but so heavy with dominance that Sabre could feel it from where he lay.

"What's the gray list?" Sabre asked, as Simone shook her head and dipped her fingers in a jar at her side.

"It passes between all the Houses," Simone said. She dabbed some of the cream on her fingers over the cut on Sabre's jaw, and Sabre gripped the rug, nails digging into the fibers. It stung like alcohol. "If you're on the list, you are forbidden from hiring any courtesan until the House lords unanimously agree to remove you."

"And she'd—ah—go on the list for *whipping* me?"

"Faces are off limits," Simone said. "Everyone knows that. Why do you think that Devon Chastain of yours hasn't broken your nose, yet, for all he threatens to?"

"He has no strength behind the blow," Sabre said. "So he couldn't."

A door slammed downstairs, hard enough Sabre could almost feel the walls tremble.

"You'll need to do something about that, soon," Simone said, placing a bandage over Sabre's cheek.

"I don't think I can control someone's temper," Sabre said, a little bewildered.

"Not that, love." Simone pulled his hair out of the way so she could wrap gauze around the bandage, so efficiently that Sabre wondered how many times she'd done it before, over the years. "The fact that he's losing it at all. We've all had our share of close calls—Clients who offer us proposals, then turn on us when we reject them. Young hotheads with something to prove. But this is personal, I'd think."

"Oh," Sabre said. "No, he's just kind."

"Is he?" Simone helped him sit up, wrapping more gauze around his chest. "Perhaps, to an extent. It's a dangerous thing, to be kind."

"And what are you?" Sabre asked.

Simone smiled. "Don't get cheeky, now, you only have one left to lose." Sabre groaned, and she pet his hair. "Can you walk?"

"She didn't whip my legs off, you know," Sabre said, but he did let Simone help him to his feet. He leaned against her, breathing in the citrus scent she worked into her hair, and she patted his shoulder. "I assume there won't be any more clients, tonight."

"No," said Laurent, striding into the room with his eyes blazing and his voice shaking with dominance. "There won't be."

Sabre made a soft sound and sank to his knees, and Simone raised her hands in the air.

"I just had him standing, my lord."

"Yes. Thank you, Simone," Laurent said. Simone raised her brows.

"I'll go, then," she said, and sidled past, holding up the skirts of her gown. Laurent sighed loudly and ran a hand through his hair.

"Sabre," he said, and turned aside, pacing down the narrow space of Sabre's room. "Would it be...better, if I...you would be safer in another House, I think."

"What?" Terror rolled through him, sharp and cold, dragging Sabre out of the drifting haze he'd settled into under the whip. "Why? What did I—Did I do something? Should I have done something differently?"

"No." Laurent turned to Sabre, held his chin in one hand. "You were on your back, covered in blood."

"Yes."

"In the House of Gold, they don't carry any tool harsher than a flogger."

"That sounds miserable, my lord," Sabre said. "And they rejected me. Here, I know you won't...I thought you wouldn't send me away."

Laurent stared down at him for a minute in silence, Sabre's breath unnaturally harsh.

"Please," Sabre said. "Lau—my lord."

Laurent let out a ragged breath and got down on his knees in front of Sabre, pulling him into his arms.

"I won't send you away," Laurent said at last, speaking into Sabre's long, red-gold hair. "I don't think I can."

* * *

THE SALVE SIMONE gave Sabre must have been magically infused, because it only took a few days for his face to heal. Sabre did get a scar, all the same. It was a pale one, like a crescent moon cradling his jaw, and while Laurent kept fussing over it, brushing Sabre's hair back in the bath and tracing it with his fingers, it wasn't noticeable with his hair down. Rose even spent an entire afternoon mixing paints to make him look like there were stars falling over his face, squinting at him thoughtfully while they sat in the kitchen.

"Laurent used to ask me to tell him stories about the moon all the time," Rose said, painting a star over Sabre's brow. "I still come up with them, sometimes. Silly things, really. I used to say I was a moon princess."

"You could be," Sabre said. "It's a shame there aren't any plays about moon princesses, or you'd be perfect for the role."

Rose stopped, brush poised over his nose. "Maybe I wrote one," she said, in a hushed voice.

"I can read it, if you like," Sabre said.

Rose disappeared into her room, which was next to the kitchen and draped with silks and handmade tapestries, and returned with a worn, leatherbound journal. She held it out reverently to Sabre, who flipped it open.

"It's probably terrible," she said.

Sabre raised his brows. Rose looked nothing like her usual, over-confident self, pacing around the kitchen while Sabre read, rocking on her heels as though she meant to ask a question, fiddling with the puff of hair on the top of her head. Finally, when Sabre got to the part where the moon princess was being chased by the bird-children of the lost Oria, Rose scraped her chair over the tile and sat so close her knees knocked into his.

"So?" she said. "Is it awful?"

"I like the line about her lost mother," Sabre said. "On page… fifteen. The way she says how it feels like a door you can't find in your house?"

"Oh," Rose said.

"I think," Sabre said, carefully, as Rose rocked in her chair, "that you might have picked the wrong profession. You're sure you don't want to do *this* full-time?"

"But, I mean. They're just stories," Rose said, in a way that meant, clear as day, that they weren't.

"Laurent loves them," Sabre said.

"I love nothing," Laurent said, from behind them, and both Sabre and Rose jumped. "I'm cold and unfeeling, just like you said when I wouldn't buy you those shoes. What are you putting him up to, Rose?"

"Nothing," Rose said, as Laurent set down the drink he'd been holding and headed over. She grabbed the book and held it to her chest. "And those shoes weren't even that expensive."

Laurent gave her a look. "Is that your play? The one with the moon princess?"

"Maybe."

"And she let you read it?" Laurent asked Sabre.

"Because there's romance in his soul, obviously," Rose said, defensively. "His whole life is basically a play, anyways."

"A tragedy, I assume," Sabre said.

"Or a romance. It depends." Rose squinted at him, then at Laurent. "I haven't decided."

"Well, *I* think your writing has promise, no matter what genre it is," Sabre said. "Maybe the House could try it out. Charon would make a good Storm King, don't you think?"

Rose closed her eyes for a moment. "I think...Yes. Maybe he would. I...I think I'm going to ask him."

"What have you done," Laurent whispered, as Rose marched off, book held tight in both hands.

"I'm encouraging the arts," Sabre whispered back. Laurent turned his face towards him, and smiled.

"Yes, I see that. Your face could feature in a gallery."

"Do you think my clients will mind tonight, if I showed up with stars on my face?" Sabre asked. Laurent grimaced. "I...*am* taking clients again? The king will notice, I think, if I don't."

Laurent's gaze went distant. "He already has. We'll be resuming your usual schedule tonight, I suppose."

He ran his hand down Sabre's cheek, tracing the pale scar that curved there, and drew away.

"Best clean up, then," he said, and turned for the hall, leaving Sabre alone in the kitchen with a hand on his cheek, chasing the warmth Laurent's fingers left behind.

* * *

THE FIRST CLIENTS of the night were Roland Garnier and Olivier Blanchet, which meant Charon was probably watching through the wall, just in case. Roland wasn't a sadist, but he despised Sabre enough to do the work of one, and that, Sabre knew now, was a dangerous combination. Roland was in rare form that night, regardless. Sabre was tripped twice as he led them up the stairs to his room, and Roland pushed him through the door, sending him crashing to the floor with a low thud that made the window panes rattle.

"You're right, Roland," Olivier said, as Sabre rolled to his side. "I think the slut actually likes it."

Roland kicked him in the side. "On your knees, whore."

"Yes, my lord," Sabre said, and Olivier smiled, foxlike and wicked. He grabbed Sabre by the chin and held his mouth open, and Roland spat in it.

"Swallow," Olivier said, almost sweetly. When Sabre managed to work his throat, he slapped him. "You know, I always liked your sister. Thought she'd spread her legs for me when you wouldn't, but watching her hang was good enough."

"You can have him now, Ollie," Roland said, holding Sabre back by the hair. "Whenever you want. Just tell me, and I'll foot the bill."

Sabre's eyes must have widened at that—he hadn't known the Blanchet estate was doing so poorly—because Olivier slapped him again, pushed him down on his back and struck him with his palm until Sabre, breathless with pain, raised a hand to stop him. Olivier sat there, breathing hard, Roland palming himself over them both, and spat in Sabre's face.

They took him together, Olivier tugging at his hair like reins while hissing about how much of a slut he was, how depraved, how desperate for cock that he'd choose the whorehouses over a hanging.

"He can always have both," Roland said, and pushed Sabre away from him, tied a rope around his neck while Sabre bounced on Olivier's cock, wild-eyed with fear. They both came too soon, after that, and left him sore and gasping, covered in sweat and come.

"Fuck," he whispered, pushing the rope off of his neck. He kicked it into the corner, taking huge, gasping breaths, and hastily cleaned himself from the basin. He didn't have much time, just enough to dress and run a comb through his hair, but his clients tended to like him disheveled.

"Do you think they're fucking?" Sabre asked the wall where the alcove was. His hands were still shaking. "I always suspected they were. I feel for the poor submissive who gets between *them*."

He didn't consider until he was walking gingerly down the stairs that *he* was the submissive in question. It was almost sad, in a way. Olivier had been sweet enough, when Sabre turned him down, but there must have been something festering under the surface.

Lord Chastain—the proper one, not his son, Devon—met Sabre in the common room. He gave Sabre a curious look, lingering on his wrinkled clothes and loose hair, but rose from the couch when Sabre bowed.

"Your manners are still atrocious," Lord Chastain said, as Sabre led him up the stairs. "I never did understand why your father chose to let you run wild for so long."

"I'm sorry, my lord," Sabre said, opening the door. "I was never formally trained."

"Clearly. Let me see your form. Kneel for me."

Sabre went to his knees. Lord Chastain hadn't bothered with form, the first time—He'd simply circled Sabre, asking him questions about his mother, his sister, until Sabre was shaking and close to tears. Now, Lord Chastain took a cane from the wall and circled Sabre again, boots thumping on the rug.

"Chin up," he said, lifting Sabre's chin with the end of the cane. "You're a submissive, not a doormat. And what, exactly, are you doing with your shoulders?"

Sabre rolled his shoulders back, and Lord Chastain sighed.

"That's three lashes. Four, for your hands. No, you imbecile, not on your thighs, behind your back. Legs like so." He pushed Sabre's knees slightly apart.

"I...apologize, my lord," Sabre said.

"I don't need to hear you talk," Lord Chastain said. He sighed again, heavily. "Over the desk. Don't drape yourself over it like a cast-off coat, boy. Count the lashes."

The cane cracked over Sabre's upper thighs, and he gripped the desk tight. "One."

"It comes from your father being a progressive, I suppose," Lord Chastain said. "This lapse in your training. Your descent into your mother and sister's treachery."

Pain flared, and Sabre had to hold onto the desk to stop himself from rubbing his cock along the side of it. "Two."

"Imagine. Making a submissive son your heir when he could have sired another. It's no wonder your mother found him so odious." Sabre tensed, and Lord Chastain leaned over the desk, holding back his hair. "You don't think so? The whole court knew she hated him. All you needed was a pair of eyes."

He caned Sabre until he was squirming, just on the edge of enough, and stopped, setting the cane aside. Sabre couldn't suppress the sound he made, then, and Lord Chastain looked at him sharply, his gray-green eyes hard.

"Did you want more?" Lord Chastain asked. "You, the son of Arthur de Valois, who suppressed the insurrection on the northern coast? Pity's sake, I almost wonder if you would have *liked* being held down by the king. A Valois, yearning for a boot on their neck. What a strange creature you are."

He stepped forward, pulling a lock of hair from Sabre's face, and gripped the lot of it in his fist. Sabre braced for the pain, and something flashed in Lord Chastain's eyes.

"To think your mother kept a masochist locked away in her estate," he said, softly. "What a waste. Get on the bed, boy. Let's see if you've learned something useful in your time here."

* * *

Laurent was not supposed to be here, tonight.

It was Charon, usually, who watched over Sabre. He knew just how much a masochist like Sabre could endure, but more than that, he knew how to tell when a submissive who was as much a painslut as Sabre was *enjoying* himself, not just enduring.

Nanette or Simone would pop in, when Charon was booked. He'd asked Laurent if he could take less clients, so that he could see to Sabre's safety.

"You know this will mean longer to repay your debt," Laurent had told him, carefully, when Charon had asked.

Charon had clicked his heels together, straightened and raised his chin—then bowed, which was apparently how Arkoudai officers showed respect. "My debt will never be repaid in money, my lord. This service eases it more than you know."

So Charon gave up a few clients a night to keep watch over Sabre, but there were some that even Laurent couldn't reschedule. Charon was with one, now, and Simone was under the weather with a cold, so that left either Nanette or Laurent. And it was Lady Cordelia's night, the young woman who was Nanette's favorite client, who came up with such elaborate character roleplay that they spent the majority of their time together gossiping, sewing, and writing backstories in Lady Cordelia's leather-bound notebook.

The last time, apparently, they'd fully dragged out Lord Danger's issues with his overbearing father and why he was so keen to join up with the navy, despite being terrified of pirates.

So he couldn't in good conscience ask her to miss that, given that Lady Cordelia's doting, older husband was more than happy to supply his young wife with all the crowns she wanted to spend on her favorite whore. Laurent therefore sat in the alcove and watched Lord Oscar Chastain suddenly start to sing a different tune.

He'd known it would happen, eventually. Some noble eager to hurt Sabre for his family's transgressions would get it out of his system, but then notice how lovely Sabre looked when he cried, how pretty he was on his knees, and instead of a *thing* they could hurt, they'd see something else. A wounded animal in need of tending. A misunderstood whore waiting for the right patron to find the *good* in him, find his bruised heart of beaten gold and polish it up to a proper shine.

He hadn't thought it would be Lord Chastain, but Laurent should have really learned not to be surprised anymore. He'd been in this business long enough to have seen just about everything, and this was fairly classic behavior; older, wiser client, suddenly aware the whore they were paying to fuck or hurt or both was a person, perhaps in need of being *saved*.

It was an act, of course. Some were better at it than others—Yves could teach lessons, if he wanted—and Laurent knew a few in the House of Gold who could pout just so, cry so pretty their clients gave them hot chocolate and cuddles instead of a flogger or a good fuck. It was a business, and people liked to feel special. Laurent hadn't been terribly good at the wounded faun act, himself, but the current top-earner in the House of Gold, Gabriel la Nuit, could have raised an army of men who wanted to protect him, if he'd wanted to.

With Sabre, though. His vulnerability was as attractive as suffering, simply because it was so *honest*. And Oscar Chastain was many things, but if there was one thing he knew how to do, it was how to find vulnerable creatures who were trying to hide, flush them out and trap them.

He had Sabre trapped, now, on the bed beneath him. Laurent had been mildly surprised that Lord Chastain had returned for another session, given he hadn't fucked Sabre the first time, and he'd been one of Sabre's first clients. It hadn't been because he'd come too quickly, either, or was too taken in by disgust to work himself up, as had happened with his son—and kept happening, according to a frustrated Sabre. It hadn't seemed as if he would, tonight, but something had changed.

And Laurent knew exactly what it was. Lord Chastain looked at Sabre and saw not the son of a traitor and a whore, but a man who moaned prettily under a cane and begged to be put so firmly in his place, untried and unsure of himself, *someone who needed to be saved*. And there was enough truth to it, wasn't there, for Sabre to sell it without even having to try?

Laurent watched as Lord Chastain pushed his trousers down, freed his cock and climbed on the bed to kneel over Sabre. He flipped Sabre on his back, stared down at him, and even through the partition

Laurent could hear how hard he was breathing, could sense the sea change that had taken him.

"They say true masochists are the rarest jewel of all, did you know that?"

"I—have heard that, yes, my lord," Sabre panted, guileless and eager and probably more than a little afraid, with it written so clearly on his lovely, tear-streaked face.

"And did you know that you were one?" Lord Chastian asked, his tone heated, his stare intense, no longer disinterested, no longer smirking.

"I was not trained for any of it, my lord," Sabre said, which was of course the truth, and would only inflame Chastain further, probably.

"What a ridiculous waste. Your mother, she had no idea what you were, a diamond in a draw of paste glass." Chastain smacked him across the face, and Sabre's moan was pained, aching, and his hips pushed up, too eager. "I wouldn't have believed it. The king must not know, or else why would he have sent you here? It's more a reward than a punishment—" Chastain went quiet, staring down at Sabre. "Maybe you weren't being punished at all."

Laurent's fingers dug into his palm, hard enough that there would be marks there, later. Any idiot with half a brain could tell Sabre wasn't only just a submissive, did Chastain think himself clever, for figuring out what Laurent could tell at a glance?

Get ahold of yourself, it's not shocking information you're smarter than a Starian noble. Even if you are one, now.

"I—my lord, I don't presume to know the king's—"

Chastain slapped him, hard enough to take the rest of his words and turn them into moans. "We won't speak of that. I said I wished to see what they've taught you here, and I do. To think Lord de Rue saw in you what no one else did. I suppose it takes a whore to know one."

Laurent smiled in the dark, mentally ignoring all of Chastain's requests for future assignations. *Takes one to know one, indeed.*

He took Sabre on his back, staring down at his face, enraptured as he made Sabre beg for it, to be mounted and fucked hard. Sabre's head tossed on the bed, and Chastain was less a noble lording over a disgraced peer's son and just a man, a dominant with a touch of sadism watching an eager masochist fall apart beneath him.

"Beg me to hurt you, Sabre," Chastain ordered, and Laurent's eyes narrowed. It was the first time any of his clients had called Sabre by his given name, and he didn't like it even though he knew it shouldn't matter. Laurent cursed himself as a fool even as he idly rubbed his cock with one hand, nails still digging into the skin of his palm on the other.

"Hurt me, please, my lord," Sabre begged, voice slurred—he hadn't come tonight, and it was making him frantic, desperate to go under.

To his credit, Chastain didn't go for the rope, which was far too obvious a choice, and instead used Sabre's long, unbound hair; he wrapped it around Sabre's neck and wound the strands like a lead over his wrist, so that every time he pulled his hand back, Sabre choked, strangled by his own hair.

"Look at you, little masochist, you could come from this, couldn't you?" Chastain's voice was wrecked, guttural, and when he smacked Sabre right on his hard cock, Sabre bucked beneath him, babbling *yes, please, please, let me.*

"You like this," Chastain whispered, speeding up, fucking Sabre so hard the bed frame rattled and the headboard knocked against the wall.

Laurent caught himself rubbing the hard press of his cock through his pants with his palm, scowled and went back to digging his nails in instead. He wanted Chastain to tell Sabre *no*, to leave him there on the bed, wrecked and unsatisfied so that Laurent could do it, finish him off, put him under.

But Chastain was not the idiot his son was, apparently, and he let Sabre come, kissing him while Sabre wailed his pleasure and came between them. Chastain came inside him after a few harsh, fierce thrusts, and all but collapsed on Sabre when it was over.

Sabre was still trying to catch his breath, likely finally under after all he'd endured that night, and Chastain didn't tell him to open his eyes. So he didn't see the pleased, smirky little smile Chastain smiled at him, but Laurent saw it, and knew it probably didn't mean anything good.

That was further proven when, instead of leaving out of the rear of the establishment as all nobles did, Chastain made a point to ask after Laurent and meet him in his office.

Laurent almost refused, but Sabre was done for the evening and fast asleep in his little bed, and Laurent was the lord of the House of Onyx and had his own responsibilities to see to. So he made himself presentable and greeted Lord Chastain with the easy, blank smile he'd spent years on his back cultivating, and said, "Is anything amiss, Lord Chastain?"

"No, no. I'm simply here to congratulate you, Lord de Rue. True masochists are quite a find. I imagine Lord Julien of the House of Gold will be beside himself, when he hears you tricked him out of one."

"Ah, but you see, the House of Gold isn't quite equipped to handle a creature such as our Sabre. But I am, of course, pleased to know that you enjoyed your time with him."

Lord Chastain had the look of all dominants who were well satisfied, but there was something else there, something Laurent didn't quite trust. The cruel, sly look of a fox watching a den of baby rabbits, figuring out best how to make off with them under their mother's horrified eyes. He slid a ring off his finger and pushed it over Laurent's desk. "Give him that for me. A token. I've heard it is useful to pay one's debt. Impossible in his case, given the amount, but he should know when he's pleased his client."

"Of course, my lord," Laurent said, smoothly, taking up the ring and placing it in the small box marked with Sabre's name, where clients could leave such baubles or tips, if they wished. His accumulated only scraps or pennies or, once, a piece of colored fabric that Sabre had finally stammered out was ripped from his sister's gown on her way to the gallows.

Other than de Mortain's gift, this would be the first he'd received.

"Sabre will be grateful, of course," Laurent added. *And I am quite*

curious as to how you know the amount of his debt at all, given no one does,
outside the House lord and Isiodore de Mortain.

"You'll reschedule my appointments so they are with him for the foreseeable future, and see that mine are first in the evening. I'm an important man and do not care to go second."

Especially not when you're penciled in after your son, you pompous peacock. "Certainly, I shall amend the schedule and send it along."

"No, no. That won't be necessary, I'll send a messenger. Do put together the requirements for travel, if you would, I'd like him to accompany me later this month to a fête I'm attending for His Majesty."

The bloody hunting party, the one the king himself had requested Sabre attend? That would cause some chaos, certainly, but Laurent just nodded and said, "I shall consult the schedule, you understand he's quite...popular."

"With the fools who don't know what he is," Chastain sniffed, as if he'd known any different an hour ago, despite all the evidence to the contrary.

Laurent's easy smile lasted until Chastain took his leave, and then he took the ring from the box and went back upstairs. He could hear the sounds of the house in business all around him—Nanette and her client laughing, the rhythmic *thwack* followed by a sob as Charon worked someone over, Yves begging *daddy, please, don't hurt me!* In such a ridiculous tone that Laurent would smile, were he in a better mood. Yves might be what Chastain called a *paste jewel*, but Laurent was fond of him, far more than most.

But he pushed into Sabre's room without knocking, staring at the mess there, the furniture knocked over, the torn clothing, the hangman's rope used as a plaything—and the submissive on the bed, bruised and messy-haired and fast asleep with a smile on his face.

CHAPTER 11

Sabre didn't often dream of his father, before his mother and sister died, but when he did, he was always in the woods.

His father loved the wild country beyond the city. He would take the queen and Adrien out with him, sometimes, when she and the king remembered they weren't alone in the world. The queen would sit on her horse and laugh as Sabre and Adrien faced off with strips of willowy tree branches, Sabre's father in the middle with his sword flashing in his hand.

In his dream, the queen's arms were red with blood, but she was still smiling.

"Arthur," she said. "Don't torment the boys."

"They need to learn how to defend themselves in close quarters, Your Majesty," Sabre's father had said. "We don't all come from idyllic farmlands."

"Neither do I," the queen said, leaning forward on her horse. "We pressed grapes on my lands. Mislian, the kind you have to freeze before they go sweet."

"Not at all idyllic, a vineyard," Sabre's father said. "Swords up, boys."

"No. I don't want to," Adrien said. "Sabre shouldn't fight."

"I *like* it, Asa," Sabre said.

"I don't." Adrien shuddered. "I don't like seeing you with a sword."

"You never have, goose. I'm not allowed to hold a real one yet."

Adrien stared at him, just as he had that day out in the woods. "I do," he said. "And it's always bad."

"Adrien," the queen said. Blood was starting to splash on the grass. "We don't speak of that, here."

Sabre turned. The woods melted away, and he was lying on his bed in the House of Onyx, looking up at Laurent. Laurent, who seemed to come from a dream himself, honorable in a way nobles couldn't afford to be, someone who would look down at a naked, sobbing wretch in the street and see something of value.

"You're new," Sabre said. "Haven't dreamed of you before."

"You haven't?" Laurent's mouth quirked. "I'm almost disappointed."

"They're all so full of death, usually," Sabre said. He reached for Laurent, hooked his fingers in his belt. "I'm tired of death. That's what the queen said, you know. Adrien told me. Tired of death. I understand why she did it, I think."

Laurent took Sabre's hands, and Sabre sighed, trying to pull him onto the bed.

"I don't think you're fully awake, yet," Laurent said.

"Of course not," Sabre said, smiling. He guided Laurent's hands to his hips. "You're here, so I'm dreaming, but it's terrible because you aren't, oh, fucking me, or taking off this damn collar. You should give me a black one, with violet lining. Yes. I'd like that."

Laurent's gaze went dark, and Sabre shivered deliciously.

"What else would you like, pet?"

"Everything, I suppose." Sabre ran his hands up Laurent's arms. "Say I belong to you. I like it when you say that. When I feel it, your hands on me…"

He stopped, horrified, as he felt the soft sheets move beneath him, the cool air of the House at night, the touch of Laurent's hands on his hips.

"Oh," he said.

"There you are," Laurent said, and leaned down to kiss him. "Black and violet, mm?"

"If you would give me a spade," Sabre said, "so I may dig a hole, here, and crawl into it?"

"You'll end up digging through Yves' ceiling," Laurent said. He took Sabre by the back of the neck, guiding him up off the bed. "You want to dream of me fucking you, do you?"

"Shouldn't I?" Sabre asked, and Laurent smacked him across the face before he kissed him again, hard and possessive. "Yes, you see, you make a good point."

"It wasn't enough to be fucked by Lord Chastain?" Laurent asked.

Sabre stared at him for a second. "Oh."

"You didn't *forget* about him?" Laurent asked, digging his nails into the back of Sabre's neck.

Sabre searched Laurent's face. "Do you want me to?"

"You mean that," Laurent said. He pulled at Sabre's hair, and ah, if that wasn't what he wanted, for Laurent's hand on him, his eyes arresting him, drowning him.

"Yes, my lord."

"Come with me," Laurent said, gripping Sabre's hair tight and practically dragging him across the room.

"Shouldn't I clean up, first?"

"You'll do as I tell you," Laurent said, and Sabre would have nodded if he weren't being pulled along by the hair, tripping up the steps. He desperately, painfully wanted Laurent to stop, to take him there on the stairway for any client to see, to drag him down to the common room and have him ride him on one of the plush chairs, to choke on his cock in front of the nobles with their useless masks.

"My lord," Sabre asked, "can we pretend I was charming and subtle about wanting you to fuck me against the window?" Laurent stared. "Or the floor, but the steps are a little narrow, and what if we fall?"

Laurent looked like he wasn't sure if he wanted to give in to Sabre's ridiculous demands or laugh. "You're honestly considering the logistics of sex on the stairs."

"I think I could manage." Sabre let out a muffled sound into Laurent's mouth as he was pressed up against the wall, Laurent's thigh slotted between his legs, Sabre groping over the dark paneling behind him for purchase.

Laurent gazed down at him as he pulled away. "Impatient, aren't we? I might leave you kneeling in the baths while I tend to myself, now."

Sabre wasn't sure he didn't want that, too. "As my lord commands."

Laurent cursed under his breath and grabbed Sabre by the collar, pulling him up the stairs. He had such a lovely voice, when he was edging into topspace, that slight accent giving his words an almost musical quality. But that's how it was with love, his father used to say, everything about the other person took a different shape—

Sabre stumbled on the steps, and Laurent paused, brows lowering in concern.

"You'll get there eventually," Laurent said, softly chiding.

"I am, yes," Sabre said. His tongue felt locked in his mouth. "You know…what I said before. It would be nice, to dream of you."

Laurent met his gaze for a long moment. Sabre stared at him, feeling oddly breathless, weightless, pained. His mother would have done more than just starve Sabre if she'd known this would happen, one day. Laurent was a noble, but to Sabre's mother, he would always be lower class, someone to pity and befriend but never love. She'd been wrong about so many things, in the end. Wrong about their line's "stewardship" over the poor, who couldn't be bothered to remember their names half the time, wrong about her plans against the king…wrong about Sabre.

And while Sabre was off riding horses through the streets with noble children who despised him, Laurent had been there, just out of reach, pulling together enough coin to run his own House, to fund his sister's acting career. If they'd met on the street, Sabre probably would have blushed and looked away, ashamed to be so close to the pleasure houses in the first place.

Sabre never would have thought this possible, if he hadn't been picked up by Laurent on the street that day. Wrapped in his coat, wretched and miserable, unknowing.

Sabre fell through Laurent's doorway, catching himself on the frame, and Laurent pulled him the rest of the way through.

* * *

IT SEEMED, really, rather stupid to fight this.

Laurent knew it, and still he thought maybe *I shouldn't be doing this,* and *it would be better for everyone if he just went back to his room.* But it was too late for that, and he knew it, Sabre knew it, hell, everyone in the house knew it by now. Laurent had guarded his heart like an iron fortress, and of course it took a disgraced noble with no artifice, a tragic story and a sweet smile to undo all his defenses and storm the gates like a conquering army.

"I watched him with you," Laurent said, pushing Sabre down on the bed, graceless, not a practiced whore anymore but a man, eager and wanting, kissing Sabre hotly and tugging uselessly on the collar that wasn't right, wasn't *his.* "And I wanted to drag him out of there and." He could barely finish the sentence.

"Are you angry when I, if I, they make me, sometimes, I can't—"

"No, sweet thing, it's not you." Laurent kissed him again, hands moving over his body, feeling the curve and muscles beneath his fingers as he pressed him into the bed. "I want you to like it, I—ah." He stopped talking, kissing Sabre instead, shifting on top of him. "You'll like it, when I take you," he informed Sabre, voice brimming with dominance.

"Yes, my lord," Sabre gasped, arching up, arms sliding around Laurent's neck to pull him closer.

Laurent hesitated only a moment before he said, against Sabre's mouth, "Not *my lord,* not tonight. My name. Use my name."

"Laurent," Sabre begged, perfect and lovely. "Please."

He didn't need to say anything else—Laurent knew what he wanted. He pinned Sabre's hands above his head on the bed, held them there not with chains or cuffs or a rope, but just a press of his fingers and a husky, *don't move those until I tell you that you may.* Sabre shifted beneath him, gorgeous and splayed out on the silk sheets, staring hungrily with his bright copper eyes as Laurent touched him, kissed him, left marks from his teeth on Sabre's chest, the sensitive area of his inner upper arms, his inner thighs. Sucked his cock with less skill and more enthusiasm than he had since he was new, until Sabre was almost sobbing, back arched like a bowstring, begging to come.

Laurent didn't let him, but he brought him to the edge three times before he fumbled like a novice for the oil, slicking up his cock and saying, "You can move your arms now, touch me, go ahead."

Sabre did, but only to grab at his shoulders and dig his fingers into Laurent's muscles, tight, little, gasping sounds of pleasure spilling from his mouth as Laurent fucked him. He was so tight, so perfect, and Laurent had to bite him again before he said something he shouldn't.

"Please, Laurent, I'm so—so close, please let me come for you," Sabre panted, legs up and tight around his hips.

"Yes," was all Laurent managed, before Sabre cried out and came between them.

Laurent watched him, trembling and breathless himself, and he lost it when Sabre *smiled* up at him, stretched like a satisfied cat—all without being under, without Laurent hurting or choking or terrifying him—and said, "Come inside me, Laurent, let me feel you."

There were very few things that Laurent *hadn't* heard in bed, at this point, given how many years he'd spent as a whore. He'd had clients ask him to do that before, come inside them, but somehow it seemed like this was the first time he'd ever heard it, and maybe it was because none of them had ever used his name, before.

Just some pretty nickname, or *whore*, even if they meant it sweetly, that wasn't his name. Just him, just his body.

But Sabre stared at him and asked him, Laurent, and Laurent was helpless to do anything else; he kissed Sabre until he could barely breathe, and the last thought he had before he tipped over the edge was, *I want him to call me by my real name*, and puzzled at what that meant for only a second before the pleasure dragged him away from thought, away from anything that wasn't Sabre, beneath him, murmuring encouragements against his mouth.

He had no idea why he'd thought that, about his name. He'd given it when he'd woken up in the sun-dappled parlor of the House of Gold. But suddenly he had a memory—black curtains in the breeze, the sound of the sea, and singing—

He sat up, blinking, and pushed his hair out of his face. Sabre wasn't asleep, but he was watching him, quiet and calm. Under, but not much. Just...content, there, with him.

"The king wanted you," Laurent said, pushing aside his strange memory, which was probably some kind of dream—he'd always wanted to see the ocean, but whores from the pleasure district didn't travel much farther than the country estates of the wealthiest nobles.

"What," Sabre said, blinking. "That's not right. He hasn't before."

"He requested you attend him during a country house party. I assume it's the same one Chastain spoke to me about, earlier, when he informed me that he'd be switching all his visits to you."

"Oh. Are you angry?"

Laurent sighed, slipped gently out of Sabre's body and rolled to his back next to him, an arm behind his head. "Yes, but only because I know what's going to happen. He's starting to see you as a person, not a whore."

"And that makes you angry?" Sabre asked, and there was something like a hint of teasing there, under his concern.

Laurent turned and fixed him with a stare. "Men who are as important and wealthy as Chastain, they sometimes sponsor courtesans. They take them, put them up in luxury and keep them there until they tire of them. It doesn't add to their debt, since the expectation is that the nobles will incur the costs of it, so it's mostly...paused. But it's never a good thing, because when you come back as you always do, no one remembers you and your debt is always sold somewhere else. To a lesser house, then a lesser one, until there's only the whorehouses and the quarries left to take it."

"This system is terrible," Sabre said.

"This system saved you from the gallows," Laurent reminded him, though he did not disagree.

"Yes. I understand...loans. That you incur them, when you live in a house and eat their food and need to constantly launder the clothes that are torn off you—"

"That might just be you, pet," Laurent said, tugging his hair, amused despite himself. "A special incurrence."

"But if someone wants you, it shouldn't make it worse. And a courtesan can't...why would they not just let you pay it back some other way?"

"Because no one trusts anyone, Sabre. Not even a little."

Sabre smiled at him. "I trust *you*."

"Men tie ropes around your neck to remind you how you almost hanged, and it's my fault, and you still trust me?"

"You didn't choose to put me on the gallows, Laurent. You didn't make my mother choose—what she did. You gave me a choice when I didn't have one."

"This was no choice, Sabre," Laurent said, softly, while Sabre's hair fell like a curtain around them. "It was me seeing an opportunity, and taking it."

"And you want me to hate you for it, and I won't. That's *my* choice." Sabre was propped up on one hand. "You think Chastain is going to do that, take me away?" He did look a little worried about that. "He's never as angry as the others."

"Noticed that, did you? He doesn't care, or he's not going to care, about your mother for long, Sabre. He's more interested in you being an actual masochist, and how, because he's a noble, his pleasure outweighs anyone else's. I don't know anymore if the king was trying to punish you or save you, if I'm honest. But if he wants you to suffer, he won't let Chastain spirit you away to his estate where the others can't have their turn hurting you. Unless he knows how bored you'd be, with just Chastain and his hounds and all those pines."

"I wouldn't be happy there," Sabre said, and they both knew why.

Laurent shook his head, once, and pressed his fingers to Sabre's mouth to keep him from actually saying it out loud. "I think he'd need dispensation from the king, and he wouldn't, if the king asked for your company at this same country party."

"They didn't invite you?" Sabre tilted his head, sucked on Laurent's fingers.

"Just my wares," Laurent answered, pulling his fingers free.

"Don't you mean *whores*, my lord," Sabre quipped, and Laurent snorted and smacked him lightly on the side of the face.

"Why would the king—do you think he means to kill me," Sabre asked, after a moment.

"Honestly, I don't know, Sabre. Emile's always seemed a shade past sane, but again, I don't know anymore if that's true or what he wants everyone to think. But no, I think if he wanted to kill you, he would have let you hang."

"He could let them all hunt me," Sabre said, shuddering a little, and Laurent knew him well enough to see the flare of heat, the interest in the idea that he couldn't quite hide.

"Oh, they do that, obviously, but it's for...a different kind of sport."

"You can just say fucking, my lord." Sabre laughed softly as Laurent pulled his hair again. "I have no desire to serve the king, who it's said...since his wife, he doesn't...is it true *you*...?"

"Finish your sentences, brat, if you're going to ask me impertinent questions." Laurent sat up, swung his feet over the bed and stood up to get some water. "He didn't fuck me. He made me pleasure myself and he watched." Laurent would not forget that night anytime soon. All that work getting him prepared, the white carriage, the horses...and Emile de Guillory had done the equivalent of hiring him to grind on a pillow on the royal bed while he sat on a chair and watched him.

"I wouldn't mind that," Sabre said, from the bed, a tangle of warm limbs and soft hair and silk sheets.

"Yes, well, I've done that before, but usually with another courtesan or...some instructions, perhaps, other than the obvious. If you want the truth, I think de Mortain paid for that and thought it might help him but it...did not, or I can't imagine how staring blankly and staying silent while a courtesan humps a pillow is—are you *laughing?*"

"I might be a little, ah." Sabre clapped a hand over his mouth, eyes bright with mirth. "This evening, it's been quite a lot."

"That's the noble in you," said Laurent, returning with the water. He held up a hand. "One joke about that and you're going back to your room."

Sabre ducked his head, but he was smiling as he reached for the goblet. "Did they ask just for me, for the hunt, or...?"

"Others, too, and I'll allow that, it's happened before. It's sex, Sabre, not—" Laurent went still, as something flashed, deep and dark like a dream, at the back of his mind.

The—skulls of the dead gods—run, the smoke will clear, the hunt, the snow—

"My lord?"

Laurent shook his head, the images like cobwebs slipping through his fingers. "I'm fine. But you, I think it best you stay here this year. If you want, I shall chase you about the empty house. Besides, this time of year, you'd be obliged to go out in the snow."

—the smoke the old gods the hunt we run—

Sabre smiled a little sadly. "I think I'll go anyway," he said, and drew Laurent down for a kiss. "I want to tell you something, a secret. Because I do trust you, more than anyone. May I?"

Laurent sighed, and nodded. "I have a feeling it would be impossible to stop you. Is this about what Chastain said, about your mother hating your father?"

"Ah, no, it's...not that. It's about Adrien's mother. The queen."

Laurent would have preferred it be about people who were not dead, honestly, but he nodded his head and settled back to let Sabre talk. Because the queen might no longer be alive, but the ghost of her still haunted the kingdom, their mad king and their son, who no one really believed would live to inherit the throne of Staria.

* * *

Sabre tried to say the words twice, lying there on Laurent's bed, but they wouldn't come. He'd made vows to his father, to the king, and they burned his throat as he rolled off the bed, running a hand through his messy hair.

"My lord," he said. "Laurent. Can I attend you, in the bath?"

"Will it make it easier?" Laurent asked.

"I think so."

Laurent kissed him, then, which Sabre took as a yes, and Sabre eased himself into the now familiar routine of service, running the bath, fetching the oils for Laurent's hair, the comb and subtly scented soaps. He kissed Laurent as he washed his hair, his back, ducked under the warm water to run his hands over Laurent's thighs. He wasn't under, when he set aside the washcloth and climbed into Laurent's lap, but he was calmer, his nerves dulled at the edges as they lounged in the heat.

"I asked the queen if I would fall in love once, you know," Sabre said, at last. "When I was young. Adrien and I, we used to read these horrible books together, about pirate princes who were, oh, half siren or something. We had notions of sailing off to find some, I think."

"And the queen would know," Laurent said, almost smiling again. "Because of royal divinity, I suppose."

"We don't have that here. It's something else." Sabre sighed. "She cut her thumb with a knife, looked at me, and laughed herself hoarse. She said she wasn't sure, but she did see me in the snow. Which is, so far, about as useless as you can imagine, because I've seen snow plenty of times by now and it's never been particularly amusing."

Laurent frowned at him, his gaze darting over Sabre's face. "You've skipped something, I think. She *cut* herself?"

Sabre took a lock of Laurent's hair, twisting it in his fingers. "Do you know anything of the Mislians?"

"Oh, who knows," Laurent said. "They're either recluses on their little island or they're setting up shop in Diabolos, pretending to be mysterious under their robes."

"And they can sing magic," Sabre said. Laurent raised his brows.

"Some of them can. Some can see the future. Glimpses. Bits and pieces, in ink, or through cards."

"Or blood," Laurent said, slowly.

Sabre let out a harsh sigh. "The queen had their blood in her family. Ages back. Sometimes, her family will throw up someone with magic. Sometimes it's so diluted that they...can't make sense of what they see, and they're locked away. Her aunt was like that. Kept in a cellar for half her life. Adrien visited once, said he heard her, crying about..." He closed his eyes tight, just for a moment. "A baby, I think. Maybe hers. I don't know. But the queen could only see it in blood, or red wine, sometimes, so she was safe. People don't really bleed around queens, you know."

"And the prince," Laurent said, in a soft voice.

"When it rains," Sabre said. "When he bathes. In his water glass."

"Gods."

"He never sees himself, though," Sabre said. "He says he's seen me, a few times. But it's only flashes, you understand."

"He saw you with Isiodore," said Laurent.

"Yes. And he saw me fall off my horse. He saw me in the woods, with a sword, and there was...something terrible. He wouldn't say."

"They aren't always true, though," Laurent said. "The world would be a frightening place if people could tell the future with any accuracy."

Sabre laughed, but it came out ragged. "He was right about the queen, though," he said, and Laurent went still. "It was raining, you see, on the night she died."

Sabre shouldn't have been awake, at the time. He was in his family's suites in the palace, playing a makeshift game with his father and a bag of candied nuts, up well past his bedtime. His mother was with Elise in their manor down the hill, and Sabre's father had even let him try coffee, which tasted foul but was made tolerable if Sabre drained it through a mouthful of sugar.

When Adrien came to them, it sounded like the palace guard was trying to beat down the door.

"Stay put, Sabre," his father had said, and rose to take his sword off the mantle before he opened the door. Adrien fell through it as it opened, a gangly mess of sobbing thirteen-year-old, his hair damp with the rain. Which was strange, Sabre thought at the time, because he shouldn't have been outside.

"Arthur," he said. "Uncle Arthur, it's Mother. It's Mother, she—"

"Show me where she is," Sabre's father said. Adrien bobbed his head like it was broken, and reached desperately for Sabre's hand. When Sabre took it, Adrien's palm was clammy and his skin feverish, and Sabre swallowed a tight knot of fear in his throat.

"She's been strange all week," Adrien said, shaking, as he trotted down the hall, Sabre's father holding a naked blade at his side. "When she pricked her thumb, and she kept saying she had to do something. Had to *change* it. For, for Father."

"What did she see," Sabre's father said.

"I don't know," Adrien wailed. "But I saw her in the window, with the rain, and there was blood all down her hands, and I went to her room and she wasn't there, and Father's gone to the stables to check but she wasn't *in* the stables, I saw her in the rain and she was in the throne room—"

Sabre looked at his father, hand gripped tight in Adrien's. "Dad."

His father's face was drawn, strangely cold. "Sabre. You need to take Adrien to Isiodore de Mortain's suites, and wait there."

But it was too late, because Adrien whimpered and tugged on Sabre's hand, and Sabre heard it—the queen's light, musical voice, humming the lullaby she used to sing while she sewed, but higher, faster, almost frantic. Adrien released Sabre and broke into a run, and Sabre's father chased after him, grabbed him round the middle just as they reached the doors to the throne room—

Where the queen knelt, a knife at her side, her arms red with blood.

There was a circle at her knees, crossed with a symbol Sabre didn't recognize, and the queen looked up, raised a hand to her mouth, and streaked blood across her cheek.

"Lianne," Sabre's father said. His voice was low, and Sabre could see it in his eyes, a heartbreak he didn't recognize until he saw it in his own face when his father didn't return from his hunt a year later. "What have you done?"

"They said it would save him." The queen swayed, caught herself on the floor, and Sabre's father threw Adrien at Sabre and ran to her side. Sabre and Adrien went tumbling onto the marble, and Sabre locked his arms around Adrien, grappling him, holding him close.

"They said it would save him," the queen said again, as Sabre's father knelt beside her, tearing strips of her own dress to bind her arms. "But all it's done is show me, show me a *boy*. Not mine, not my Adrien. Just a boy, one of theirs, *worthless—*"

"Lianne, who said this? Who did you go to?"

"They swore," the queen said. She looked over Sabre's father's shoulder, her gaze drifting strangely, slowly, like a doll in a theater. "No. No, he shouldn't be here, he shouldn't see—"

"Sabre, remove the prince from this room immediately," his father snapped.

"No." Adrien fought like a cat as Sabre tried to drag him up, scratching at him, struggling to break free. "No, she'll die, Sabre, she'll die."

There was no holding him. Sabre hissed in pain as Adrien punched him feebly in the eye, and Adrien stammered out an apology as he stumbled across the floor towards his mother, who was slumped on Sabre's father's shoulder, whispering in his ear.

Then the doors slammed open, and the king appeared like a spirit of the storm, just in time to hold his wife as she died at the foot of his throne.

* * *

"Adrien wouldn't speak for weeks," Sabre said, pressing his lips to Laurent's shoulder. "My father swore us to secrecy, and I swore a vow to the king, but there was no need, with Adrien. Something broke in him, I think. He went into himself, after. And the king...ah, well. That was when the executions started."

Laurent was strangely still, his hands flat on Sabre's lower back under the water. "She was trying to change the future."

"That's what we think." Sabre sighed. "But all she saw was a boy. The Mislian who gave her the spell—Isiodore found him. Father disapproved of what they did. Said any confession he gave was worthless, under the knife. I didn't ask what he meant."

"No one spoke of a Mislian when they spoke of it to me," Laurent said, again in that strange, quiet voice.

"They wouldn't have. Father said he was looking for someone. To kill them. But he couldn't find them, so when the queen asked for a spell…"

"Was it the boy?"

"That's what Adrien believes." Sabre wrapped his arms around Laurent's neck. "He's tried looking for him himself, you know, in bowls of water. Nothing. It doesn't come on command, I guess, unless you have the spell for it. And Adrien never could sing. But the king thought the Mislian was after the queen, and him, and Adrien. He never learned what the queen saw that made her so desperate, and he's been jumping at shadows ever since."

"And you knew this," Laurent said. "You knew this all along, and your mother and sister—"

"Never even asked," Sabre said. "Not once." He ran his hands down Laurent's chest. "I do wonder about him. The boy she saw. I hope he survived just to spite them."

"Stranger things do happen, apparently." Laurent sounded a little like he was in shock, distant and hollow, and Sabre kissed his neck.

"Sorry. It's a horrible story. Most of them are, in that family. Our family. My mother killed my *father*, Laurent. We're all just circling disaster, and the only thing I can figure is I'll probably find snow to be enlightening five minutes before I'm ambushed by rabid deer in the woods."

"Remind me never to have you read my fortune," Laurent said, and Sabre smiled into his shoulder.

"You know," Sabre said. "I actually forgot. There was *one* thing the queen told me, when I asked her who I'd marry, but I figured she was probably just having a bit of fun at my expense."

"Let me guess," Laurent said. "They'd be wealthy beyond your wildest dreams."

Sabre sat up to kiss him properly, slow and lingering. "Oh, no," he said. "Not remotely. She said I'd marry the sun."

CHAPTER 12

Sabre had forgotten, over the years, how powerful a secret could become.

It didn't free him to speak of it. He didn't emerge from the baths with a lighter soul and a new perspective. Instead, it was as though he'd wrapped Laurent up in it and tied it round him like an old scarf. When he woke to find Laurent idly stroking his hair, Sabre didn't fumble or hesitate when he drew Laurent's hand to his mouth and kissed Laurent's palm. Something had shifted the night before, and he didn't think either of them knew how to change it back.

He still dreamt of the gallows, but when the House opened for the night and Sabre led noble patrons to his door, he thought of how Laurent felt under his hands, the soft light of his desk lamp as he hummed to himself, marking down the House earnings for the evening.

"Do you know who he was, before he became a courtesan?" Sabre asked Rose one morning, while Sabre took down laundry and Rose paced through rows of colorful sheets, staring at her journal. "Laurent."

"A nerd," Rose said, pushing aside a crimson pillowcase. "Is *effervescent* better than *ephemeral*?"

"Well, they don't mean the same thing, exactly."

"Yes, but the way they sound," Rose said. "Effervescent. Effervescent. Maybe not. Why are you worried about what Laurent was, anyways? People forget their childhoods all the time. I know *I* did. I could meet my mother in the street and I'd never know."

"That doesn't upset you?" Sabre asked, folding a sheet.

"Not really. She wasn't the one who sang to me when I was sick, or taught me how to read and write. It was all Laurent. Even if he *is* a nerd. Listen to this monologue and tell me what you think."

Sabre unpinned sheets and towels to the sound of a moon princess lamenting the loss of the bird-children to the Winds of Nothingness, her voice rising as Rose paced and gestured and spun on her heels.

Elise could have used a friend like Rose. She'd grown quieter, after their father's death, isolating herself from other noble ladies, slipping into her mother's shadow even as Sabre seemed to shy from it. He didn't think Isiodore was right about her, exactly. She hadn't been a lost cause—She'd just been lonely, and her mother was the one who was there for her when Sabre was off on jaunts with other noble heirs, or visiting Adrien and training with Isiodore. Perhaps she'd even been lied to, told that the king arranged her father's death, a lie Sabre would never believe. Still, lingering on the possibilities did nothing but drag Sabre down into a pit, and he forced himself to watch Rose instead, tracking her movement through the clotheslines.

"Does it get lonely at all?" Sabre asked. "With Laurent working all the time."

Rose snorted. "He's never out of my hair. Also, I know what you're trying to do."

Sabre froze, holding up a damp gown to the clothesline.

"You're trying to get me to say he's nice," Rose said, marking something in her journal, "because you want an excuse to mope around and stare at him like he hung the stars. Don't lie," she added, when Sabre opened his mouth. "I've *seen* you two."

"There's no reason for *him* to stare, though," Sabre said.

Rose gave him a long-suffering look. "Nanette's right. Men are hopeless. I'm going to ask Simone about the monologue, instead."

No one, it seemed, was immune to the Rose Charm Offensive, because even Margritte was signed up to take a role in the revised, slightly shortened *Princess of the Moon* play, which was slowly starting to take over the common room. Even a few clients were starting to comment on the enormous black curtains covering her haphazard set, and a number of them already invited themselves to see what, exactly, Yves in a north wind costume would look like.

"She's going to be heartbroken when she realizes she's a dominant," Laurent said, painting his face on the morning of the play. He was dressed in what Rose insisted were supposed to be rags, to show off how destitute and tragic he was as a shipwrecked prince, but even ripped, gray window curtains managed to look scandalous on Laurent.

"It won't stop her from having ten children, though," Sabre said, braiding colored glass in Laurent's hair. "Did you feel it earlier, when she came in with the costumes? Her natural dominance is coming through. She's going to be a terror."

"*Going* to be?" Laurent asked, and smiled at Sabre through the mirror. "Prepare for tears, in any case. She had her heart set on being a submissive."

Sabre grimaced. It was different for everyone, really. Some thought it was a compulsion, a magic that ran through the water or the earth itself—others thought it was just biology, an imperative that passed on through the blood, like yellow hair or brown eyes. Some people, like Sabre, had an inkling of whether they'd skew towards dominance or submission early on, but it hit most like a shipwreck on the shores of puberty, making an utter mess of an otherwise awkward stage in any young person's life. Rose, it seemed, was heading directly into the shipwreck phase.

"Well, she and I could have a talk about ruined expectations, then," Sabre said. "I was supposed to be a dominant, as the eldest. So was Adrien—He tried to hide it for a while, but any time someone praises him, he looks like a puppy in a window. Isiodore thanked him, once, and I thought he might die."

"When I was in training in the House of Gold," Laurent said, "I was asked to prepare tea for the courtesans, and I told them to prepare it themselves. You can imagine that went over well."

Sabre trailed his fingers down the beads in Laurent's hair. "That can't have been pleasant, though, hiding who you were."

"I made it worth it, in the end," Laurent said, but there was a hardness to his mouth, and Sabre tried to imagine what that would have been like, holding so much of himself back for so long. He'd heard of the practice, of course, of submissive firstborns trying to hide their inclination to serve, but his father had forbidden it, as it never lasted very long before resulting in a scandal. His father was a submissive, anyways, and he'd inherited just fine.

"I don't think I can picture you as a submissive," Sabre said.

"Oh? And how *do* you picture me?" Laurent asked.

"In that costume? I don't think my imagination needs the help," Sabre said, and Laurent's smile took on a wicked air.

Which was why, when they inevitably arrived just a minute shy of late, Sabre's shirt was undone, his hair was a mess, and Laurent's pale face was slightly flushed, as though they'd run down the stairs and Sabre had tripped out of half of his clothes.

"*Why,*" Rose said, as Sabre buttoned up his shirt. "Okay. Okay, no. It doesn't matter. Sabre, you're—"

"In charge of the curtain," Sabre said. Even Charon had earned a speaking role, but Sabre's inability to act was so horrifying that his job consisted of pulling a rope three times an hour.

"Good. No distractions," Rose said. "This is *serious.*"

"As the grave," Laurent said. Rose narrowed her eyes.

Sabre took a seat by the rope pulley and watched, with mild amusement, as the small audience sprawled on the common room couches politely applauded. There weren't many nobles in attendance, save for Lady Cornelia and the younger daughter of Lady Fournier, who had a pale green wig and a pleated bonnet that made her face look perfectly round. She applauded loudly as Rose stepped in front of the curtain, and kept leaning over as though trying to see who was waiting on the other side.

Rose stared at the common room like a rabbit frozen before the hawk, hands clenched around her journal.

"Th-thank you for coming," she said, after a long, painful silence. "To the play."

Sabre applauded, and Rose turned to push jerkily through the curtain. Simone, dressed in a lovely silver gown with fairy wings, kissed her on the cheek, and Rose covered her face with both hands.

"They'll be eating out of your palm soon enough, Rosie," Laurent whispered, and Rose groaned slightly.

Simone was the first on stage, depicting the mourning moon queen with the kind of grace and talent that probably didn't belong on a stage made out of window hangings, and when she died tragically off stage left, Lady Fournier the younger burst into tears.

"She's so beautiful," she sobbed, as Simone lay artfully in a field of paper flowers.

Charon stepped into the middle of the stage. His face was painted with harsh white lines down his cheeks, and he was wearing a fur stole over one shoulder.

"I am the storm," he said, which wasn't, in fact, his line. "My lover is the wind, which I also am."

Yves leapt onto the stage to a smattering of applause. "Oh, storm king," he cried, flinging himself onto Charon's bare chest. "I have thrown the moon princess from her bower, and the queen has died of a broken heart!"

Charon blinked down at him, then looked at Rose, hovering behind a painted castle. "Am I to punish him, then."

A number of the audience members sat up in their seats, but Simone, half rising from her death pose, flapped a hand for silence.

"Off stage!" Yves said, a little desperately. "Punish me off stage, oh storm king."

Charon, who seemed to have remembered at last what a play was supposed to be, shrugged and carried Yves off to general applause.

When Laurent appeared, flopping himself down onto the stage with a dramatic sigh, Gwydion whistled, and Rose dropped from Percival's arms in her puffy white moon gown.

"What's this?" she said, in a wooden voice, gesturing broadly to Laurent. "An orphan prince, cast off and unwanted, pale and hideous as curdled milk. What tragedy to have befallen someone so graceless and inconsequential!"

"Oh!" Laurent cried, kicking his leg up. Rose slapped it down. "Woe! Woe, that I should languish in misery, alone and ugly."

"That's fine," Rose said, resting a hand on his head. "I'll take you in, because that's what princesses do, even if you're so terribly afflicted."

Sabre held back a laugh as Laurent swooned in gratitude.

The play ended at the first act, when Yves was turned into a flock of birds by the storm king and sent to carry Laurent away, with Rose and Pirate Queen Nanette swearing revenge. The audience applauded, with Lady Cordelia standing with a delighted grin as Nanette bowed, and more than one person whistling at Laurent in his rags. When the courtesans turned to applaud for Rose, Rose stared at them, took a single, gasping breath, and sobbed on Laurent's chest.

"They actually applauded for it," Rose cried later, sitting in the kitchen with a basket of pastries and flowers while most of the House ran in and out, changing out of their costumes. "Someone even, even laughed, during the scene where the pirate queen made a joke."

"You did great, Rosie," Laurent said, softly, feeding her another pastry.

"Lady Fournier cried when the queen died, you know," Sabre said.

Rose turned to Sabre. "You're so nice, Sabre, and I didn't even give you a *role*."

"Oh," Sabre said, as she flung herself into his arms. He held her gingerly, patting her shoulder. "I didn't mind."

"You officially have my permission," Rose whispered, half sobbing into his shirt, "to marry Laurie. If you *have* to."

Sabre glanced quickly at Laurent, whose face hadn't changed—Perhaps he hadn't heard. "Ah. Thank you, Rose. That's very…magnanimous of you."

"Yes," she said, wetly. "I know."

* * *

DEVON CHASTAIN WOULD PROBABLY HAVE BEEN HORRIFIED if he knew his father was there two hours ago, with Sabre riding him while Oscar pulled his hair and smacked him, over and over, until Sabre cried and came all over them both.

Devon was not fucking Sabre at the moment. He had Sabre with his hands bound behind him, which Laurent knew Sabre hated, kneeling with a short lead clipped to his collar. Devon was standing behind him, caning Sabre, whose cock was standing hard between his legs as he bit back a moan with each smack.

"You really…you really just *take* it. What kind of, of *whore*," Devon snarled, hitting Sabre harder. Sabre seemed to be enjoying himself. Laurent, who stopped pretending to have a vested interest in watching Sabre's appointments with clients since everyone in the house knew which way the very obvious wind was blowing, still felt himself on edge as he watched. He knew Sabre did like this, that whatever strange biology made submissives want to kneel made masochists want to hurt, but he didn't *like* Devon Chastain.

He didn't like Oscar Chastain, either, but for an entirely different reason. Oscar was getting the lovesick look of a client who was taking his transactional relationship too far. Devon looked like if Emile wanted him to execute Sabre by hand, he'd revel in it. There was something so personal about Devon's snarling, vicious sadism. Most of Sabre's clients now did genuinely enjoy hurting him, but not because of his family, not anymore. They liked how the humiliation made him gasp, grind against their boot, how the pain made him pant for it and beg to be fucked.

True masochists were rare, but Devon didn't seem to care or appreciate that—if anything, what made Laurent the most nervous about him was that he seemed to be *angry* at Sabre for enjoying his attentions, because clearly he wanted to hurt Sabre and have Sabre *hate* it, not like it.

"You're so fucked up," Devon said, and he was aiming his strikes too high, on Sabre's back. The look on Sabre's face was close to blissful. "How can you like this, you—you're nothing, you're not even, they should add money to your debt, you're not supposed to *like* being punished."

"Yes, my lord," Sabre said, swaying on his knees. He was staring, Laurent knew, at the place behind the wall where Laurent was watching. He liked showing off for him, Laurent knew.

"I don't know why you act like you like this," Devon was saying, throwing the cane down in disgust and going for his belt. "It's just to make me look foolish, isn't it?"

"No, my lord," Sabre said, blinking. "It's not an act."

Laurent startled as Devon moved quickly, wrapping the belt around Sabre's neck above the collar and starting to pull. "Think your former whore of a boss could save you before I choked you to death, like you should have on the gallows? Fuck, why didn't you just die like your fucking sister? I bet you would have gotten off, wouldn't you."

Sabre didn't struggle, and his erection didn't flag. There was an easy way into the room, and he knew it; Laurent wouldn't let this angry noble choke Sabre to death, and Sabre liked the edge of fear, he wasn't even trying not to choke and was, in fact, leaning forward a bit as if he wanted to feel more of the bite of leather against his neck.

"You think you're better than me, don't you?"

Sabre didn't say anything, he couldn't, he was still choking.

"You do. You and the prince both, so eager to fucking take it, be treated like the whores you are, and my father *fucking fawns* over my *brother* and he's no dominant, he's—like you, you know, a *submissive.*" Devon said the word like it was a curse. "And the heir. As if I'm nothing. That's what you think I am, don't you? That I'm nothing."

He stopped choking Sabre and went back to hitting him with the belt. It had Sabre moaning, rocking forward on his knees, inelegant and showing his throat—not to Devon, that lout, but to *Laurent,* watching behind the plaster.

"My brother, you, the *prince,* your *boyfriend,*" Devon sneered, sounding like a schoolchild. "All of you. Fuck you for being—useless. Tell me you're useless."

Sabre looked mostly annoyed by the fact Devon had stopped whipping him to talk, but he was amenable enough to the demand, saying, "I'm useless, my lord," and Laurent couldn't help but bite back a smile at how he was pretty sure Sabre was rolling his eyes.

Maybe he'd help, after this. Devon would pin Sabre down, come on his face, leave Sabre unsatisfied. Laurent was good with a belt. He'd string Sabre up, maybe tease his cock with a feather, belt him until he was begging and—

He pushed that aside as Devon reached down to undo Sabre's bindings around his wrists. He picked up the cane, and seemingly heedless of Sabre's free hands, started to hit him again. "You are. You're useless, just like your sister and your mother, nothing left to even *bury*, and your—your father, he was just as useless as you. Like father, like son, your father couldn't even ride a *horse*, properly, weak, cowardly creature that he was—"

Sabre, who would simply kneel and let the nobles lash him with their whips and their words, apparently had found his limit. He caught the cane with his hand and got to his feet, turning to stare Devon Chastain right in his wild, bright eyes. "I am the son of a traitor, and I've never denied it. I'm a whore who craves the lash and I won't deny that, either. But my father was not weak, and he was certainly no coward."

Devon stared at Sabre, hands fisted at this sides. "You *dare*, whore—"

"Yes," Sabre interrupted. "I do. There are rules. Even here."

"You're not—you think I care? You should swing, and you *will*," Devon hissed, hauling off and smacking Sabre across the face. "I was so. Furious, when I saw them take you down. You deserved to hang and you *will*, you fucking whore, when your boyfriend's not around to protect you. And you can stop me with the cane, as if I fucking care, but you can't do anything about *him*. You think you're not in prison, here, because you're a sick fuck who likes being hurt? See how much you like it after the hunt, whore. When you hear the prize I caught. I'll be in the front row this time to watch you die, and I'll make it last and *no one* will stop it this time."

With that, Devon pushed Sabre, hard, and stormed toward the

door. He wrenched it open and thundered down the hall. He'd leave by the back, Laurent was sure of it.

He pushed the alcove door open and said, to Sabre, "Well, I suppose that noble bearing of yours was going to show up, sometime. Would you like me to put him on the gray list, then?"

"Am I allowed it," Sabre asked, staring at the door where Devon had disappeared.

"I am the lord of this house and a noble, so, yes."

"He said he was going to hurt Adrien, and that I'd hang."

"He was mad that he didn't get to come all over your face," Laurent said, studying him.

Sabre glanced at him. He looked, for the first time, a little regretful. "Oh. I'm sorry, maybe I shouldn't have...but my father was no coward."

"And you're not worthless, or sick," Laurent said, heading over to close the door to the hallway. "The things people say, here, to you. They don't matter."

"This mattered," Sabre said. He exhaled, slowly, and met Laurent's gaze. "You told me to keep something for myself. That's what I'm keeping. My father."

Laurent sighed. "What Devon said about your father, it doesn't make it true just because he said it."

"I'll take his abuse, even if he's not really that good at it. But that was too much. And I...my lord." Sabre went to his knees, stared up at Laurent with wide, bright, pleading eyes. "May I go to the hunt? Devon threatened him, you heard him—"

"Hush, pet," Laurent murmured, and laid a hand on his head. "I'll have someone keep an eye on Adrien—I'll go, how's that, I can get a favor from the lord at the House of Gold. You can stay here, help Rose with the second act of her play. But you needn't be anywhere near any of these people, all right?"

"No one can protect Adrien but me," Sabre whispered. He bowed, pressed his forehead to the floor in the most submissive pose Laurent had ever seen from him. "Please, my lord. Please let me go. I've lost everything else."

Laurent sighed. "You're taking lessons from my sister on dramatics, I see. And you're certainly better at it when you're not acting." He went down on his haunches, laid a hand on Sabre's bowed head. "I know what you've lost, Sabre. And I won't let you lose Adrien, too. I know he's been a true friend to you, and you need to trust me that I'm better equipped to deal with this, all right? I'll bring Charon. Yves was invited, there will be three of us—"

"Please, my lord," Sabre begged, to the floor. He was trembling. "I don't think anyone can save him but me. And I think he knows it. Devon, I mean. He said that, about hanging, so I wouldn't go."

Laurent sighed and stroked his hair, quiet for a moment. "I won't put you around Emile if I can help it, Sabre. You really are just going to have to trust me, okay?"

Sabre lifted his head. His eyes were calm, clear. "I trust you more than anyone, Laurent."

"Good boy," Laurent said, ruffling his hair, even though it wasn't really an answer. "Now, come with me and let me show you how a dominant uses a belt on a willing painslut who needs it."

"Yes, my lord," said Sabre, who followed him on all fours, crawling with as much grace as Yves, who must have taught him how...and if Laurent were thinking a little more clearly, he might have noticed that, and had the faintest suspicion about what was to come.

CHAPTER 13

The House of Onyx lay quiet on the morning of Lord Chastain's yearly hunt. The carriage bearing Lord de Rue, Charon, and Yves to the Chastain estate was already winding its way through the city, and the courtesans who remained closed their curtains against the midmorning light. Sheets swayed in a soft wind outside, and the only sound came from the slight creaking of the office door, its lock bent, the table scattered with the colorful contents of Lord de Rue's correspondence drawer.

In the heart of the city, Sabre crossed the square where the gallows once stood. His father's signet ring shone on his forefinger, and Lord Chastain's favor hung heavy in his pocket, thumping against his thigh with every step. His long hair was unbound, with none of the ribbons young nobles tended to favor, and if his mother were to see him as he climbed the steps of the palace, she would have chided him for being underdressed in just a white shirt and simple trousers.

She would have said worse, he thought, if she knew what he was there for.

Sabre stopped to bow when a guard approached him at the doors, which he never would have done a year ago.

"Sabre of the House of Onyx," he said, and the guard rocked back

199

on her heels, glancing at the door. "Here to keep my appointment with his majesty the king."

He handed the guard the invitation to Lord Chastain's hunt that he'd stolen from Laurent's desk, and she went ashen.

"Oh. Are you sure?"

"Yes," Sabre said. "Unfortunately."

The guard sighed heavily. "Right. Sure. It's been that kind of morning." She gestured for Sabre to follow, and turned off down a side hall, which Sabre hadn't used before. He'd always known that servant passages were everywhere in the palace, but it was another thing entirely to see them himself, the gleaming veneer of the palace stripped away to reveal cheap paint and faded rugs. They passed servants in the palace livery, who barely gave Sabre a second glance as he was led in a wide spiral to the attendance hall, where the guard pushed Sabre gently against a pillar and pointed at the ground.

"Stay," she said, as one would to an errant pet.

"Would it be easier if I sat down?" he asked.

"No, it'd be easier if you went *home*. Or to the pleasure district. Wherever you live." She paused. "*Do* you live there, in the houses? I've never seen inside one of them before."

"Yes, we do," Sabre said.

"Rent free?" she asked, and sighed when Sabre shrugged a shoulder. "Ah. Of course. Forget I asked, then."

She knocked politely on the high doors to one of the audience chambers, straightened her shoulders, and disappeared through the door.

Sabre waited, leaning against the pillar, while a patch of sunlight slowly crept along the floor at his feet. With nothing to distract him from the weight of what he was doing, his heart was starting to race, and he kept twisting his father's ring on his hand, struggling just to breathe without gasping. When the door opened again, he jumped to attention, and the guard didn't even have to give the order to send him forward, moving as though drawn on a line through the hall and into the audience chamber.

The chamber, like the throne room itself, was built like a sun, with a rounded ceiling and thin gold plates fastened to the windows, which made the light that spilled over the marble floor look like sunlight through a honeycomb. The king stood facing the window, a hand on a dark wooden desk, already dressed for a hunt.

Sabre forced himself to ignore the treacherous rolling in his stomach and dropped to his knees.

"I heard you had a fondness for pain," King Emile said, his back still turned, "but even I would call this excessive."

"You requested my presence, Your Majesty," Sabre said. He couldn't hide the way his voice shook.

"That doesn't mean I particularly *need* it," said Emile. He turned, adjusting a golden pin on his cuff, and Sabre looked down. It was unsettling, seeing his own features on the king's face, now. "You seem to be thriving in your new status. Half of my court has seen fit to visit you, if gossip is to be believed. Would that be correct, by your estimate?"

Sabre looked down at his hands on his thighs. "No, Your Majesty. Not half, yet."

"Then they're over-ambitious. What a shock. I may never recover." He stopped before Sabre, and Sabre shivered as he lay a hand on his shoulder. "Are you still bent on proving your family's innocence? How has that gone for you, I wonder?"

Sabre couldn't seem to gather enough breath. "I. Can't prove what isn't there, Your Majesty."

"Ah, I thought Isiodore would tell you. Your mother—" He clicked his tongue. "I'm sure my inventive and *loyal* courtiers have told you much of what you missed that day, when you were safe under my boot, but they didn't tell you what she looked like when I called you down, did they? Your mother, I mean."

Sabre closed his eyes. "No, Your Majesty."

"Oh, she was furious. I suppose she wanted you all to die together." The king touched Sabre's hair, so like his father's, like the king's. "A last revenge, perhaps, letting me watch Arthur de Valois' legacy die twice."

"You were there?" Sabre refused to look up. "When my father died?"

"Lord Chastain always invites me to those ridiculous hunts of his," Emile said. "Your father was an exemplary rider. More beast than man on horseback, Isiodore used to say. How strange, then, that he would fall while chasing a fox."

Sabre turned his gaze to the honeycomb pattern on the floor, the way the light seemed to sparkle on the marble.

"And why would you accept my invitation to Lord Chastain's hunt, when your Lord de Rue already sent his deepest regrets on your behalf?"

Sabre was trembling at the king's touch. He knew it, knew Emile could feel it, and wondered if some small part of the king regretted it, turning his young cousin into a man who would swallow terror in his shadow.

"I made a vow, Your Majesty," Sabre said. Emile said nothing. Vows were worthless, he supposed, to a man whose cousin's wife plotted his murder. "I have something of yours."

"If we're being metaphorical," Emile said, and his fingers traveled down Sabre's shoulder to the collar at his neck. "You do."

Sabre took a shivering breath, and dug in his pocket for the ring. "Lord Chastain gave this to me. The son of a traitor."

Emile picked up the ring and held it to the light. "Foolish, possibly, to give a favor to a man who has so clearly lost mine."

"Or cunning," Sabre said, and looked away as the king glanced at him, his gaze cutting. "I'm sorry, Your Majesty, I should not have spoken out of turn."

"Probably not," Emile said. "But then, your father was the same. Eventually, the blood will out. Let's see which sort runs in your veins, mm?" He tipped Sabre's chin up, and Sabre looked into eyes gone glassy and vague. "Well? We're due to leave in an hour. I can't have you underfoot in the meantime, so come with me and I'll, oh, chain you to the carriage until we're ready. You'll feel right at home, I'm sure."

"Y-yes, Your Majesty," Sabre said, bowing slightly over his knees. "As you wish."

* * *

THE LAST TIME he'd been to one of these fêtes, Laurent had been one of the hunted. And he'd thought the whole thing a bit of a bore, if he were honest, but maybe that was because he wasn't really one to enjoy being treated as prey instead of predator.

But no, as it turned out, it wasn't all that fun to go as a guest, either. At least when he came there dressed as a fox to be hunted, he was paid for his time. This was Charon's first time at the hunt, and he looked mildly interested at seeing the snow-covered pines on the way to Lord Chastain's country estate. Yves, who'd been invited every year, was clearly thrilled to be there. As he'd told Laurent, he simply got caught quickly and spent as little time in the snow outside as possible. Charon would, he imagined, be hunting the few nobles who wanted to be caught and ravished in front of the fire.

Laurent had no idea what he was going to do, other than shadow the prince and make sure nothing happened to him. How he, a noble who'd sworn off having anything to do with politics, ended up in this situation was anyone's guess. Except it would only take one guess, wouldn't it? The reason was back in the pleasure district, probably doing laundry and being run ragged by Dot and Laurent's sister.

"Do they do this in Arktos?" Yves asked, batting his lashes up at Charon, whom he was sitting next to in the carriage—and by sitting, it was more *pressed up against*, as if he were freezing and needed Charon's warmth. And maybe he did, given his fox costume involved some clever usage of fur and very little else. His eyelashes were glittered. He looked ridiculous but adorable, which was absolutely intentional, and he *did* have a warm cloak, fur-lined, that he could have worn over his skimpy outfit but was, mysteriously, packed away in his traveling trunk.

"Chase each other for sex? Not quite so literally," Charon said. If having a half-naked, glittery-lashed Yves using him as a human furnace bothered him, Laurent couldn't tell. "And the desert, of course, there is no snow there."

"Just those little dragons," Yves said, smiling. "I would like to see those, someday. I still think you're making them up."

"I am not, and they are a nuisance, seeking heat always." Charon glanced down at him, pointedly. "Hmm."

"Don't you dare, I'm not a nuisance," Yves laughed. "I'm surprised Sabre isn't here, but I guess it's for the best. Some of those nobles might actually try to kill him. That Devon Chastain is crazy."

"Don't say anything like that once we're there," Laurent admonished, leaning back against the velvet-padded seat of the carriage. It was rented, because he'd declined the offer to have one from Lord Chastain's estate sent to fetch them. Not after that story about Sabre's father and his hunting accident—he was going to double-check anything that had to do with horses while he was there.

"My lord, please. What kind of whore do you take me for, huh, I know not to complain about the clients. I'm insulted you'd even say that. But I'm also not wrong, about Devon."

"He could use someone to whip him, I think," Charon said.

"He's a dominant," Laurent pointed out.

Charon shrugged. "Doesn't mean he couldn't use it."

"That's probably true of all nobles," said Yves, then added quickly, "present company excluded, of course."

Laurent had been whipped before, but in the House of Gold, it was usually with the softest leather floggers, the ones with the widest strips. Or made of silk, which hurt more than people thought if they were in the hands of someone who knew how to use them. Laurent did, and he let himself think about using one on Sabre for a moment before putting it out of his mind.

"Did you know, in Lukos, they find their life mate and live in the snow for months," Charon said, peering out of the window. "It snows so much they can't leave their homes."

"That sounds dreadful. Or amazing. Depends on the lifemate, or whatever." Yves was almost bouncing in his seat. "Do you want to go there someday, Lukos? People do, or they try. I had a client tell me that, I think."

"I would like to see a land like Arktos, but full of snow. And the wolf-people. Someday, perhaps."

"I'll go with you," Yves said, beaming up at him. "If you promise to keep me warm."

Laurent rolled his eyes, but he wondered if he should keep an eye on this. Yves was flirtatious as a rule, it was why he was so good at his particular skill as a courtesan, but sometimes the way he looked at Charon seemed more...honest, than his other flirtations. Or maybe Laurent was just projecting, since he'd done the most ridiculous thing he could have ever imagined by falling in love with a courtesan of his own *house*.

Because of course he loved Sabre. He wouldn't be here, heading into the snow—which he didn't like—to look after the *crown prince of Staria,* if he didn't. And everyone knew it, of course. Their house was small, and while Laurent had done that on purpose, wanting to establish right away a sense of camaraderie rather than competition, it meant things didn't go unnoticed. Everyone knew Nanette spent her nights in Simone's bed, that Yves wanted to climb Charon like a tree and then kneel and make his weird tea for him, and if anyone claimed Sabre *slept* in his bed in his room, they'd be lying through their teeth.

"Both of you, stay away from Devon Chastain as much as you can," Laurent said, as they turned onto the long drive up to the estate. "And if you hear anything about the prince—"

"We'll tell you, we know," Yves said, smiling. "It's sweet you're doing this for Sabre."

"And don't talk about *him,* if anyone asks, play coy—"

"Oh, no, however will I manage that?" Yves gasped, and put a hand on his chest.

Laurent smiled despite his rising tension. "Bat those glittery lashes at someone else, you brat."

"I intend to," Yves said. "Just have to do my usual, find the noble who is complaining about the weather the loudest and cozy up to him. What about you, Charon? I bet you'd be good at hunting, and you'll have some poor noble version of me who wants to get caught."

"It is all right, I will catch them quickly, do what they wish."

Charon did sound a little wistful, though, when he added, "but it would be nice if they gave me some sport, first. "

"I think you'd need a different kind of noble for that," Laurent said, dryly, as the carriage came to a halt in the drive. A few moments later there was a sharp knock on the door followed by a footman there to greet them and take their trunks.

Yves, already primed and ready to be adored, allowed the befuddled young man to help him out of the carriage with a beaming smile and a flutter of lashes, a swish of his tail. "Yes, please *do* show me to the fire before I freeze my cute tail off."

"Um," the footman squeaked. He looked to be all of seventeen or so, and was entranced by Yves immediately. "I, yes, I—Mr. Ah, that is to say—"

"You're adorable, sweetie, I'm a whore. You can call me Yves or whatever else you want. I'm technically part of the help, you know," he said, linking his arm with the footman's. "Charon can get the trunks, it's fine. Show me to the warmth, good man, what's your name, again?"

"I didn't, ah, say it," the footman said, as Yves dragged him toward the front of the estate.

"Is he sure he is a submissive," Charon said, sighing.

"He's going to get a reminder if he doesn't behave," Laurent said, and then laughed despite himself. "Which he'll like, so. I can help you with the trunk."

"It is fine, I have it." Charon glanced over. "The prince must be here, yes? That would be his carriage, I imagine."

Laurent glanced over at the carriage near the front of the line, emblazoned with the starburst insignia, and shook his head. "No. That's not the crown prince's carriage, that's the king's. Do me a favor, and if he wants you to hunt him, don't. Damn and blast, I wish I could have told Yves that His Majesty was here. I live in perpetual fear he'll try his bratty act on Emile and we'll all be sent to haul marble until we die."

"It would weigh less than this trunk," Charon said, dryly. "My lord. I will make sure Yves turns his charms elsewhere."

"You have a lot to handle, I'm sorry, I should have brought Simone, too."

"She would not have liked this," Charon said, but didn't elaborate as to why.

Laurent saw Yves already hanging off someone else's arm—a noble's, this time, at least—in front of the fire, chatting easily, while the footman hurried up to help Charon with a dazed expression.

"I'm so sorry, my lord," the footman squeaked, at Charon.

"That's me, technically, but it's all right. Hurricane Yves does this to everyone. Just let us know where our rooms are, please." Laurent made a note to leave a few extra coins for the footman, who was now half in love with Yves, probably. Last year, he'd apparently snuck off with a chambermaid after the noble who caught him in the hunt had fallen into a pleasant sleep in front of a warm fire.

Laurent changed into proper noble's hunting attire that he had to admit looked dashing; it took some work to get his hair in the proper queue with the black ribbon, which he normally didn't wear, since he liked to flaunt the traditional style of dress when he could. But he wasn't here to make waves, he'd leave that to Yves. And Charon, who got more than a few eager looks as they made their way to their rooms. Laurent had one close enough to the courtesans that he assumed it was supposed to be a slight, but was glad of it. He didn't intend to "catch" any of the courtesans, his own or any of the others brought for the event from the other houses.

It was odd to be there, attired as a noble, and he very nearly went down the back stairs instead of the grand staircase without thinking. The estate itself was very much like its lord; elegant, cold, and not inviting in the least. The decor was traditional to the point of boring, and while everything was clean and shining, the portraits showed a generations' worth of men and women with expressions of either haughty disdain or dourness, not a single variation between those two things.

Laurent had no idea who his ancestors were, but if they were nobles, he hoped they weren't *these* kind of nobles, though he was starting to think maybe there *weren't* any other kind. At least in Staria, and whatever else he was, he was definitely not from Staria. Laurent found his way to the large group gathered in front of the fireplace, and paused next to a window that overlooked the sweeping expanse of the back gardens. They were manicured, but bare in the winter, and the snow was beginning to fall harder, faster, as the light waned. The hunt would need to start soon, while there was still some light left.

The snow made him feel uneasy. Laurent put a hand on the window, and felt the cold glass even through the leather of his gloves.

Hunt run run the smoke go faster we have to go faster the dragon I can't see

The image was there and gone, leaving only the impression that even if he wasn't here to be hunted, this year, somehow...he still felt like a prey. It wasn't a sensation he enjoyed.

"One has to wonder if this farce is enacted because there are no foxes left to hunt," a voice said, from behind him.

Laurent turned and tried not to stare. The man behind him was tall, pale as the snow outside with eyes almost as colorless as his snow-white hair. He was immaculately dressed, down to a sleek cane with a silver top, and looked as if he'd been formed by the snow itself.

Chills raced down Laurent's spine as he remembered his manners and bowed to the only other duke of Staria. "Your Grace. I would imagine the foxes have gone to ground, given the weather, but I doubt it would matter for an event such as this. What a surprise to see you here."

Sebastian d'Hiver did not often leave his manor house, far up on the northern coast near the cold winter sea. His family estate used to be the summer home for the court, since it was cooler there, but that practice had long since fallen by the wayside.

"I received an invitation for a winter hunt, but I suspect the prey shall not be to my liking. You are a noble now, they tell me. Lord— something they've made up, I imagine."

D'Hiver was an odd man with a cold voice who they said went mad as a child and murdered his family in their ballroom. Nanette's client, Lady Cornelia, had sworn her lady's maid knew a girl from near d'Hiver's estate that used to take the laundry to and from the manor, and the girl swore the staff told her all sorts of tales about how d'Hiver never ate, or slept, or did much but wander about talking to something only he could see and going through a set of double-doors with no handle that only opened for the duke.

Nonsense, probably, but d'Hiver never came to court and yet there was no particular ill will that Laurent had heard of between him and the king—if anything, Emile seemed to forget he existed. Maybe that was on purpose, and d'Hiver was just clever enough to play off his odd looks and strange demeanor.

Maybe Laurent should try that. They did look a bit alike, he'd had someone ask him once if he was from some offshoot of the d'Hiver family. He could pretend to be related to a mad duke if it meant the royal eye landed elsewhere. Something to consider.

"It probably is made up," he said, now. "Laurent de Rue—clever, isn't it, to name a former whore *lord of the streets*? It should have been, oh, *de lit*, since I spent more time in a bed than anything."

If he thought that would shock d'Hiver, it didn't. The duke's gaze slid past him to the snow. "There is something to be said for earning your title, Lord de Rue. And you are hardly the first noble to earn your title on your back."

Laurent was startled into a laugh. He'd heard d'Hiver was as cold as his name implied, being the duke of winter, but he was strange and striking, and that wasn't a lie. "Well, good to know I'm in such austere company, then."

D'Hiver stepped forward, toward him, though Laurent told his immediate panicked reaction it was just to look out the window. "I have never met a Mislian before," he said, to the snow. "But I know one who has. You would do best to avoid me, Lord de Rue, lest that one think you intend something you do not."

"I'm—" Laurent bit that back and bowed, mystified. "As you wish, Your Grace. Happy hunting."

D'Hiver smiled out at the snow. "There isn't much here that we find worth hunting."

Right, definitely time to go. Laurent made his excuses, which did not get him anything other than a brief nod, and headed into the room where everyone was gathered.

And then he forgot about d'Hiver, their strange interaction, and the fact he'd called him *Mislian*—because Emile de Guillory, the king of Staria, turned and walked immediately toward him. He was holding the lead of a leash, and on the other end of the leash, was Sabre.

"Ah, Lord de Rue," the king said, his cold eyes fixed on Laurent like a wolf spotting a sheep. "It would seem you misplaced something." He held the leash out.

Laurent took it, smiled politely and bowed. He wasn't sure what to say, but now wasn't the time. "Thank you, Your Majesty."

"Perhaps don't thank me just yet," Emile said, oblivious of the stares and the whispers that started up the second he walked in with Sabre de Valois on a leash. "Keep a better eye on your pets, de Rue, else they'll have to be given to someone else."

With that, Emile turned on his heel and walked out, leaving Laurent standing and holding Sabre's leash, speechless and suddenly very, very eager to leave.

* * *

When Sabre dropped to his knees at Laurent's feet, it was with a ragged, broken sigh of relief he was fairly sure half the room could hear.

Across the room, Adrien was staring at Sabre like he'd materialized out of the fireplace as a bad fairy sent to personally torment him. His face was unnaturally pale, and his fingers were curled tight around the stem of his water glass. Beside him, Isiodore looked utterly unaffected, speaking softly to Marius, Lord Chastain's oldest son and heir. Devon, who was dressed like the prince Adrien never really managed to look like, smiled at Sabre from the door.

Sabre was *not*, however, looking at Laurent, who had to tighten the leash around his fist for Sabre to even stare at his fine leather boots.

"My lord," Sabre said, in a soft voice.

"Lord de Rue," said Lord Chastain, from behind Sabre. Sabre kept his gaze fixed on Laurent's shoes. "Your people certainly know how to make an entrance."

"Yes," Laurent said. There was a chill in his tone that Sabre recognized. "They do."

"We can, of course, provide a suitable costume," Lord Chastain said. Sabre tensed as he lay a proprietary hand on the back of his head. "Perhaps a deer."

"No."

Sabre looked up, despite himself, as Adrien, still pale and strung tight as a bow, pushed himself away from the fire. Lord Chastain's smile didn't waver, but his eyes were cold, as they had been when he first visited Sabre at the House of Onyx.

"Your Highness," he said. "Did you have a suggestion?"

"He'll go to the woods in what he has," Adrien said, and for a moment, his voice was sharp, short, like his father's. He met Sabre's gaze, and Sabre remembered what Adrien had told him, when they were boys. A vision of Sabre, in the woods, with a sword. "He isn't here to be hunted. He's here as my father's guest. Not yours."

If Sabre weren't there to ensure the opposite, he would have *killed* Adrien with his bare hands. Adrien just stared at him, frowning slightly, entirely unmoved.

"A coat, at least," Lord Chastain said, stroking Sabre's hair indulgently. "I insist."

"He won't be wearing one," Adrien said, with a certainty only Sabre had ever heard. It must have taken Lord Chastain by surprise, at least, as he stared at Adrien a moment before smiling faintly.

"As Your Highness wishes, of course," he said. He turned his smile to Laurent. "It seems the prince has already staked a claim on his prey for the evening."

"Except I told you," Adrien said, and there was a hint of fear in his voice, now, a wildness in his eyes that made Sabre think of his mother, kneeling over a sigil of blood in the throne room. "He isn't prey."

"Save us, he's smitten with a whore," Devon said, and Adrien turned on him, eyes bright. The *fool*.

"Here, now, Adrien," Marius said, striding over to take Adrien by the shoulder. "Ignore my little brother, he was raised feral. I know you and Sab were old chums, once, but I have it on good faith that he'll be a poor match for your tastes. Have you met the wolf in the corner? From Arktos, if you can imagine."

Adrien cast Sabre one last, hard look from over his shoulder as he was led away, and Lord Chastain finally removed his hand from Sabre's hair.

"I can take him, then," Devon said, setting his wineglass on a table. "If he's free."

"Thank you for your concern, Lord Chastain," Laurent said, and Sabre lowered his gaze again. He caught a glimpse of Yves, draped over a noble's lap and pretending not to openly stare at Sabre. "But he is not. I thought entertainment was meant to take place *after* the hunt."

"Except my son has already made it clear, Lord de Rue," the king said, and Sabre stiffened. He hadn't seen him come back, but he was already sauntering towards the drinks table. He held a glass to the light and set it back down. "Your newest acquisition came with me, so I suppose you can take him at your discretion."

Sabre's breath caught, and Laurent tugged at the leash, just hard enough to ease the familiar terror threatening to rise at Emile's slow, bored drawl.

"Your Majesty," Devon said. "I would love to—"

"I can't imagine why you're addressing me," the king said, and Devon rocked back on his heels, a hot, furious blush rising to his cheeks. "He wears *my* collar, last I saw it. Do you not? Show them for me, de Valois."

Sabre didn't miss the way the room hushed at the sound of the king using Sabre's last name. Laurent pulled at the leash, and Sabre tipped his head back, tugging at the neckline of his shirt to reveal the gold collar at his throat.

Emile didn't even bother to look.

"And tell them what you did to earn my collar," he said.

Sabre couldn't think. He could feel Laurent at his back, see Charon watching him, Adrien with his hands fisted in his cloak, but he couldn't push past the thought of Emile's boot on his back, his mother and sister hanging behind him. The rough weight of a rope at his neck. This wasn't how it was supposed to go. He was supposed to be watching Adrien, watching Laurent, not being laid bare for a room full of courtesans and nobles alike.

"Have...have I, Your Majesty?"

"You don't think you've earned it?" the king said, and, for the first time since the queen died in his arms, his eyes no longer looked cold and dead as cut glass. He crossed the room towards him, and Sabre didn't realize he was squirming on his knees to get away until Laurent grabbed him by the back of the neck, squeezing hard.

Sabre only barely stopped himself from reaching for Laurent in return.

Emile grabbed Sabre by the chin. "It's a shame you have your mother's eyes," he said, as Sabre trembled beneath him. "Oscar. Have one of your painted whores fetch me a blindfold."

Sabre couldn't breathe. Laurent kept a steadying hand on his neck, but Sabre gasped painfully when a servant handed a black cloth to the king.

"Your Majesty, please," Sabre whispered. "Please, I need my eyes."

Emile actually laughed. He leaned in close, and Sabre ground his teeth as he tied the cloth over his eyes.

"They're hunters, little bee," he whispered, and Sabre shuddered at the tone of the man he used to know, the man who would laugh while the queen herded Sabre and Adrien about like restless sheep. "There's no sport in it until you're on the saddle." He drew away. "Well, de Rue? Show us what the boy has learned."

"Please, Your Majesty," Sabre said.

"Adrien." Emile's voice was hard again, ringing with natural dominance. "Stay where you are."

"Up, pet," Laurent said. He couldn't disobey the king any more than Sabre could, even with his title, and Sabre knew it. Still, Sabre relaxed just a little under his hand as Laurent took him by the hair. He pulled Sabre through the darkness, and guided him to what felt like a flogging post. He stripped Sabre coldly and efficiently, and Sabre could hear the voices rise around him, his name weaving through the crowd like a cold wind.

"You should whip him, my lord," said Devon, and Sabre could almost feel Laurent rolling his eyes.

"I can provide a flogger, Lord de Rue," Lord Chastain said.

"I have my own. Charon. The fur, then, and the chain flogger, thank you."

Sabre would have wept, if he could. Charon probably would have had no use for the chain flogger there—Even Adrien, whose submission seemed to be etched in his bones, likely couldn't handle it—but it was one of the few things that could bring Sabre out of the terror, the dread of being blindfolded with Adrien surrounded by enemies, the dark night and the hunt to come.

"He's already panting for it," Devon said. "It's sick."

"Devon," Lord Chastain said, in a sharp tone.

"I don't envy him, regardless," said Marius. "Do you, Prince Adrien?"

"I'd rather not," Adrien said. Sabre sighed.

"Lord de Rue?" The king's voice, soft, smiling.

"Yes, Your Majesty."

"Make sure I can hear it. I'll be outside when you're done."

Laurent lay a hand on Sabre's lower back, and Sabre braced himself, still shaking slightly, the taste of copper on his tongue.

"Funny to see him on the other side of it," someone said, and Sabre tilted his head, trying to make out the voice. "Do you remember Lady Hamish's fête? He spent half the night between her thighs."

Laurent's hand pulled away, and Sabre arched back on the post. "My lord," he said, before Laurent could answer. "My lord, please. Please, make me hurt, for you."

There was another brief hush, expectant, eager.

"I can't watch," Devon snarled.

"Please, my lord," Sabre said. He gasped at the heavy, soft fur of the flogger on his backside, and pressed his cheek to the post.

"Let us hear you, pet," Laurent said, and Sabre moaned as his skin started to heat, as the pain built like a wave, slow and deceptive until it was almost enough to tip him over, his cock rising as the crowd watched. In the dark, it felt hotter, sharper, the pain rolling through him until the first moan shivered in the air.

"Please," he begged, grabbing at the post. "Please, please, Laur—my lord, *ah*—" His moans went breathy, pushed out of him with every strike, and he had to stop himself from grinding against the post.

"Scream for me," Laurent said, as Sabre panted into the wood. "You'll do it, won't you, my whore? Show them how badly you want it, how good it feels."

"Yes, my lord," Sabre said, and cried out as the chain flogger struck his sensitive skin for the first time. He knew it wouldn't do more than mark him a little, but it felt like knives after the soft, heavy fur, and Sabre started to rut against the post, mindlessly, lost in pleasure.

He screamed at the fourth strike, and jerked against the post, thighs tensing. "My lord, I—I'm close, please."

Laurent lashed him again. "You could come from this, couldn't you? Show them. Show them what you are, Sabre. Come for me. *Cry for me.*"

"Lau—*lord*—" Sabre sobbed as he brought himself off on the flogging post, his skin on fire, the terror pushed back by Laurent's hand. Laurent ripped the blindfold off as Sabre came, and Sabre got only a glimpse of Lord Chastain in the back of the room, heat in his eyes, before Laurent turned him around by the shoulder and kissed him.

Sabre kissed him back, melting into it, the familiar press of his mouth, the slide of fingers under Sabre's collar. Then Laurent tugged, sharply, and Sabre gratefully dropped to his knees a second time, breathing hard, forehead pressed to Laurent's thigh.

"My lord," Sabre whispered, looking into Laurent's eyes for the first time since he'd been led in on the king's leash. "Should I—"

"I think," Lord Chastain said, as the room filled with scattered applause, "that as thrilling as this has been, we've kept the king waiting long enough. The sun is set—Gather at the gates, my lords, ladies, and esteemed guests, and we will have ourselves a hunt."

CHAPTER 14

*L*aurent did not want to do this.

And while he could cheerfully strangle Devon Chastain himself, there was something to be said for the clarity of topspace, which he'd easily slid into by putting Sabre under with the flogger. But it made his already alert senses feel like he was buzzing, like the times he'd been given *exalte*; that strange powder drug that nobles liked, the one that made you feel like your heart was racing too fast, your mind keeping pace with it, so it was like topspace times a thousand. Laurent hadn't minded it too much back when he'd been forcing himself to be a submissive, as it was the closest he could get, with most clients, to topspace.

He hadn't touched it since, and yet.

Laurent had a few moments before he had to send Sabre out with the others, and he used them mainly to stroke his hair, murmur a few words and try and gently ease him up enough to pay attention to his surroundings. Being in topspace might be a momentary boon for Laurent, but he would have preferred Sabre not be drifting like he was, right before the hunt.

"I would have thought," Isiodore de Mortain said, appearing next to Laurent and attired as if he really *were* going hunting, "you would have had the good sense to *keep him at home.*"

"Your Grace," Sabre said, still kneeling, his face pressed to Laurent's thigh. "Lord de Rue tried to keep me at home, but I didn't listen."

Laurent cast his eyes heavenward. This was not going to help. "Pet, be quiet."

"Perhaps being a good whore doesn't mean you're good at managing them," Isiodore said, and laid a brief hand on Sabre's head. "Stay alert, Bumblebee. Nothing here is meant to go well, for you."

He left with another nod to Laurent, who glanced down at Sabre. "We're going to talk about this, you know. When we're home. I've half a mind to add another thousand crowns to your debt."

"Go ahead," Sabre said, so softly, staring up at Laurent with a look so nakedly honest that Laurent felt his world shift, dangerously so. "I don't mean to leave you, my lord. I lo—"

"No," Laurent said, putting his fingers on Sabre's mouth. "Don't. Not here. This isn't the place for it. Later, when we're home, in my bed. When you're safe."

Sabre kissed his fingers, and Laurent sighed and tugged on his hair. "Go on. Charon will keep an eye on you, and I will, too."

"Prince Adrien," Sabre said, glancing over at the crown prince, who was obstinately standing by the fire and not leaving the room.

"Yes, him too, go on, now." Laurent tugged the leash, and Sabre rose to his feet. He unclipped it. "Take this to the king, and bow when you present it. Don't look him in the eyes. Something isn't right, here."

Sabre nodded, but before he could leave they were joined by Lord Chastain, who was smiling in a way Laurent absolutely didn't trust—it was far too sweet, too eager.

"Sabre," he said, warmly enough that Laurent would think him acting, if Chastain had any talent for it. Which meant it was genuine, and yet another threat to be on guard against. It would do Sabre no favors to be caught by Chastain *or* his youngest son. Perhaps Marius, a submissive who seemed more interested in Charon, could be persuaded to intervene?

"My lord," Sabre said.

"Don't worry about the hunt." Lord Chastain reached out and took Sabre's hand, which made Laurent wonder if the man had honestly lost his mind, or if he'd slipped into the fantasy where Sabre really did need his protection, and wanted it. "I know it's frightening, but it's only for—" he stopped, abruptly, and his voice went cold as the grave. "What is that, on your hand? I would have thought, if you were to wear a bauble, it might be the favor I gave you. Unless your lord didn't see fit to give it to you, along with my invitation to be my guest at this event?"

Laurent had given Sabre the ring, of course. And he glanced down, wondering what Sabre had chosen—not all clients gave their courtesans gifts through the house lord, but Laurent had not expected Sabre to earn many of them, if any. But the ring on Sabre's hand wasn't some noble's casual trinket, but a signet ring, with the noble crest of the de Valois family, and a deer. His heart pounded in his chest as Lord Chastain stared at it like it might leap off Sabre's hand and bite him.

"It belonged to my father," Sabre said.

"It belonged to a traitor," Lord Chastain snapped, all warmth gone. "And you would do well to remember who enjoys the king's patronage, and who hanged at his command."

"My mother was a traitor," Sabre said, his voice clear, that same inherent noble pride he'd displayed with Chastain's son, a few days ago. "My father was always loyal to his cousin, the king. He wore this the day he died, on a hunt. I thought it would bring me good luck. If you'll excuse me. I heard the bell."

Apparently no one had ever explained to Lord Oscar Chastain just how much steel was in the spine of a submissive, because he seemed speechless as Sabre took himself off to join the "foxes" outside.

Lord Chastain's hands fisted at his snide. "Devon!" he snarled, as if Laurent wasn't there, as if he'd forgotten Laurent was a lord, not another thing to be chased, carried off and fucked. "Attend me, there is something we need to discuss before the hunt."

"Finally," Devon Chastain muttered, and as Laurent tried to discreetly sneak behind them and listen in...he was stopped by Sebastien d'Hiver, of all people, who looked like a frost creature come to life, cold as a statue with eyes as empty as glass.

"You," he said, pointing to Laurent with his cane.

"Your Grace," Laurent bit out, between his teeth, as Chastain and his son moved to speak privately near the door. Devon started to smile, and apprehension dug in tight to Laurent's nerves and wouldn't let go. "Is there something you require?"

Sebastien had a disturbing tendency not to blink. He also stepped in far too close, and the apprehension paled for a moment to the *dread* at being so close to him, though Laurent couldn't really fathom why.

"That was quite the demonstration you provided," D'Hiver said, in his odd, flat voice. "Tell me. That one, who just left with the lord of the hunt—what is his name?"

This is what d'Hiver wanted to talk about? Who someone *was*? Damn and blast, his timing was horrendous. "Are you—do you mean, his son, Devon?"

"Ah, yes." D'Hiver's eyes went vacant and he tilted his head like he was listening to something. "We thought the rage was from the whore tied to the post, that's why we came to see. But it wasn't him. It was that one, that Devon."

Who's we? No. No, he wasn't asking that. He didn't want to know, and he needed to be out there, keeping an eye on the *man he loved* who had just walked out like a man bleeding climbing in a pool with hungry sharks. "He's...yes, not very fond of Sabre."

"So much hate, that one. We'd hunt him, I think. Yes."

"He's—a hunter," Laurent said, helpless in the face of d'Hiver's weirdness and the dread that poured off him like a cologne. "Devon is, I meant. He's not a fox."

"Oh you're all foxes, to us," D'Hiver said, waving a hand. "Thank you for your assistance, you may go. We thought about hunting you, but then we realized you don't know who you are, do you?"

"What?"

Of course, when Laurent would have welcomed a few seconds longer of conversation with the Duke, he simply...turned and walked off, muttering something softly and smiling at nothing.

Laurent shivered and went outside, immediately seeing Yves—who was smiling up at a noble but who did keep glancing over at both Sabre and Charon, often—and Sabre, who wasn't looking at anyone.

Devon Chastain was smiling with something sick in his expression, an eagerness that made Laurent want to drag Sabre back to his room and forgo this whole thing altogether. And there were...so many people, so many more than were here before, in the room when he'd flogged Sabre. Weren't there? Some he didn't recognize, and they were laughing, dancing in the snow and—

We have to go, you must follow—look at your feet not out of its eyes, its dead but it will make you see what it—the smoke, don't breathe the smoke, whatever you do—run, run, it's staring I hear the horses and—

"...His Highness, of course," Lord Chastain was saying, to the king.

Emile, standing next to his fearsome black horse, sighed and said, "I will fetch my son." He disappeared into the house, and Laurent could hear the dominance in his tone if not the words themselves. When Emile reappeared, Adrien was there, pale faced and wild-eyed in the snow.

He immediately left his father's side and came to Laurent's. "My lord, you have to get him out, don't let him—"

"Adrien, you will *come here, now,*" Emile called, and several of the submissives—noble and not—went to their knees in the snow, simply from the strength of the king's dominance. For all the power the crown gave to him, Emile was mostly a quiet man who rarely raised his voice. Laurent had heard when he executed his royal guard out of paranoia that they were plotting against him, he never said a word, simply shot them all and left the room in silence. Somehow that was worse than if he'd done it in a rage.

Adrien couldn't fight that tone in his father's voice, and he turned and trudged toward Emile's side with the dread of a man heading to the gallows.

"Now the prince is here, let's get started," Devon Chastain called, still smiling his sick, twisted smile at Sabre. "I'm eager for the hunt. Let the foxes go, would you, father?"

Run run they're coming Solas run don't breathe the smoke don't breathe don't run run don't look out of its eyes—

D'Hiver's voice, *you don't know who you are, do you.* Calling him a Mislian.

The sun that morning, in the House of Gold. The woman who told him—who told him—

Tell them your name is Laurent. I would ask your forgiveness, but if I have done this right, you will forget I ever existed.

Don't breathe the smoke, Solas!

Tell them your name is Laurent.

Do you see that, there? It's the symbol of the old gods, the ones we tore down from the sky—

Laurent stumbled at the sound of the gun, heart in his throat, but it was only the sign that the hunt had begun and even though every instinct in his body was telling him to run...he remembered he wasn't a fox, was a hunter, and whatever this strange surge of memory was, now wasn't the time to get lost in it.

But as he searched for Sabre's familiar, beloved form in the snow...he found he was holding his breath, and he could still hear his mother's voice in his head telling him, over and over, *run, run and don't look back.*

* * *

THE GUN FIRED. Courtesans raced through the dark woods, their costumes glittering in the fading light of the sunset, but the only thing of Sabre's that caught the sun was the collar at his neck and his father's ring. He registered the flash of color out of the corner of his eye, a shadow that could have been Yves, but he didn't run far enough to tell. He stopped well before the shadows started to blend into a false midnight, turned on his heel, and waited.

Devon would come first.

He came like thunder, his horse a black shadow bursting through the trees, kicking up clods of dirt and tossing its head as Devon spurred it faster still.

Sabre didn't run. He stood there, quiet as he'd never fully managed to be in the practice courts with Isiodore, watching the horse bear down upon him, the terror a distant thing in his mind. It was like being under, in a way, like going so deep he'd come out the other side.

Devon's horse was not trained for war. It was trained for speed, agile and nervy, and when it saw Sabre unmoving in its path, it veered in panic and stumbled against a pine. Snow fell from the upper boughs, making the air glitter as Devon was thrown from his horse. He rolled in the broken earth with a ragged cry, and groaned as he struck the roots of a tree, the bark stripped and rough. He got to his hands and knees with his face a ruin of blood, and spat at Sabre's feet.

"You *whore*," he said.

"Hello, Devon," Sabre said.

"Don't you try to—" Devon drew his sword, ornamental but sharp enough to cut a man's throat if it had to, so long as no one put any pressure on it. "Don't you act like you're—like you don't know what you are. What you've done."

Sabre just stared at him. Waiting.

"We knew your mother's plans would fail," Devon said, "because she kept *you*, the prince's pet *whore*, mooning after him while his father killed half his own *guard*—"

Devon swung too wide, and Sabre stepped into range, ignoring the sharp pain of the blade slicing across his arm. He struck Devon full in the face, with all the strength of years of training with Isiodore, and Devon went down like a marionette cut from its strings, cursing thickly through a mouth full of blood.

"My mother failed because she was no better than the king, in the end," Sabre said, stepping on Devon's hand. Devon yowled in pain and fury, animalistic and low, as Sabre took the sword from where he'd dropped it in the snow. "If she did love me, it wasn't a weakness."

"She hated you," Devon said. "You and your father, *Adrien,* submissives feigning a right to power…"

Sabre looked down at Devon, trembling with rage in the snow. "Maybe you're right," he said. "But I don't care. Not anymore." He turned on his heel.

Devon's scream echoed through the trees at Sabre's back, a lonely, wretched howl of a broken creature, as Sabre disappeared into the woods after Adrien.

He passed two nobles riding through the trees, but they shied to the side when they saw the blood on Sabre's sleeve and the sword in his hand. One of them tried to wheel around, but Sabre ran past them, towards the lighter, open part of the forest Adrien tended to like best, and the tremor of hoof beats faded into a gentle, distant thrumming.

"Asa!" he shouted. "Asa!"

"Sab!" Adrien's voice was faint, too distant. Sabre took off through the snow, pushing at trees, ducking branches, ignoring the burning pain of his sword arm as blood trailed down his hand.

This must have been what his father felt, that night, as they raced to the throne room. Sabre knew now what the panic and grief in his eyes meant, that fear that he was already too late, that all he could do was bear witness. He pushed himself forward, and staggered over a patch of wet snow and into a pool of dying light.

Adrien's horse stood against the last line of the setting sun, eyes rolling as Adrien, surrounded by smiling, laughing people in fox costumes, clung to the saddle. There were three foxes, all of them reaching for Adrien, tugging at his cloak, his boots, his belt. He looked to Sabre, panic in his eyes, and one of his captors turned to stare. She wore a mask over her face, and her red hair spilled out the sides, tight curls gone dark in the growing shadow.

"It's him," one of the others said. He wrenched at Adrien, who fell from his horse with a soft cry, and drew a blade from his belt. "Kill the whore first. The prince dies with the king."

The woman reached Sabre first. She was fast, faster than Devon, but Sabre was trained by a man who didn't care for honorable combat, and he kicked snow in her face, grabbed her hair, and pulled at her mask. She snarled, groping for something at her waist, and Sabre looked at Adrien, who was scrambling back on his hands and knees in the dirt.

"Does she live," Sabre said.

"What?" The third fox, reaching for Adrien, hesitated, hands out.

"No," Adrien said. "I saw her body at your feet."

Sabre grimaced and dragged the sword over her belly. She screamed, high and horrible, and Sabre had to wrench the sword out of her as the man reaching for Adrien turned to tackle Sabre head-on. The sword bent uselessly as Sabre tried to thrust it into the man's arm, and they rolled together in the growing mud and snow, Sabre's arms locked around his neck. The woman lay dying behind him, moaning softly.

"Does he live," Sabre said.

"No," Adrien whispered.

Sabre's stomach twisted as he felt the man's neck crack beneath him. He rose, looking at the last fox, who fell back against a tree, his mouth a black pit of horror in his face.

"Does he live," Sabre said, again.

Adrien was weeping. "No."

Sabre lay the man's body in the snow, when it was done. His shirt was tacky with blood, his hands thick with it, and Sabre almost wanted to crawl into the dark of the woods, disappear into it, cover himself with the shadow of it until he no longer felt like he was dragging his own body along by the throat. He turned to Adrien, and stood over him in the snow. He was panting and bloody and marked in a way he couldn't think about, yet, and he leaned down to take Adrien by the arm.

"I'm sorry," Sabre said.

"So am I," Adrien whispered. He wouldn't look Sabre in the eyes. "I didn't. I didn't want you to—"

"I know," Sabre said. He looked up. The horse was gone, but there were figures between the trees, now, nobles on horseback, courtesans holding each other, the sound of voices drifting through the dark. "Fuck. Give me your sword, Adrien."

"It's decorative," Adrien said.

"I just killed three people with a decorative sword, Asa," Sabre said. He unsheathed Adrien's sword for him and approached the horses, holding Adrien tight by the arm.

"You said you'd kill the whore, Lord Chastain," Sabre said, raising his voice as he dragged Adrien forward. "Kill the whore before they kill the prince. You should have picked another whore, I think."

"Yes," drawled the unmistakable voice of the king. Sabre pulled Adrien another step across the snow. "Terrible luck, Oscar. Look at what a mess he's made."

One of the horses shifted slightly, and Sabre stepped around Adrien to keep him at his back. His blood-slick hand slid over Adrien's arm.

"First he kills my guests," Lord Chastain said, "then he cries treachery. You should have let him hang, Your Majesty. Him and his bitch mother."

"And you should have killed him when you helped his mother kill Arthur de Valois," the king said, "but then, you never were a very observant man." Lord Chastain moved to turn his horse, and the king's voice snapped out sharp and cold. "Apprehend him. *And* his sons, Isiodore. Both of them."

There was a thundering of hooves as Isiodore turned to chase Lord Chastain's horse into the dark, and Sabre watched them disappear, swaying slightly in the circle of watchers. Someone dropped down from their horse—Laurent, it had to be—but Adrien was still there, weeping silently, out in the open.

"Your Majesty," Sabre said. "Your son."

"Yes, de Valois, I see him. Bring him here."

Sabre staggered forward. The king came into focus through the trees, somber and watchful, and Sabre pushed Adrien towards him, leaving a smudged, bloody handprint on his coat.

"I don't believe I'll require another vow, this time," the king said.

"No, Your Majesty," Sabre said, his voice hoarse. "Not this t—"

Lightning cracked in the distance, sharp and sudden as the door to the gallows dropping beneath his feet. Sabre fell to his knees as something struck his back, a white-hot ball of pain that seared through him like fire. He went tumbling into the snow, and behind him, Devon Chastain dropped his gun to the ground, turned his bloody face from Sabre's body shuddering at the feet of the king, and disappeared into the night.

CHAPTER 15

*R*ight at the moment when Laurent's heart felt like it finally could return to normal, it broke.

He knew, logically, that Devon Chastain's shot was meant to kill. Sabre was an easy target, his back to the woods, on his knees, unprotected. And that someone would catch him, bring him to justice.

But all he cared about in that moment was Sabre, bleeding out in the snow.

The prince was shouting, and there was chaos all around, but Laurent moved in a daze to where the man he loved—this stupid, foolish, brave man who was more noble than the rest of them combined—was gasping, making a horrible sound that could likely only mean one thing; the bullet from Devon's gun had hit his lung. Either he'd done it on purpose to make Sabre suffer, or he wasn't steady enough with his hand to have hit Sabre's heart. Either way, while someone was already running for the house and a doctor, Laurent knew it was too late.

He crouched on the snow and gathered Sabre to him, stroking his hair off his already too-pale face, turning waxy.

"It's okay," Sabre said, and Laurent couldn't imagine what the look on his face must be, for Sabre to cough that out with his dying breath, choking and coughing up blood. "I. Saved him. My...father would. Be. Proud, I—I think."

"Yes," Laurent said, and his voice was just as harsh, as if he'd been struck with Devon's bullet, instead. Tears fell unchecked from his eyes. "Sabre, I—I'm sorry I didn't keep you safe."

"N-no," Sabre said, and he was *smiling*, the idiot, even as his body started to shiver and shake in Laurent's arms. "Never felt. As safe as I did. With you."

Laurent could barely breathe through his sobs. "We'll get you some help, it's—"

"Too late," Sabre coughed. He reached blindly for Laurent's hand, but barely had the strength to squeeze it. "Is it okay if I. Say it, now."

"I love you," Laurent said, helpless, lost.

"I love y-you, too." Sabre coughed, and the light was leaving his eyes, too fast. "Thank you for. Saving me."

"But I didn't," Laurent whispered, leaning down, as if trying to hide the end of this from anyone, even himself.

"You did," Sabre whispered. "You did. Hold me until I—until it's. Over."

Laurent lifted his face, stared down at him, slid his own shaking fingers through Sabre's hair. It wouldn't be long. Minutes, at the most. And the only person Laurent had ever loved would die, here in the snow, shot by a noble who Laurent would see dead if it was the last thing he—

"I know what you're thinking," Sabre managed. "Let it be. Promise you'll. Live for you, don't...don't do something. Foolish."

"Shh, love," Laurent said, because he couldn't lie, even to the man he loved while he died in his arms.

"I'm glad that it's your face—" Sabre said, and coughed again, and Laurent felt something shift inside him, something forgotten and suddenly found, and while his heart ached and his tears fell and he realized that this was the end of it, the precious thing he'd found in the last place he'd ever expected it—

Laurent remembered all the things he'd forgotten, and who he was.

It didn't come to him with the sudden break of a summer storm, but a gentle, easy sigh, like a breeze stirring the leaves. There was not knowing and there was knowing, and it rushed over him like a gentle spring rain.

Solas, said his mother, pulling him to the House of Gold. *They won't find you, here. They can't find you if you don't know who you are. And you won't remember who you are, because love can't come from this place, where you sell your body. You would hate me for it, but gods willing, you won't remember me.*

His mother had sold him to the House of Gold, not for the money, but for the safety to be found in treating sex, and love, like a transaction. The block she'd put on him to hide him from those back in Mislia, magic so complex he couldn't fathom the shape of it, stacked up like bricks that now came tumbling down because he had, in the end, found love.

"Hush, love," said Solas, who was also Laurent, in the language he thought he'd left behind. "The last thing you see may be my face, but gods willing, it won't be for some time, yet."

The magic was there, when he reached for it. Warm and bright, not like the dark siphoning thing the mages who made their pacts with demons used, the ones that turned their hair to pitch, bleeding ink through the whole of their eyes. This was older magic, from the older gods they'd slain in Mislia, the dark mages who ruled it, now. And Solas, born with the gift only one in a thousand would ever inherit, taken from his home so he would not be slain in the mages' rituals for power, bled dry of the magic none of them, with their demon-touched spells, could do.

But Solas, the exile who could heal and bring life in a place clouded by darkness and death, had remembered who he was. And the magic poured bright and hot from him over Sabre, and it was easy even though he hadn't done it in so long, even if Solas hadn't remembered any of it for almost two decades.

There were some soft murmurs behind him, but he didn't care. He'd always been reckless with it, hadn't he? That's why his mother took him to Staria to save him, in her way. He wondered what happened to her, but only vaguely; the magic was working, he knew it was, could see the way the light came back to Sabre's eyes, could feel the warmth of him, again.

"What—am I dead," Sabre whispered.

"No," Laurent said. "No, you're not." He felt something, on the hand resting on Sabre's back. Small, and whole, and warm from where it had been, lodged in Sabre's body. A bullet.

"But I can breathe, and. It doesn't hurt. And you're. Glowing."

"Just a little longer," Laurent said, even though he wasn't sure how he knew. But it was only a few seconds before it faded, leaving them there in the snow; Sabre covered in blood but alive and whole, and all of Laurent's missing pieces finally clicked back into place.

"How," Sabre whispered, reaching up and touching him. "How did you do that?"

"Turns out, I'm Mislian," Laurent said. He shook his head. "It's a long story. But I remembered it, and I...my name. I remembered my name."

"Is it something awful," Sabre asked, smiling a bit, his eyes bright now with tears of his own.

"Back from the brink of death, and already you want to be punished," Laurent managed, through tears of his own. Happy ones, at least. "It's Solas."

"Solas," said Sabre, trying it out. "Hello."

There was a laugh from behind them. Laurent turned, and saw the prince there, on his knees in the snow. His face was tear-streaked but there was a smile, an inescapable fondness as he looked at his cousin and said, "Didn't she—she told you, when we were children. That one day, you'd marry the sun?"

"I don't think courtesans in debt to the crown can marry," Sabre told his cousin, sitting up. He blinked. "Everyone's gone."

"As touching as your farewell scene was, a surfeit of emotion makes others uncomfortable. And they have actual prey to hunt, now."

Laurent felt a chill as he recognized the king's voice. His dislike of Mislians was well-known, following the queen's death. Perhaps they'd been spared only for Sabre to live, and Laurent to die on the gallows. Or here, before his beloved, in the cold snow.

"Your Majesty," Laurent said, as he and Sabre both got to their feet. If he was going to die, he wouldn't do it on his knees. He bowed. "I seem to have recovered the memories I lost. I assure you, I didn't—"

"Yes, yes," Emile waved a hand. "I despise Mislians, but if one sold you into the pleasure houses, likely you do, too." His cold eyes bore into Laurent, and Laurent understood what he was hearing, *you will hate them for it, because I said so.*

"Yes, of course," Laurent said, bowing.

"And a man is easy to keep in line, when you know what he values most," Emile said, eyes shifting to Sabre. "Strange that it would be a whore, but perhaps your people know no better."

Either Emile was testing him, or he really was that terrible about Mislians. Either way, Laurent was smart enough to know an out when he heard it. "Yes, well. As you know, I was one, before. And I will take Sabre's debt, if you wish it of me. He's proven his loyalty, and—"

"No," Sabre said, going to his knees again, bloody and foolish as ever. "Laurent earned his freedom, paid his debt. Mine is my own, and—"

"Would you stand up," Emile interrupted. "Before some other traitor comes from the woods and shoots you, and I'm forced to see that again. I will forgive that forbidden magic once, because your lord used it to save you, and you saved my son. But that is the extent of my mercy. Come here, Sabre. That collar of mine doesn't belong around the neck of a noble."

Sabre startled, but he approached the king—a little warily, but Laurent could understand that. The king reached out and flicked his fingers over the collar, which unlatched from around Sabre's neck.

"Your father's ring, you still have it?"

"Yes, Your Majesty." Sabre held his hand out, which was bloody. He scrubbed at it, wincing a bit, and Emile sighed, again.

"I will make certain it is known that you have performed a great service to the crown. To ferret out a group of treasonous snakes, you infiltrated the ranks of the pleasure houses at my behest. Your...proclivities...made you the perfect spy for the crown, you see. And you did as we had planned, found the traitors who would have slain my son. Now your noble name is restored to you, wiped clean of suspicion. Your oath isn't necessary, but you may thank me for my mercy, Duke de Valois."

"Thank you, Your Majesty," Sabre said, prettily enough, and bowed.

"And Lord de Rue, it simply isn't done for the consort of a noble of Duke de Valois' status to live entirely in the pleasure district. You understand, it might send the wrong message. I'll see to it your family's estate and your suite in the royal palace are redone for your use. Now, I believe we are done here. I have every faith in Isiodore's hunting skills, and it would seem I have to find a suitable tree for a hanging."

And with that, having just undone months of misery and returned to Sabre the life he himself had stripped away, the king of Staria strode off toward the estate.

"I..." Sabre said, staring at his hand, at his father's ring. "I don't know that I even wanted that."

"He can't stand to be wrong," said the prince, who Laurent had all but forgotten was even there. "It was the same when Mother died. He let everyone think he did it in some fit of madness, rather than have the truth out, that she was practicing forbidden sorcery and it went wrong." Adrien looked exhausted but far less unsettled than he had any other time Laurent had been around him. "Lord de Rue. Thank you for saving him. Not just here, but before."

Laurent said, somewhat wryly, "All part of the king's plan, don't you know?"

Adrien smiled a bit, and standing there in the snow, he looked a little like his father, perhaps. But he embraced Sabre, murmured something that made Sabre blush, and then clasped Laurent's hand in farewell before heading back the way his father came.

Sabre moved to him immediately, and Laurent took him in his arms. "I thought I'd lost you. And you, with your *I'm glad your face is the last thing I'll ever see.*"

"I thought it was nice," Sabre said, into his shirt. He was crying again. So was Laurent. There was no one there, it was fine.

"Nice, he says."

"I'm sorry, m'lord. I'll try and come up with something better, the next time I lay dying in your arms."

"Cheeky brat," Laurent said, and took his face in his hands. "First, I love you, and I'm sorry I didn't let you tell me, before. You can say it whenever you want. Second, you're a noble again. You don't have to call me that, anymore, and you can probably do better than a disgraced Mislian whose mother sold him into a pleasure house to hide from mages who will, probably, try and find him again. I might have to leave."

"Then I will go with you," Sabre said, fiercely. "Wherever you are, I will be there."

"This better not be out of gratitude," Laurent said, but he smiled, fingers moving up and down Sabre's back, as if reassuring himself there was no longer a wound, there. But there was drying blood, and they both needed to be in a bath, and naked in front of a fire. Sooner rather than later. "I didn't save your life for you to owe another debt you think you need to pay."

"You saved my life because you love me, and I will share yours because I love you, too." Sabre reached out and took Laurent's hand, brought it to his mouth and kissed his fingers—then took it and pressed to his now-bare throat. "And I want your collar as soon as you have one made for me. A nice one. Black, lined in purple velvet. I want to go home and watch your sister's plays, and run the curtain. I want you to put me under. I want to never sew another button on a shirt again."

"I think I can manage that," Laurent said, and kissed him, there in the snow and the darkness, which no longer seemed so terrifying, anymore.

* * *

Lord Oscar Chastain was caught near the edge of the forest, summarily hauled back to his estate by Isiodore de Mortain, and hanged from a tree near the edge of the property as a traitor to the crown at dawn the next day.

Laurent and Sabre stayed abed.

Marius and Devon Chastain, however, eluded capture. It was only a matter of time, really, as there was nowhere for them to go, and news of their disgrace was likely already back in the capital. Along with it, the shocking news that Sabre de Valois was never a traitor, and had in fact put his life and honor on the line to prove his innocence by finding the last of the conspirators. If anyone really believed that, Laurent would eat his favorite hat and wear nothing but Yves' short glittery shorts for the rest of his days. But the nobility would know better than to speak of it, and would treat Sabre as they now did Laurent—as if he never was a whore, as if he were always one of them.

It was all exhausting, really.

The last shock of the weekend came when Emile sent the footman —the one who was enamored of Yves—with a deed to the Chastain estate, which now belonged to *Laurent,* who stared at the paper with shock and a deep sense of horror.

"What am I supposed to do with this," Laurent said.

"I'd put it in a safe, were it me, m'lord," the footman said. "Can I stay on, though? The staff, we're all a bit worried."

"No one is losing their jobs," said Laurent, sighing. He could feel a headache threaten. One of the reasons he'd liked his title was that it didn't come with property other than the House of Onyx.

"Well, um, about that," said the footman. "Lord Chastain, none of us are real sure we can be in the same, ah, business as—"

"Wait," Laurent held up a hand. "What did you just call me?"

"That's how it works," Sabre said, from where he was lounging in the bed, naked and wrapped in furs and delightfully disheveled. "You are a proper Starian lord now, Laurent. You own an estate, so you're Lord Chastain."

"No, no one ever calls me that, do you hear me?" He fixed the footman with a look. "And I'm not turning this into a—everyone can keep the job they're already doing."

"Oh, thank the spirits," the footman said, and bowed, leaving in a hurry.

Laurent stared at the paper, and then at Sabre. "When we marry, can I take your name?"

"I was going to take *yours*," Sabre said. "But not Chastain."

"Why would Emile *do* this to me?"

"A reminder, probably. How his favor should be courted and not lost." Sabre yawned. "Come back to bed, my lord."

"But I have a—*this*, now," Laurent said, waving a hand. "Am I expected to, to leave the House of Onyx?"

"I wouldn't think so. Do what every noble does, who doesn't want to manage his estate. Hire someone." Sabre tilted his head. "It's a working farm, you know. Dairy, a few other things. I think."

"Gods help me, none of you know anything," Laurent said. "At least I have an excuse, I'm in disgrace from a totally different country."

"About that," Sabre said.

"I'll tell you when we're home." Laurent might own this estate now, but he didn't trust that it was safe to speak freely, here. "And as fetching as you look there, pet, with your *hurt me, fuck me* eyes, we need to get going. I've had enough of country living for a while."

Lord Chastain's body was gone, at least, by the time they left for Duciel. The majority of the carriage ride back was Sabre telling Yves what happened, and Yves gasping dramatically and practically hanging off Charon's lap. Charon had apologized profusely for not stopping Devon—so contritely that Laurent had to tell him to stop or he'd erase all his debt and make him run the farm he now owned.

"You should hire my family," Yves said, when Laurent tried that. "They're exemplary dairy farmers, it'd be a scream. When I'm old and no one wants me anymore, I'll come here and, I don't know, learn how to make cheese. You can come, too, Charon. Everyone can, from the house."

"You could do that, you know," Sabre said.

"Sabre! You are supposed to say, *Yves, don't be silly, you'll never be old and everyone will want you, especially after I manage to introduce you properly to my cousin the crown prince—"*

"You do not want to be in that family," Laurent interrupted, firmly.

"The cheese would likely be preferable," Sabre agreed. "But I only meant, m'lord, that you could make it a choice for those with debt who are no longer...sought after, in the pleasure houses. An alternative to the quarries. It would allow for an easier transition. Perhaps give former courtesans a skill or two, for when their debt was repaid."

"Aw." Yves batted his eyelashes at Sabre. "Our lordling, a revolutionary."

"Let's not call him that," Laurent said, sighing. "But Sabre, that's a good idea. I think that is exactly what I'll do. Yves, if you're serious, I'll send a letter to your father. The only thing I know of cheese is that it comes from milk."

Laurent turned to look out of the window, watching as the city came into view, the spires of the palace gleaming gold in the sun. There was still so much unsettled, the missing pieces of his life there to examine, Sabre's reinstatement, the fact that Devon Chastain was still missing and would, he assumed, try to finish what he'd started once he'd learned Sabre was not only alive, but back in the king's favor. Marius Chastain, who would perhaps take issue with the fact that Laurent now owned his father's estate.

The bullet, tucked away in Laurent's things, kept as a reminder of how quickly things could end.

But with the sound of Yves' easy laughter, the sun bright and the little snow melting beneath it, and Sabre's hand held tight in his own...it was easy to put it aside, just for a time, and be happy with what he'd found. A family, a life, and a future that was his to make...with the man he loved, who not even death could take from him. A new foundation on which to build something steady, something lasting, to weather the storms that were sure to come.

*I*t had been quite some time since Sabre de Rue last set foot in his family home in the shadow of the palace.

The carefully maintained gardens at the gate were overgrown, thistle and mint pushing up against the iron fence as Sabre lifted the latch and slipped through. He had a small staff who came in once a week to keep the house from collapsing under the weight of its own consequence, but none of them were gardeners, and wild roses brushed Sabre's dark jacket as he turned the key in the front door and stepped inside.

The manor was empty. The front hall was cleared of furnishings that had been in the de Valois home for hundreds of years; Old clocks generations of children weren't allowed to touch, ancient books arranged by color behind glass, chairs that were dusted off and polished but never used. The drawing room had a couch for the staff and a tray for tea, but the rug where Sabre and Elise used to read poetry to each other was gone, and the painting of dogs running about in a distant, unknown countryside was just a blank space on the wall.

He ran a hand over the dent in the wallpaper where Sabre, age seven, had driven a wooden sword through a stand of plate armor and upset half the household. There was the mark on the glass window where Elise had thrown a stone at twelve, and scratches on the banister where countless children sat and watched their noble families mill about below, the murmur of hundreds of dinner parties rising like steam through the halls.

Sabre stopped in the ballroom, where the king's guard had caught him months before, dragging his family through the streets to the square. He crossed to the high windows where Elise had stood in her blue gown and ribbons, her hands trembling, and looked down at the street below, the fine houses of fellow nobles who had gladly beaten him, whipped him, hissed curses into his ear, as soon as they had the chance.

"You know," he said, running a line down the dust on the window. "You and Mother might have been right about Staria. Not exactly the way you meant it, perhaps, but we can't just go on as we are."

He thought of his room with Laurent in the House of Onyx, of Rose revising scripts in the kitchen, teenagers in debt to the Houses along the street, running dangerous gambles for a chance at a comfortable life.

The quarry cart, rolling down the streets with the marble that formed the manor in which he stood.

It took being unmade for Sabre to learn the shape of who he was, in the end. That didn't mean it had to be the same for the rest of the world.

He turned to look at the empty ballroom. "Perhaps you'll be a school, one day," he said. "Or a theater. Another option, before people sign their debt into a House's ledger." He smiled. "The neighbors will be thrilled."

He sighed and turned his back to the ballroom, leaving it empty, bathed in early morning light.

The square before the palace was starting to thin as the day wore on, and Sabre passed a hat stall where the gallows used to be, children selling flowers, a herald reading news from the palace. Sabre stopped to buy a flower for Rose, who had a fondness for her namesake, and turned toward the pleasure district.

"Hey, kid," Nanette said, when Sabre came in through the front door of the House of Onyx. She was wearing a heavy red sweater over her catsuit, and was reading one of the salacious novels they sold on the street, something about Arkoudai warriors slinging Katoikos nobles over their shoulders. "You just missed Yves' mother. She made us *sweaters*. Did you know Yves' legal name is Darling? *Darling*."

"I'm not surprised," Sabre said, sidling around the cart of masks in the foyer. Gwydion was in the common room with Rose, reading through her latest edits while Simone listened and mended an enormous lavender gown. Rose patted Sabre absently on the cheek when he handed her the flower, then turned back to her script, papers shuffling over her dress as she moved.

"Laurent's upstairs," she said. "And so's a copy of Act Three."

"I'll have my notes on your desk in the morning," Sabre said, and smiled as Rose waved him off.

He ascended the stairs through the House, lightly sliding his hand along the banister. Music played from Yves' room, a guitar of some sort, soft, hesitant strings plunking away through the wall. Laughter rang out from the baths. Through the window, laundry dried in the sun, and the white, heavily pregnant cat Rose had just adopted off the street basked beneath it, content.

Sabre stopped at the door at the top of the stairs. He'd knelt there, once, waiting for permission to enter, too afraid of love to think it could be given, too eager to turn away.

He opened the door. Laurent looked up, still dressed in his morning robes, the light of the open window pooling into his eyes.

"Good morning, love," Sabre said, stepping inside. "I'm back."

THE DUKE'S DEMON (STARIAN CYCLE #2)

The story will continue...

Enjoy a preview of *The Duke's Demon*, book two in the Starian Cycle!

* * *

It wasn't very difficult, hunting people in the snow. Especially when they were bleeding.

Sebastien d'Hiver was not a man who hunted for pleasure, simply because animals were very little sport at all. Even the cleverest of them were predictable, following their instincts even to their own detriment, creatures of habit to the end.

He'd thought people might be different, and sometimes, they were. Not always, though. And not this time, either.

The man he was hunting was injured, yes, but it wasn't even the trail of blood or muddled bootprints that made him easy to track. It was the rage, so hot that it burned bright like a beacon to the thing that lived in Sebastien, that urged him in soft whispers to *go, my host, find that one and feed.*

It was unusual enough that he'd come here, to this fete with the nobles who spent so much time arranging new and boring ways to fuck someone. Sebastien did not share their same desires, but he did not begrudge them, either; he'd only come out of interest, once he'd heard the former whore would be there, the Mislian. But that one had no notion of who he was, and when he'd learned it, it turned out he was some other kind of Mislian, possessed of a different magic. No demon tethered to him, like the others.

If there had been, Sebastien would have taken him. Hunted him for the thrill of it, perhaps, then bound him in chains and carried him back north to the Abbey. No one would have looked for him, there.

Just as no one would look for this one, the noble with wrath pouring unchecked from him, leaving a trail easier to follow than the bright drops of blood on the snow.

Sebastien tapped his cane on the ground, thinking. The demon wanted him to pin the noble down, siphon his rage, cut him slowly into pieces and sup on his fear, his pain. But those were easy things to find, really. Everyone screamed under the knife, but it took a special soul to harbor so much anger that Sebastien took notice of it.

He was being hunted for something having to do with the one who came under the lash, earlier, in the room with the fire. Sebastien had been drawn there, thinking it was the man blindfolded to the post who was angry, but no. It was the man in the corner, with the too-bright eyes and cold smile, and his thoughts were so easy to read that Sebastien didn't know how they went unnoticed. There were others in the room who could use magic, his demon told him so. The prince, who saw the future in water. The Mislian, whose magic was older than Staria itself and trapped under a fog of someone's making. Even the king, who was shut off to it, had something there. Or maybe he was just mad. It wasn't always easy to tell.

The particulars didn't much matter to Sebastien. The d'Hiver estate, called the Abbey for reasons long lost to history, was far enough removed from Duciel that most people forgot he existed. Technically he was the third highest-ranking noble in the kingdom, but that didn't matter a bit to Sebastien. It was likely why the king merely let him be—he wanted no part of any of it, the court or the politicking or the games that were never very interesting. It made his demon restless, and it was harder to satisfy its particular desires when someone paid too much attention to you. The small village around the Abbey knew better. Sebastien was pleased about that.

The snow was falling faster now, and there was some commotion —he could hear a horse's hooves, shouts, the rustle of people who realized the game was up and something else had taken its place. Sebastien tilted his head, and the demon clicked soft in his mind, hissing soft, telling him where to go to find their prey.

Not that he needed the guidance, per se. The prey in question was crouched in some of the underbrush that hadn't yet fallen to the ground, and he was doing a rather poor job at concealing himself.

"Here, there," Sebastien said, crouching down, poking at him with the end of his cane. "They're searching for you. You're making it very easy."

Devon Chastain, whose father would, likely, be hanged as a traitor before noon tomorrow, was crouched feral and snarling behind the bushes. His face was bloody, his eyes were wild, and he bared his teeth at Sebastien in something close to a snarl. "Do you think I care that you're a duke?"

"Not particularly, no," said Sebastien, who didn't particularly care that he was one, himself. He was never supposed to be. Etienne had been meant for it, but he was long dead, buried in the ground near Sebastien's home.

"At least I killed him," Devon muttered. "Before I die, at least I know that bastard watched his whore lover *die* and couldn't save him."

Sebastien shivered slightly, enjoying the rush of rage that trickled out of this exhausted, hunted young noble like wine. He wondered if he should tell him that de Valois was alive and well, his status returned. Perhaps he would save that for later, when some of the anger in him had dimmed. "Yes, well done, are you going to stay there, then? Your wounds aren't fatal."

"How the fuck do you know?"

Sebastien smiled at him. "We know death when we see it, boy. Now come out of there before we do it for you."

Devon Chastain blinked at him and asked the one question that no one ever should, when Sebastien spoke in tandem with his demon. "Who's *we*? I only see you, here."

Sebastien held the cane out, pushed the end through the bushes. "Come out and I'll show you," he said. "Stay there, and I'm afraid they'll find you."

"Isn't that—what are you offering, then?" Devon reached out, curled his gloved fingers around the cane. "Safety?"

"No," Sebastien said, and laughed. "Nothing of the kind. But it will spare you the noose, and I think you are wise enough to take a chance when it's offered, are you not? Any sensible person would, I should think. Do decide soon, won't you? They're on their way. We haven't got long."

"And if I. Turn you in, tell them you offered aid to a traitor—"

"Ah, no, I'm afraid that won't work. I'll be gone before they arrive, and any number of people will claim to have seen me. And no one will be inclined to take the word of a traitor, the king is rather in a poor mood. Well? We've no more time, make your choice." Ah, but the spike of fear amidst the rage was an added delight, wasn't it? This one, he would have to treat carefully. A fine meal not to be wasted.

Devon snarled and held onto the cane, and Sebastien rose smoothly to his feet and pulled, hard enough to bring Devon out of the underbrush *and* ensure he was scratched up a bit more—why not throw a dash of pain in there, to spice it up even more?

"Now," Sebastien said, brusquely, beginning to walk. "We shall find my horse, and be on our way." He took off his coat and presented it to Devon. "Put that on."

"I don't need your *fucking* pity," the angry noble hissed at him, ignoring the proffered coat.

"Wonderful, I have none to give you. But my horse will not take you on his back if you do not have the scent of me, so it would be best if you listened and did as I said. Otherwise, you're free to suffer as much as you like, around me."

"They say things about you," Devon said, shrugging into the coat. "That you're...insane."

"Oh, no," Sebastien said, scanning the treeline and moving toward the horse that waited, needing no summons other than Sebastien's silent wish that it appear. "It is nothing so mundane as that, my angry little fox. You'll learn the truth soon enough."

"You're bringing me back to them," Devon hissed, beginning to pull away. "There's no—" he stopped, as Sebastien's horse, a black stallion, came trotting out of the forest and stopped right in front of them.

Sebastien climbed up, patted the horse on its flank. "This is Mari Lwyd. I wouldn't do that," he admonished, when he noticed Devon staring at the horse's eyes. "The less you look, the less it stays with you."

"What the fuck *are* you," Devon asked, and Sebastien tasted his fear in a long, slow inhale...and smiled.

"The devil you don't know," he said, and held out his hand. "It shall remain to be seen, which is better."

As a longtime reader of fantasy, Iris is committed to writing fun, escapist dark fantasy featuring decadent, kinky stories, intricate worldbuilding and unforgettable characters.

Loved the book and want to help indie authors like Iris produce more unique content to enjoy? Leave a review on Amazon, Goodreads or wherever you like to review books. Don't forget to tell a friend!

Connect with Iris:

Twitter: @irisfoxgloveauthor
    Email: irisfoxgloveauthor@gmail.com

If you're interested in receiving information on new releases, as well as exclusive excerpts from upcoming books and bonus content, sign up for Iris' newsletter!

www.ingramcontent.com/pod-product-compliance
Lightning Source LLC
Chambersburg PA
CBHW032016150726
47990CB00005B/1985